THE

AFTERWARD

E. K. JOHNSTON

DUTTON BOOKS

DUTTON BOOKS

An imprint of Penguin Random House LLC, New York

Copyright © 2019 by E. K. Johnston

Visit us online at penguinrandomhouse.com

Library of Congress Cataloging-in-Publication Data
Names: Johnston, E. K., author.
Title: The afterward / by E.K. Johnston.
Description: New York, NY : Dutton Books, an imprint of Penguin Random House
LLC, [2019] | Summary: In the aftermath of a successful quest, Apprentice
Kalanthe and Olsa-the-thief-of-the-realm must cope with their newfound
fame and find a way to overcome the forces that would drive them apart.
Identifiers: LCCN 2018017857 | ISBN 9780735231894 (hardcover) | ISBN
9780735231900 (epub)
Subjects: | CYAC: Fantasy. | Heroes—Fiction. | Celebrities—Fiction. |
Knights and knighthood—Fiction. | Robbers and outlaws—Fiction. |
Love—Fiction.
Classification: LCC PZ7.J64052 Aft 2019 | DDC [Fic]—dc23 LC record available at
https://lccn.loc.gov/2018017857

Printed in the United States of America

1 3 5 7 9 10 8 6 4 2

Design by Anna Booth and Maggie Edkins
Text set in Bembo Std.

To David and Leigh Eddings,
I really wish I had written you a letter.

– I –

CADRIA

*A*nd so it was in the days before, when the Old God brought ruin to every corner of the world. Great were His injustices and mistreatments of all living things: the birds in the sky and the beasts on the ground, and the humans who laboured in His service. He cared nothing for their pain and suffering. Worse, it pleased Him to inflict horror wherever He could. When He saw the bright wing of a cormorant diving towards the sea for its dinner, He would send scalding water to burn bird and fish both. When a horse pulled a plough behind it, He would strew the path with rocks, to dull the blade and to pain the horse's hooves. For humankind, He reserved his most particular kinds of violence, but, ah, remembering those days causes even the bravest of storytellers too much grief. Better to tell of what came after.

Seven godlings, born of the Old God's discarded human toys, found one another in the ruin of the world. They knew that should any of them stand alone, their small power would be instantly obliterated, but they did not give up hope. They practiced working together, uniting in concert to increase their chances, but still they feared it would not be enough.

When all seemed truly lost, the youngest of them found a green stone, the sort that humans called emerald. It was of inconsequential size and not particularly striking to behold, but the godling thought that it would suit their purpose, and called upon the others to fill it with their strength. Over and over, the godlings put their power into the stone, until it sang to them with the promise of better days to come.

The Old God felt the stirring of this new power and came to find them, but He was unprepared for their new strength. Godlings no more, they had only to touch the Old God with their gem, and they undid Him. Thus peace came at last to the world, with the Old God vanquished and the new ones much kinder in their treatment of it.

But, alas, that was not the end. The Old God had fled, yes, but some of His servants remained, and though they faced a long wait to restore their Master, wait they did. Finally, after long millennia, one such servant took it upon herself to bring her Master back, even though it would release ruination on the world once more. To that end, the Old God's Servant ensnared the King of Cadrium, centre of the world and beacon of knowledge, in a spell so vile that it ate away at the king's very life.

Fearful that the loss of her king would bring about a war violent enough to resurrect the Old God Himself, Sir Erris Quicksword went on a desperate Quest to find the godsgem again, that same emerald the new gods had used, lost all this time from history's record. With her rode three champions, each particularly skilled in multiple aspects of the knightly arts, along with the greatest living Mage, and two others, so that their company might number seven, the same as did the new gods.

Great were their trials and tribulations upon the road, yet through mastery of themselves and of their surroundings they did manage, not only to find the godsgem itself, but also to take it to the Old God's altar, rebuilt in secret by His cruel servants, and there destroy Him utterly.

It was in those final moments, when the Old God was at His most powerful and the knights at their most vulnerable, that the wisdom of the new gods showed itself. Sir Erris dealt the killing blow—yes, her sword was as quick as her name foretold—but, without the aid of her companions, picked for their skills but also for their number, she would have been overmatched.

At this most important time, the weight of destiny fell upon the shoulders of a mere apprentice knight. Kept aside during the fighting to guard the Mage's back, the apprentice saw the battle unfold and knew when the moment for her to act had arrived. As she watched her companions quail in the face of the Old God's rising, Kalanthe Ironheart did not falter. She was able to distract the Old God, giving time to Sir Erris and allowing her to use the godsgem to put to rest the Old God, once and for all.

With King Dorrenta unensorcelled and the world made safe once more, Sir Erris and her six companions returned to

Cadria and to the honours and privileges they had earned. Erris herself was married to the king, as had long been both their wish, while the other knights and the apprentice resumed their duties in the palace. The Mage returned to the Mage Keep with the godsgem under his protection, to consult with his fellows how best to conceal within their sanctuary.

The seventh companion disappeared, and little is known about her. The common folk say she was lowborn like them, and a thief besides, but it is far more likely that she was, in fact, one of the seven new gods, keeping watch over Sir Erris's Quest to ensure no misuse of the godsgem.

In any case, with peace returned and the kingdom stabilized, it seemed that the time for great tales was done. The horror and grief of the past was gone, driven out by the light and goodness of the new gods; and under the protection of the knights who served them and the king both, it seemed unlikely that such darkness would ever return.

And they all lived happily ever after.

*A*s a rule, Olsa Rhetsdaughter avoided breaking into a house through the nursery. More generally, she avoided housebreaking, especially now that she operated without protection, but as the rain poured down on the city of Cadria, she was almost grateful to escape the soaking cold. She was used to sleeping rough—had slept rougher, as a point of fact, than she would tonight. But she hated the wet— how it permeated everything from her clothes to her hair to the slick stone of the wall she was scaling—and hated it all the more now that she didn't have reliable access to a good fire. There would probably be several of those inside the house, as the wealthy owners warded off the damp.

Once she reached her destination, she paused halfway over the sill and surveyed the layout of the room as best she could in the dark. Her preference for a job of this sort was a musty attic or, in a pinch, an unoccupied guest room. There were just so many obstacles in a nursery: toys strewn on the floor; more than the usual number of beds; the family cat; and, of course, the children themselves. Children were restless sleepers.

Children required lamps left lit in case they woke up in the dark. Children *asked questions.*

"Are you Olsa-thief-of-the-realm?" The voice was high enough and young enough that she couldn't tell whether it was a lad or lass who spoke, but the question froze Olsa in her tracks halfway across the room. Dammit, she'd done such a good job of opening and shutting the window too.

"No," she hissed. "I'm a demon that preys upon waking children in the night. Go back to sleep."

"I think a demon would be taller," said a second voice. This one was almost certainly a girl. "Also, demons are usually on fire."

Olsa sighed. All she wanted was a quick, easy job, and those were increasingly hard for her to come by. She'd taken this one because it had been a slow week, because her percentage of the take was high, and because the family she'd be stealing from employed one of the best cooks in the city. She'd been planning her detour through the kitchen on her way out in almost as much detail as she'd been planning the actual heist.

"Yes," she said, flopping gracelessly into the chair by the fire. She was probably destroying the fine upholstery with her soaked tunic and hose, but the fire was warm enough that she couldn't bring herself to care. "I'm Olsa."

"Oh, tell us about the godsgem!" said the little one, a girl after all, bouncing across the room to sit in front of her, as though Olsa were her nurse. "Papa is a gem merchant, so I've seen lots of pretty stones, but they say the godsgem is the prettiest."

"She knows Papa is a gem merchant, Ildy," said the older girl. She was at the age where she felt it imperative to remain dignified at all times, so she didn't bounce, but she did come closer and take a seat. "Why do you think she's here?"

"Be quiet, Mina," the little one, Ildy, said. "I want a story."

"If you'll both be quiet, I'll tell you," Olsa said.

It wasn't the best plan she'd ever had, but short of diving out the window right now and making a run for it, she couldn't think of anything else. She was caught, but it was better to be caught by these two than by their parents or whatever burly servants they had kicking about the house. Also, it was a very good fire. Olsa decided it was worth the risk.

The girls settled in front of her, their white nightgowns tucked neatly under their legs. Soon, they would be too old to sit on the floor. Their skirts and stays would require chairs. Olsa wondered if either of them had ever sat cross-legged in their lives. She'd had to teach Kalanthe how to do it, and Kalanthe wore trousers half the time anyway. Money made a person very strange, and Olsa was more aware of it now than she had ever been.

"The first time I saw it," she began, "I thought to myself 'I could see a roomful of gems, all piled up on top of one another, and be able to recognize this one immediately.'"

"What does it look like?" asked Ildy.

"Hush," said her sister.

"It's not large and it's not cut very well," Olsa said. "From the stories, you'd imagine an emerald the size of my fist, cut with so many facets that the reflected light goes off in all directions at once. The truth is that the godsgem is much smaller, and almost raw."

"That doesn't sound very special at all," said Mina.

"You hush," said her sister.

In spite of herself, Olsa smiled.

"It doesn't look like much," she continued. "It doesn't have to. As soon as you see it, you know it's special. It sings, you see. Imagine the most beautiful hymn you've ever heard at the temple. The kind they sing on festival days, where the different sections of the choir layer their voices over each other's in more than four parts. Now, imagine that, but a hundredfold. The most complicated and the most beautiful music you've ever heard, so much so that you can barely stand to listen to it, because you know that once you start, you'll never want to stop."

"That sounds dangerous," said Mina.

"Of course it was dangerous," said Olsa. She shook herself a bit to try forgetting what the godsgem had sounded like. Of course it didn't work. It never would. The song would haunt her for the rest of her life. "That's why they sent all those knights to find it."

"Quicksword and Stonehand and Fire-Eyes and Silverspoke," said Ildy, rhyming them off like a psalm. Olsa had seen them all naked, so she was somewhat less impressed by them. "And the Mage, of course."

"And Ironheart," said Mina. "And you."

"Why did they send you?" Ildy asked.

"I asked myself that question a lot," Olsa said. "The truth is that I'd done Sir Erris Quicksword a couple of favours. She needed a spy, and I was available. Only the men I was spying on got wind of it, somehow, and sent some footpads to cut my throat. I escaped them, but I knew I needed better sanctuary. I didn't much fancy shutting myself up in the temple, so I went to Quicksword herself and she took me with her. Then I stayed because I didn't have anywhere else to go, and because the gods like it when the people on a Quest stay the same."

"They say the king picked those knights and you because you each matched a facet of the new gods," Ildy said.

"Don't be foolish, Ildy," Mina said. "Everyone knows that the king had given instruction to let Sir Erris make her own decisions, and that meant picking her companions, and she picked the ones she thought it would be the hardest for the Old God to tempt."

"You don't know the half of it," Olsa said. It wasn't Kalanthe's soul she was thinking of. "But, yes, Erris picked who went."

There was a creak in the hallway, and Olsa tensed. Neither of the girls reacted, and presumably they weren't supposed to be out of bed at this hour. They wouldn't get in nearly as much trouble as Olsa would, but no one likes to be punished. Perhaps it was the cat. Olsa knew from casing the house that the family cat was enormous, and it wasn't in the room with them.

"Tell us about Kalanthe Ironheart," said Ildy. It was more a plea than a demand. She wasn't old enough that she was used to being obeyed without question yet.

Olsa paused. Both Mina and Ildy were leaning towards her now, eager to hear a story about the Apprentice Knight. Kalanthe, like herself, had only been on the Quest because of circumstance. Young though she was, she was the same size as Sir Erris and could wear her armour. It was decided that if she came along, she could be used as Erris's double if the occasion called for it. Since the knights were much older and the Mage was mostly unapproachable, Kalanthe and Olsa had spent a lot of time together. It hadn't been very much fun at the start, but, well, it didn't much bear thinking of, to be honest.

"Ironheart will be the perfect knight someday," Olsa said. She was plagiarizing a little bit, but maybe these girls hadn't heard that particular ballad yet. It was easier to think about Kalanthe if she didn't have to use her own memories to do it. "Tall and strong and dedicated. Pure of heart and sure of arm."

Less pure and less sure when it came to other areas of expertise, but that was hardly fit for young children. Also, it was exactly the sort of memories Olsa did her very best to avoid thinking about.

"At the very moment when Sir Erris Quicksword needed her, Ironheart was there," Olsa continued. She could see the scene in her head, replaying as it always did when she thought about Kalanthe and tried not to think about Kalanthe at the same time. Which happened fairly regularly. "In an act of sheer defiance and bravery, she threw her axe at the Old God's altar."

Both girls gasped, their faces lit with glee. They knew the story after all, it seemed, though they hadn't heard it from someone who had been in the room where it happened.

"You know the Old God's power," Olsa went on. "Dark and cruel, it could not be broken by so simple a thing as a knight's axe, even when the knight was good and righteous as Kalanthe Ironheart."

She was very proud of herself for saying that last part with a straight face.

"But it was enough to split the Old God's attention," she said. "For a fraction of a second, He turned His awful face to Ironheart."

It had been a terrible moment. Olsa had been certain that Kalanthe was going to die for her bravery.

"And in that moment, Erris Quicksword struck," Olsa said. "Like her name says, she moved so quickly I could barely see her arm. Instead, it was a blur of motion as her blessèd sword came down on the altar and, with the power of godsgem, smashed it to pieces."

"And that was the end of the Old God," Mina said. "And the start of the new age with our King restored."

"Something like that," Olsa said. She wasn't particularly fond of the new age. She was a lot hungrier in it.

There was another creak from the hallway. This time, Olsa was sure it wasn't the cat. She hated leaving a job undone, but there was no way she'd be able to ditch the children and complete her thievery now. That chance had been lost as soon as Ildy woke up, and now it was time to abandon the house completely. Another failure and another night as the most famous person in the realm who wasn't going to get any supper. At least she was warm and her tunic had dried out. She looked back towards the window, her escape, and counted out how many breaths it would take her to cross the room to it and jump.

Without warning, the door to the nursery slammed open. Though she was prepared for it, Ildy and Mina were not. Both girls screamed at the noise and kept screaming when, instead of the familiar faces of their parents, the nursery filled with soldiers-at-arms in the uniforms of the city watch.

Olsa dove for the window, but as soon as she had it up, she saw the torches below and knew there was no escape that way either. She looked about for another rooftop, but found nothing. That was why she'd had to scale the wall to the nursery window in the first place. The chief gem merchant of Cadria took few chances when it came to home security.

She turned around to face the watch. The girls' mother had come in and was soothing them. Mina looked calm, but Ildy was furious. Olsa did her best to swallow a smile. It appeared she had made another noble friend, for all the good it was about to do her.

"Olsa Rhetsdaughter," said the leader of the watch, her tone more resigned than anything else. "You are under arrest."

The state of the prison had not improved much from her last visit. Ever since his healing, King Dorrenta had embarked on a massive campaign of public works, including the sewers and the aqueducts, amongst other things, but apparently he had not yet turned to prison reform. The cell Olsa was dumped into smelled like piss, and the straw that covered the floor was at least a week old and starting to rot. The torches were burning tallow, which didn't help clear the air, and the pervasive damp of old-city stone made everything chilly. Olsa wrapped her arms around her knees and glowered.

They hadn't chained her to the wall because, much to the disappointment of the watch leader, she hadn't resisted her arrest. Mina had given her a cape, insisting that it belonged to Olsa and therefore ought to be arrested with her, even though it was abundantly clear that Olsa couldn't possibly own anything so fine. The cape was made of the hide of some animal Olsa couldn't identify, long strips sewn together, and lined with fur. It was much too short for her and since its primary function seemed to be keeping water off its wearer, it didn't do a lot to keep Olsa warm. Still, there was fur, and every little bit helped.

Her trial wouldn't be until the morning, and long hours of boredom stretched out between now and then. To keep herself entertained, Olsa tried to puzzle out what the cape might be made of. The average street thief would have given up after a few minutes, but the average street thief didn't have Olsa's advantages. She had gleaned her primary education from the Thief Bosses, of course, and could tell good coin from bad as well as any, but her education hadn't stopped there. Once the Bosses had seen her gifts at basic thievery, they had increased what they taught her, including how to determine the quality of materials and work. The fine stitching on the cape she held indicated the latter, and the fact that the work had been expended indicated the former. Whatever the cape was made of, it was expensive and worth the best of craftsmanship.

It wasn't a cow. Cow leather was something any urchin born in Cadria would be able to identify on sight. And the pieces were too small for a bear. No, it had to be something else.

Her mind's eye saw a tall figure with black skin and sparkling plate armour. At almost seven feet, with the broad shoulders typical of a knight and tightly braided hair, Sir Uleweya Fire-Eyes feared very little. Her helmet was crowned with bone, which she said absorbed the shock of an axe to the head, and the steel of her armour always glinted as she moved. Unless it was covered in blood, of course. Then she stopped gleaming for a while, until she had time to polish it again. She made a very imposing figure, and even without her armour, she was intimidating. Her eyes were dark brown, except when she was working her specific kind of magic. Then, as her name indicated, they were afire with the power that allowed her to see great distances, even at night.

Olsa hadn't spoken to her very much at first because she had an excellent instinct for self-preservation. One night, though, when it was Sir Uleweya's turn to keep watch, Olsa couldn't sleep. It was raining, which it did very differently in the country than it did in the city, and which Olsa found to be unnerving. She wanted to sit by the fire, where it was warm, but the lady knight sat there, and Olsa didn't want to interrupt.

"You might as well come out," Uleweya had said, after several moments but without actually looking at the place where Olsa was standing. Someone with magic in her eyes still had at least four other senses.

Olsa did as she was told and went to stand by the guttering fire. They'd rigged a cover for it, but rain rarely fell straight down, so some of the water made it through.

"Here," said the lady knight, and held out her cape so that Olsa could sit next to her and be protected.

This was far, far more than Olsa had been willing to cope with.

"Oh, stop being an idiot," said Uleweya. "We are on a Quest. I don't want to carry you if you catch your death. Sit down."

Olsa had sat. Immediately, she stopped getting wet. She'd never encountered a cape that did that before. Even the thickest wool got damp eventually and would take forever to dry. She'd tried to turn around and look at it, but there wasn't enough space.

"It's sealskin," Sir Uleweya said, her eyes dancing in the firelight. "Great big creatures that live in the oceans to the north. You can't grow anything up there, and importing food would be too expensive, so they kill seals instead. Wonderfully nutritious meat, very useful hides."

"How did you get it?" Olsa asked, and the lady knight launched into an explanation involving pirates, an endless night, and a series of close escapes that might have been not entirely accurate, but was highly entertaining nonetheless. Uleweya's family had money but no land, so after she was knighted, she had served the realm by travelling widely and had seen a great many things. Several of her stories may have actually been true.

"Seal," Olsa said now, to the oppressive quiet of the dungeon. "And some kind of fur to make it more comfortable. I wonder how Mina got it?"

"No talking!" said a guard from outside her cell. She rattled the bars of her door, as though to remind Olsa that she was trapped by them. She stuck out her tongue, even though she couldn't see her. Prison was the worst.

Retreating to the peace of her own mind, Olsa began to replay the story that Fire-Eyes had told her. She wasn't searching for inspiration, but rather was attempting to distract herself from the boredom of her cell, much the way

Sir Uleweya had been attempting to distract a frightened young thief from the unknown wilds when she'd told the tale in the first place. Usually, Olsa thought her Quest had been pretty useless—personally, anyway. There was no denying she had helped to save the realm. Still, every now and then, even though the knight had probably forgotten her, she was reminded that parts of it would be with her forever.

Or at least until her inevitable hanging.

Daylight pierced Olsa's eyes as she stood before the court. The room, as she had expected, was packed to the rafters, just as it had been the previous two times she'd been tried here. The three times before that, there hadn't been a trial at all. Instead, she'd sat in her cell for a few hours, and then the door had been opened and the magistrate informed her that she had been pardoned by the king and was free to go. Apparently, the king's mercy was extended only three times. He hadn't come to any of her trials, nor had Sir Erris. So much for royal gratitude.

The courtroom of the royal palace of Cadria was a vast room with a vaulted ceiling, much like the temple, only decidedly less ornate. Along one wall was the bench where the magistrate sat, surrounded by messengers, scribes, lawkeepers, and the magistrate's own security force. To the left and right were the viewing galleries, where any member of the public might come to view a trial. Usually the seats were empty, but for Olsa they were crowded, and those with good views were employing great effort to fend off those who found their view obstructed by one of the numerous support columns. The rear wall was reserved for any wealthier citizens who might choose to watch the proceedings. Olsa, her hands now chained as much for appearance as anything else, was led to the wooden box in the middle of the room, and stood there with great aplomb while the crowd got their fill and the magistrate lamented her existence. There was no sign of Ildy or Mina, though Olsa saw the girls' father sitting with his own lawkeeper and guard close to the magistrate's bench.

"Olsa Rhetsdaughter!" The magistrate had a booming voice—probably thanks in part to her knight training—and rarely required use of her gavel at all to get everyone's attention. As soon as she said Olsa's name, there was instant silence from the crowd. "You have been brought before us again today. This is your sixth arrest and your third trial. What have you to say for yourself?"

This would be the part where, if she wanted to, Olsa could give up her coconspirators. She'd been hired for this job, after all, and everyone in the room knew it. The chief gem merchant of Cadria was too unlikely a target for a random robbery, particularly in his own house. Olsa could tattle on her employers and throw herself on the court's mercy, but there would be no mercy for her on the streets if she did. Thieves who turned in court didn't long survive the turning.

"It was raining, sir," Olsa said instead. "And I saw the fire through the window. I was cold."

"So you climbed three storeys to break into the nursery?"

the magistrate said. Olsa could tell Knight of Laws was just as frustrated by all the show as she was.

"Yes, sir," Olsa said. "Nothing like a good climb to stir the blood."

A good number of the crowd laughed, but the magistrate didn't so much as twitch. The gem merchant leaned over to his lawkeeper and whispered something. The woman nodded and stood.

"Sir, if I may?" the lawkeeper said, and the magistrate gave her permission. "The thief spent an unknown amount of time with this good man's daughters. The gods only know what she told them, but we request that sedition be added to the charge of robbery, as surely no one of her character could impart any wholesome information to children so young."

"I object!" Olsa said. Thievery was one thing and something she was surely guilty of, but she would not have her name besmirched with crimes she hadn't actually committed.

"You are out of order," the magistrate said severely, though she shook her head at the guard who would have struck Olsa for speaking out of turn. She considered the request for a moment, consulting the papers before her. The crowd grew restless. "The request is denied. I spoke to the girls myself, and they do not seem harmed by their association with this . . . person."

Olsa relaxed a little bit, though there were still the other charges to deal with. She wasn't exactly the magistrate's favourite person. She thought the lawkeeper might protest, but she only sat down again and shuffled her own notes.

"If there is no other evidence to be offered?" the magistrate said. Neither Olsa nor her accusers moved. "Then hear the decision of the King's Court."

The crowd dutifully rose to their feet as though the king were present, though he was not. Olsa guessed that if he were, there would be a lot more soldiers in the room. Still, with everyone on their feet it made her feel a little less exposed. She pretended they were standing for her, a hero of the realm.

"Olsa Rhetsdaughter, this is your sixth arrest for thievery," said the magistrate. "Three times you have been pardoned and twice you have been exonerated, yet the pattern before me is a clear one. You are a thief, you have shown no desire to rehabilitate yourself, and you continue to flaunt the King's Law in your every action."

Personally, Olsa thought this unfair. She did a great many things without thinking about the king at all. She forced herself to pay attention.

"For the crimes of thievery, housebreaking, and conspiracy, the court finds you guilty," the magistrate declared. "And in accordance with your past record, we sentence you to be hanged by the neck until you are dead."

At this, the crowd began to buzz. Everyone knew she had been on that Quest, even if they didn't know what she'd done while she was on it. Surely, surely, the magistrate would not execute such a person as her.

Olsa stood very still, facing the magistrate and willing herself to ignore everyone else in the room. For the first time, the magistrate's façade cracked.

"Unless"—and here the old woman sighed as though she regretted having been made to get out of bed this morning—"you can find someone who is willing to speak for you."

Olsa smiled sweetly at her as, right on cue, a familiar voice sounded.

"I will speak for her."

BEFORE. . . . .

The first time I saw her, I couldn't tell if she was a lad or lass. Her night-black hair was unevenly cut—like she'd done it herself with a blunt knife—and stuck out in short tufts that were already starting to curl even though they were barely long enough to comb properly. Dark eyes flashed as she took in her surroundings and sized us up. She was covered in red dirt—the kind that came off the cheap roof tiles used in the poorest neighbourhoods inside Cadria's walls—but her skin under that was darker than mine. Her clothes were so old and misused that it was hard to tell what was patches and what was original cloth—or if any original cloth remained at all. I couldn't fathom why Sir Erris would bring her, even to get a seventh companion. Surely there must be other knights or mages that would be better suited.

"This is Olsa," Sir Erris said. "She's a thief, who does work for me in the city. Her face has become known to our enemies, and they have tried to kill her. We're taking her with us."

And that was that. The other knights obeyed Sir Erris, and who was I to question her.

I was about two years away from becoming a knight in the king's name and service, at which point I would have earned the right to speak to them unbidden, but even then I would be far below them in rank. These were champions of the realm, known throughout the Kingdom of Cadrium and possibly even to the continents beyond. It would take me many years to be good enough to call them my sisters, or my friends.

Mage Ladros, whose white hair and lined face made him look venerable instead of vulnerable, was the only one of our party who might have gainsayed Sir Erris, and he chose not to, instead reorganizing his pack in final preparation before we set out. I watched him carefully. Of all the knights on the Quest, only Sir Erris and I had any plain magic to speak of—Sir Uleweya had some sense magic with her sight, but that sort was like breathing; either on or off. Plain magic, my sort, was like a fire, always needing fuel. I was mostly untrained, and so I hoped that by watching Mage Ladros, I could learn a bit, and so not fall behind in my studies while I was on the road.

My yearmates were all envious that I was chosen to go. They would have laughed to hear my worries: that I would lose time at my schoolwork while on a Quest with four living legends. Or maybe they would have said I was afraid. They would have been wrong with the latter. I wasn't afraid of very many things, and with the company I was keeping, there was no reason to be. Either we would be successful, or the Old God would kill us. It was almost reassuring in its finality.

The thief was staring at me. Maybe she was wondering why I was included as much as I had wondered at her. At least I would be useful. I was a competent swordswoman and good with bow, whether I was shooting game or enemies. I hoped Sir Branthear would show me how to use an axe, if we had any spare time on the road for teaching. And I was the same size as Sir Erris, which meant that I could wear her armour—with the visor down, of course; Sir Erris was pale-skinned and her hair was red—to distract our enemies while she committed acts of stealth or magecraft.

I wondered what the thief could do for us, and I continued to wonder the whole first day of our ride, while she eyed each bush and shrub as though it might conceal the deadliest of enemies.

"What is your problem?" I asked finally, unable to stand her jumpiness any longer.

To be honest, my own silence was growing difficult to bear. I was not overly talkative but I was used to talking, and holding my tongue unless I was spoken to was nerve-wracking.

"There's so much space," the thief said. "No walls or houses in sight. No roofs, no stone work. Nothing but trees and grass and whatever that is."

"That's a rosebush," I told her. "It's not blooming yet, but when it does it will be very pretty."

"That's what roses look like?" said the thief. Olsa, her name was Olsa, and if she was the only person I could talk to, I'd do well to call her by her name.

"Of course," I said. "What did you think they looked like?"

"Red, usually," Olsa said. "Sometimes yellow or pink. I saw a white one once, when I was at a lesser temple and, um, working."

Stealing from funerary offerings, is what she meant. This was going to end in disaster.

"That's what the flowers look like," I told her. "This is what they look like without flowers on."

"So it's still a rose even when it's not a rose?" Olsa said.

Ahead of us, Sir Terriam began to laugh, her massive shoulders shaking with mirth.

"Our thief is a philosopher, it seems," she said. "You watch yourself, apprentice. She'll steal more than your purse."

"I wouldn't," Olsa said. She wasn't talking to me, but directly to the lady knight. I tried to catch her eye to warn her off, but she was giving her full attention to her horse. "I don't steal from my own crew. That's how you get your throat slit."

"She's not your crew," I hissed. "And she deserves the respect of your silence."

"Apprentice Kalanthe, I appreciate the deference, but I don't think that's going to be sustainable long-term." Sir Terriam slowed her horse and pulled alongside me. I straightened in my saddle. "I know that in the palace, your oaths include respectful silence, but out here on the road, if you notice something and wait for us to call on you, we might all die."

"Silverspoke is right," Sir Erris said. The woman had the sharpest ears of anyone I've ever met. "I don't imagine either of you will abuse the privilege, but don't hold yourselves to the courtly quiet out here. Your necks are at risk too. You should be able to ask questions about the Quest we're on."

Mage Ladros laughed to himself and for a moment I wasn't sure why, but then Olsa launched into a flurry of questions about what we were doing and why we were doing it, and I realized that he had anticipated the oncoming storm if Sir Erris had not. Sir Uleweya was also concealing a grin.

"Olsa, stop," Sir Erris said, but her tone was oddly fond. "I can't answer more than one question at a time anyway."

"Sir Knight, if it pleases you, I'll answer her questions," I said, surprising myself at my forthrightness, even if it had been as good as ordered. "As many of them as I am able to, in any case. And then we will ask you the questions we cannot solve ourselves."

"Where did you find this girl, Quicksword?" Sir Terriam said. "Finishing school?"

"Apprentice Knight Kalanthe is the best of her class." Everyone had heard Sir Terriam's question, and Sir Erris answered in the same carrying tone. I know I flushed at her words, but I couldn't help it. "She is green because it is her first true mission, but we have great hope for her once she wins her full knighthood."

Sir Terriam looked at me for a long moment, and then spurred her horse ahead to join with Sir Branthear at the front. I hoped I had not just lost her good opinion of me.

"Very well, Kalanthe," Sir Erris continued. "I think that is a good idea. You can keep her from pestering the rest of us too much, eh?"

"Yes, sir," I said.

"Don't I get a say in this?" Olsa asked.

"No," said Sir Erris. "Loosen your hold on the reins, lass. If you harden your horse's mouth like that, you'll never be able to control it in a skirmish."

Olsa obediently loosened the reins, but I could tell that her tight grip had been the result of her discomfort with the exposure of the countryside. I pulled my horse alongside hers. Now that she was dressed better, I could see that her figure was good. It was nowhere near as developed as mine, probably due to underfeeding, but there was no reason she couldn't be trained a bit, at least in horseback riding.

"Hold on with your knees, Olsa," I said, using a voice I might have used with a girl much younger than she. "Push down with your heels. That will make sure your legs are in the right place."

She bristled at my tone, but followed direction. She wouldn't thank me tomorrow morning, when her whole body clenched with the strain of newly used muscles, but in the long run, her riding would be improved. Her seat was already better.

"That's perfect," I told her. "It's easier for your horse if you sit properly, and then it's easier for you if it's better for the horse. Most knights spend years learning to ride, so don't worry if you're not as good as we are overnight."

"Thank you, your ladyship," she said, voice over-honeyed.

"Kalanthe," I said.

"Do you have a knight-name yet?" she asked. "Or do they give that to you when you win your title officially?"

"We usually have our sobriquet long before that," I said. "We live in close quarters for years, after all."

"So what's yours?" she asked again.

I sighed. It wasn't that my sobriquet was bad, it was just so misleading. I felt it didn't describe me at all, and yet it had met with near-universal approval the first time one of my fellow apprentices had said it.

"Ironheart," I told her, hoping I wouldn't regret it. "Kalanthe Ironheart."

"That's much more suited to ballads than my last name," Olsa said. "There's not a lot that rhymes with Rhetsdaughter."

So she was illegitimate on top of everything else. The gods had given this poor girl no advantages at all, except perhaps her light fingers and her acquaintance with Sir Erris. Maybe that was all she needed. I could help her from here, in any case.

"I don't imagine there will be any ballads about me for a while," I said. "Sir Erris rides to save the king, and that is far more worthy of song than the apprentice and the thief who ride with her."

"You're probably right, Kalanthe." She said my name like it was a secret, a sweet on her tongue. "Now, I know about the godsgem and the Old God and the poisoned king, but if you could tell me about the clues we're following, I would appreciate it. I don't like travelling blind."

I spent the rest of the afternoon telling her the stories and hearthtales about what had become of the godsgem after it had been used on the Old God and laid Him low. She listened to every word I said, asking questions with none of the hesitation I would have felt talking to my teachers, and pointing out logistical errors in the more fantastic of the legends we were hoping held literal truths. At one point, I told a story that contradicted one from earlier in the lecture, and she recited it back to me verbatim to point out the inconsistencies.

"You have an excellent memory," I told her. I could recite lessons with practice, but not the first time I had heard something.

"People rarely tell a thief a thing more than once," she replied. There was the slightest edge to her voice, a challenge I didn't feel like meeting, so I let it pass and kept talking.

The other knights listened, even Sir Terriam, smiling indulgently from time to time, and Mage Ladros did not interrupt, so I supposed I made no errors.

Finally, as the sun was setting, Sir Erris called a halt. We each unsaddled our horses, brushed them, and set them at their pickets, and then turned our attention to setting up camp. Olsa, who, it turned out, had never left the walls of Cadria at all, was quite useless at tent pitching and was dispatched into the forest to collect firewood instead. Given that I knew she was afraid of animals that might lurk there, I was strangely proud of her for doing as she was bid without protest. The rest of us made quick work of our tasks, and Mage Ladros set wards for safety around us so that we would not be surprised in the night.

"Whose turn is it to do the cooking?" Sir Branthear asked, as the last tent peg was driven home.

"Yours," said Sir Uleweya, though I wasn't sure how she'd arrived at that conclusion.

Still, Sir Branthear accepted it and turned to the food packs. Olsa came back with firewood, and soon enough we had dinner in our bellies.

"We'll be making an early start," said Sir Erris, when we were done eating. "You should get to your beds."

The others nodded and drew lots for the watch. I went away from the fire to relieve myself before I went to bed, and when I returned, only Sir Branthear was visible, her naked axe on her knees as she settled in. She nodded at me, and I headed to my tent.

I had set up my sleeping space the way we had been trained, tying the knots on the tent flap the way the knight-masters taught us for use on the trail. They weren't common sailors' knots, adapted as they were for being untied while wearing gauntlets, and it wasn't usual for someone who wasn't a knight to know how to tie them. I knew I had fastened the flap with just that sort of knot, even though there was no real call for it. I also knew that someone had untied it and refastened it almost perfectly. Slowly, I pulled the loop that would release the canvas, and let the light from the campfire spill across the floor.

On my bedroll was a splash of colour. When my eyes adjusted to the dim light of the tent, I saw that it was a single red rose.

Kalanthe still woke early most mornings, but that didn't mean she had to like it. Any time of day, the life of a knight was harder than most she might have chosen, but she only truly had second thoughts when she had to get out of bed before the sun was up. After the Quest, she had been awarded her own rooms in the palace, away from the apprentice barracks. Though she would hold that rank until her birthday, still some months away, the knight-commanders decided that returning her to her previous comrades would be counterproductive for everyone. She studied alone, or with tutors, and practiced arms with Sir Erris. It was meant to be a great honour, her quasi-promotion. It helped if she reminded herself of that when the loneliness set in.

She's always been the odd one out amongst the other apprentices. Most of them came from wealthy families and could pay the knight fees outright. It was an expensive process, and Kalanthe's family was wealthy, but not *that* wealthy. They could not afford armour and horses for her without a loan. Her parents made it clear that they were happy for her, and proud, but everyone knew that she must marry so that the bride-price could be used to pay off the debt. Most of the other apprentice knights had no plans to marry, or at least no plans to marry until much later in their lives. They would spend the years of their knighthoods travelling at the behest of the crown or seeing to their own estates. Kalanthe always felt the weight of her future, and it was heavier than any armour.

Her solution was to be the best. She studied hard and trained hard. She listened to every piece of advice her teachers gave her, and she quickly rose to the top of most of her classes. That was an excellent way to build a reputation, but a terrible way to make close friends, and so Kalanthe had very few of these. It didn't bother her. She was not destined to be a leader of other knights nor would she hope for a position of command in the King's Army. She would be a knight at court, or wherever she and her spouse decided to live. It wasn't particularly glamorous, but Kalanthe was determined to make the best of it.

Then, on that fateful day when Sir Erris had come into the hall where the apprentices took their meals, Kalanthe's life had turned upside down again. When she finally returned to the palace more than a year later, Kalanthe had new scars, new stories, and new skills. None of the other apprentice knights could match her, which meant they didn't often try, and she mostly faced her old classmates in carefully choreographed training duels. So now she waited, agonizingly, for her birthday. Then the king would knight her officially, and she would be free to travel under her own colours. Free, at least, until her wedding.

So she continued to rise early, to dress and brush the grit out of her eyes, and go to the practice field in the hope that Sir Erris would be there to spar with. More often, as the business of court kept the newly married queen away, Kalanthe practiced the bow instead. She was getting distressingly good at it. Soon she would have to take up something new, though what that might be she hadn't the foggiest idea.

On this particular morning, however, Kalanthe didn't make it to the practice field. Instead, as she was tying on her hose and preparing to don the bulky linen undertunic she wore beneath her informal chainmail, there was a knock at the door. She pulled on her tunic, called out, and a messenger came into her room.

"Good morning, Lady Ironheart," said the messenger.

She hated that name, but until they could call her "Sir Kalanthe" she was stuck with it, at least in the palace where formality was studied and practiced. Sir Erris said it spoke of her determination, but Kalanthe knew that wasn't the spirit in which the name had been given. The other apprentices had called her Ironheart when the tutors were around, but alone in the barracks it was always *Ice*heart, and Kalanthe despised it.

"Good morning, page," she replied. Her voice was even and kind. The page had clearly been awake longer than she had, and that meant he deserved the best of courtesy, regardless of his rank in relation to hers.

The boy straightened and puffed out his chest a bit at her manner with him. She was happy to let him. Iceheart indeed.

"I have a message from the magistrate for you, my lady," said the lad, and handed over a sealed note.

Kalanthe was momentarily confused as to what business she and the magistrate could possibly have, but then it dawned on her: the only business they ever had with her. She sighed.

"Thank you, page," she said, and handed the boy two of the tokens he could exchange for coins with the page-master, indication of a job well done. "Please go two doors down from here and fetch my lady's maid. Tell her I'm sorry, but I'll need her immediately this morning."

The lady's maid was a new addition since her return to court. Triana was delightfully practical and good at several things Kalanthe was not, so they got on very well. Kalanthe required no help to get into her training-armour, though, and thus usually let Triana sleep in on the mornings when she got up to practice. Today was not going to be one of those days.

"Yes, my lady." The page bobbed his head and set off at a trot. He was smiling and turning the tokens around in his hand.

When he was gone, Kalanthe shucked the linen tunic and began to untie the hose. Triana arrived just as she was peeling them off and took in her nearly naked mistress with aplomb. That was another thing Kalanthe appreciated about her lady's maid: she had the good sense to ignore Kalanthe's barracks-trained sensibilities.

"What is it, then?" Triana was wearing a simple wool gown overtop the linen shift that served as her nightdress. Her dark blond hair was in a single braid, but not pinned up for sleep.

"The magistrate has summoned me to court," Kalanthe said, and sat down at her dressing table. "I'll need to look the part. And quickly."

"Right," said Triana, and disappeared into one of the larger wardrobes. "Those underthings will do fine, but if you could start combing your hair out, I'd appreciate it."

Kalanthe suppressed a giggle, despite the immediacy of the situation. She was more than capable of dressing herself and taking care of her own hair, but Triana seemed to think she was hopeless at both and was determined to take her in hand. Obediently, Kalanthe picked up a comb and began to untangle her black hair from the braid she'd put it in for the morning's now aborted training session.

By the time she was done, Triana was standing behind her with a suitable collection of clothes, and Kalanthe stood to put them on. Being a knight excused her from some of the fashion of the court women—hoops and tight-laced corsets for starters—but she still had two underskirts overtop her shift, then the dark-grey undergown, then a bodice, and, finally, a sky-blue overgown. It was, Kalanthe had come to understand, armour of a different sort. And it certainly smelled better.

"Sit, please," Triana said, and when Kalanthe was settled, the maid began to do her hair.

The style was simple, like the gown, and lacked ornamentation that would have been unsuitable for both the hour and the solemnity of the king's court of law. Usually Triana wove gold wire or ribbons into Kalanthe's hair—the bright metal highlighting the lustrous black mass of it—but today she settled for coiled braids along the crown of Kalanthe's head.

"I suppose it's too early in the day for face paint," Triana mused, tying off the end of a braid and tucking it into the loop behind Kalanthe's left ear.

"I should think so," Kalanthe said.

She didn't much care for the stuff, but she had to admit that Triana was very good at applying it. It had been the first argument she lost with her new lady's maid, as a point of fact. Triana was determined to show her what was possible with a few well-placed strokes of the makeup brush, and Kalanthe, equally opposed to the idea, had finally acquiesced out of exhaustion. The first time she'd seen her own face with Triana's handiwork, it had nearly taken her breath away. It was undeniably her, but her eyes were so much sharper, her lips more vivid, and her cheeks—

"I left you the scar," Triana had said, her voice almost reverent. "You earned it."

"Thank you," Kalanthe said. "I—I didn't know it could look like this."

"I'll get better, my lady," Triana assured her. "Your colouring is very different from mine, so I'll have to experiment a bit with the powders to get it right."

With several months of experience since then, Triana had found a colour palette to suit her mistress's dark-brown skin. They would not be using it this morning, though.

"Except a bit around the eyes, I think," Triana said thoughtfully.

"Triana—" Kalanthe protested.

"It's early!" Triana said. "You need to look awake."

Part of Kalanthe's training involved learning to pick one's battles. As with the rest of her lessons, she'd been good at that, so she lowered her hands and let Triana work. It didn't take very long, and when the maid was done, Kalanthe could barely tell she was wearing any makeup at all.

"You are very good at this," she said, not for the first time.

"My lady flatters me." Triana smiled. "As if you would go into battle in any state less than complete readiness. Now stand up, so I can straighten the gown, and then you'd better be on your way."

Kalanthe stood as patiently as she could while Triana made the final adjustments. Now that she was ready, Kalanthe's mind was full of the task that waited for her. She hadn't seen Olsa in weeks, not since the last time the thief was arrested. She wondered if Olsa was hurt this time, if she'd finally resisted her arrest. She knew the city watch was frustrated. They did their jobs, but Kalanthe had noticed that Olsa's escorts for her last court appearance were the type who usually guarded violent, unrepentant criminals, and they would not hesitate to rough her up if she gave them the opportunity. She imagined it would be so again today. It was a sure sign that the watch commander's patience was wearing thin, hero of the realm or no.

Quiet fury replaced concern as Kalanthe neared the court-room and heard the buzz of pretrial speculation. Olsa had no reason to keep doing this and yet persisted in breaking the law. She took more and more risks, and when she was arrested she refused to give up her employers. Kalanthe respected loyalty, but she could not condone what Olsa was doing.

Yet, she knew in her heart that condoning it was exactly what she was about to do. She would not let Olsa go to the noose, Ironheart be damned, even if it seemed that Olsa was determined to end up there. Kalanthe chewed on her lower lip as she took her seat at the back of the room in the seats reserved for nobility. She couldn't abandon Olsa, not after the Quest. Not after everything that had happened on the Quest. She wasn't the only one with scars.

The magistrate was on her feet, reading the sentence. Then she paused, and she asked if there was anyone present who would speak for the accused. At least she did Kalanthe the courtesy of not looking at her until she had risen to her feet.

"I will speak for her."

. . . . AFTER . . . .

Olsa knew better than to be smiling when Kalanthe came down to fetch her off the wooden box, but she was so pleased to see her that it was a struggle to keep her face solemn. It wasn't just that Kalanthe had spoken for her freedom, though that was of course very much appreciated. This was the first time Kalanthe had stayed. The previous two times, she'd left the courtroom immediately after her declaration, and Olsa had simply been deposited outside the great wooden doors by the guards and sent on her way.

As the apprentice knight drew near enough for Olsa to see her clearly through the crowd, she clamped down on her burgeoning smile even harder. Kalanthe was furious, though she walked at a measured pace and nodded politely to all the guards and nobles that she passed on her way. It was a gift Olsa did not share: when she felt something, she showed it on her whole body. Kalanthe could keep her fury behind her eyes, where only those who knew to look for it might see. Olsa gave serious consideration to running.

"You." Kalanthe's voice was hard, but her hand shook just a little bit as she pointed at where Olsa stood. "Come with me."

Olsa held out her hands to the guard who stood closest to her, and at Kalanthe's nod, she unlocked the shackles. Freed, she flexed her fingers and rolled her wrists. She hadn't been locked up very long, but her dexterity was her livelihood. She looked at Kalanthe, ready to take her cue.

"This way," Kalanthe said, her voice not softening a whit. "And no talking."

It was going to be like that, apparently, at least until they were out from under the eyes of their less-than-adoring public. Olsa did her best not to sigh. She hadn't expected Kalanthe to embrace her as a sister, but *some* warmth would have been appreciated, considering their history. She matched Kalanthe's steps as best she could, though the apprentice knight was using her stride to its fullest advantage and forcing Olsa to half run to keep up with her. They made their way out of the courtroom, down several corridors, up a twisting stairwell, and finally through a sparsely decorated hallway, lined with sturdy doors. Kalanthe stopped in front of the second-to-last one and opened it, gesturing for Olsa to precede her into the room.

There was a fire burning in the hearth, which made Olsa relax in spite of herself. The walls were lined with shelves, many of which had books on them, along with assorted knickknacks that Kalanthe had collected and kept over the years. There were two comfortable-looking chairs and a small table in front of the fire with a thick rug between them, and a writing desk over by the window with a more utilitarian seat tucked underneath it. There was a covered tray on the small table. Kalanthe moved to the fireplace and picked up a teapot from the warmer by the wood crate.

"Sit down, Olsa," she said, still distant and cold, though Olsa could tell that her fury had abated somewhat. "I don't suppose they gave you breakfast?"

"Not really," Olsa replied. "Is this your office?"

Kalanthe didn't reply but took the cover off the tray. Underneath was breakfast for two, and entirely more food than Olsa had seen in one place for a good long while.

"You might as well eat, then," Kalanthe said. "And it's my sitting room. I don't really need an office yet."

"It's very nice," Olsa said, and then immediately thought about how stupid that sounded.

"Is that your professional opinion?" Kalanthe asked, delicately spreading jam on a piece of toast.

"Don't be silly," Olsa said. "I only meant that it's cozy and it suits you. Besides, there's too many guards to break into the palace."

She attacked her breakfast, and Kalanthe did her the courtesy of staying quiet. Olsa didn't get to eat her fill so often that she wanted to mix food and the interrogation she suspected was coming. Kalanthe poured her a cup of tea.

"If you drink that, you can eat as much as you like and you won't throw up," she said.

Olsa looked up at her, startled, but saw the truth in Kalanthe's eyes. There was kindness there, if no particular sign of affection. Olsa was not so starved that she would accept one in the other's place, but she would accept all help with regard to her digestion. She reached for the tea and downed it before diving back into the bacon and eggs.

"Is it one of yours?" she asked, her mouth full. Kalanthe had never cared about that sort of thing when they were alone.

"Yes," Kalanthe said, a small, proud smile on her face. "It's new, but I've tested it, don't worry."

All magic tasted the same, but Olsa experienced it so infrequently she wondered if she might be especially attuned to Kalanthe's. She felt it at work already, in any case, a warm blanket in her stomach that calmed her innards, even as she packed them full of more food than they usually saw in a week. Kalanthe watched her eat without further comment, her face a blank mask that Olsa detested. Once upon a time, they'd shared nearly everything from feelings to bedrolls to mortal peril. Then Kalanthe had gone back to court and left Olsa to her own ends, and now here they were, eating breakfast in Kalanthe's own room, but talking as though they were only acquaintances.

She was still beautiful, though. The scar on her cheek, the one that Olsa hadn't tackled her in enough time to avoid completely, stood out against her brown skin, but was no longer the angry red of when it had first been inflicted. It looked like it was as much a part of her as her nose or her mouth. Olsa immediately returned her attention to her plate. It didn't do her any good to think too much about Kalanthe's mouth.

"You have to stop, Olsa," Kalanthe said gently when Olsa had finished all the food on the tray. She'd eaten most of Kalanthe's breakfast as well, save for two pieces of toast, but it didn't seem like Kalanthe minded.

"Stop what?" Olsa said, looking down at her empty plate as though she were expecting Kalanthe to tell her she ought to have left a polite portion uneaten.

"Stealing," Kalanthe said. "Thievery, housebreaking, whatever you want to call it. It has to stop."

"Oh, well, in that case I will stop immediately," Olsa said, feeling her temper rise. "If my lady Ironheart bids me to."

"Don't do that, Olsa," Kalanthe said.

She got out of the chair and went to the door. Olsa wondered whether she was going to call for a guard, but Kalanthe only placed both hands on the wood and said a string of words too softly for Olsa to hear them. More magic. The air around them hummed, making all the hair on Olsa's neck stand up, and then Kalanthe came back to her seat.

"There," she said, still as placid as a milk cow. "Now we can yell at each other and no one will hear us."

"That'll preserve your reputation well enough, won't it?" Olsa said. She didn't want to hurt Kalanthe, not exactly, but she couldn't deny the small flare of pleasure she felt when she saw Kalanthe's calm demeanor crack. She'd scored another hit.

"My reputation is not what we're concerned about," Kalanthe said. "We're talking about you. The king stepped in three times to save you from the noose, and now I've stepped in three times as well. How many more times do you think the knight-magistrate will let me? She sent me a note this morning, or I would have missed your trial altogether. What happens if she doesn't do that next time?"

"They won't execute me, Kalanthe," Olsa said. She immediately regretted saying the name. It felt like a memory on her tongue, and she needed a clear head right now. "They can't execute a hero of the realm."

"They can't execute you *publicly*," Kalanthe said. "They can skip the trial or hold it in the dead of night. You'd just disappear, and the people would think you'd gone off to seek your fortune in another city."

Olsa's blood ran cold. She'd heard of such things, of course, or rather, she'd *not* heard of them. Thieves disappeared all the time, with no one the wiser. It only stood to reason that someday the courts would be so frustrated with her they'd just skip the trial outright. And her targets were increasingly high profile. The Thief Bosses weren't exactly setting her up to win.

"What would you suggest I do instead?" Olsa said. "I have no trade and no skills that are particularly marketable, unless the king is ill again."

"Surely you can think of something else to help you capture the thrill of it," Kalanthe said.

"The *thrill* of it?" Something in Olsa hardened. She thought Kalanthe knew her better than that, but apparently the apprentice knight was even more a ladyship than Olsa had ever guessed. "You think I steal for fun?"

"You can't possibly need money already," Kalanthe said. "The king's reward was worth more than that."

"I spent the king's reward immediately, same as you did," Olsa said. "Only instead of paying off part of my debt and hiring a lady's maid to prepare me for paying off the rest, I bought myself out of the Thief's Court."

"What?" This was Kalanthe, the real one, at last. The girl who talked to Olsa when she afraid on the road and kept her as safe as she could while the other knights were busy. This was the Kalanthe that had earned Olsa's loyalty, and more besides.

"They owned me, before, more or less," Olsa said. "And now they don't. I work for them because I want to eat, not because I have to."

Kalanthe was silent. It was true that her part of the king's reward had also gone immediately. She'd used it to pay off a little more than half of her debt. Now she no longer needed to marry a person who was ludicrously wealthy, only someone who was fabulously so.

"I suppose there's one more thing I could sell," Olsa continued. "I imagine there's any number of people who would pay good coin for a few hours with the—"

"Stop it!" Kalanthe said. The magic around them shimmered. "I'm sorry. I didn't know."

"I do what I must, Kalanthe," Olsa said. "The same way you do."

"And what if I'm not here next time?" Kalanthe said. "What then?"

"If you go on a Quest without me, I will murder you," Olsa said, a glimmer of her humour showing through. Kalanthe was unmoved.

"What if I'm married?" There were tears in Kalanthe's eyes. "What if I'm gone to my new home on my spouse's estate."

"Already swelling up with his child?" Olsa said rather indelicately.

"It would be expected," Kalanthe said. Hers would be a marriage for heirs.

It hung there for a long moment between them, both their hurts exposed.

"No one who marries you will expect a normal wife," Olsa said.

"I don't think they'll take too kindly to you hanging around either, though," Kalanthe said. "Olsa, I need you to be safe."

"I'll never be safe," Olsa said. "I was born on the streets and I'll die there, or in the noose. It's only a matter of when."

"I refuse to accept that," Kalanthe said.

"How come your fate is so set and mine is so flexible?" Olsa said. "Why don't we both just run off?"

It wasn't the first time she'd suggested it, but even if it had been, she knew what Kalanthe's answer would be. Kalanthe wouldn't leave the court and her family, and Olsa wouldn't leave her apprentice knight. Ironheart, they called her. More like Iron*head*.

"You know I can't, love." Kalanthe said the word like she always did, like it was as easy as breathing.

The breaking part of Olsa's chest broke a little more. Then she drew herself up.

"Thank you for the breakfast and the pardon, lady," she said. "Would you summon a page to show me to the gate?"

Kalanthe went to the door and broke the spell. A page arrived, carrying the sealskin cape Olsa had entered the prison with. She was glad to see it again. When they took it from her this morning, she wasn't sure that it would be returned. She took it from him and hesitated. It really was much too small.

"Would you please see that this is returned to Mina, the gem merchant's daughter?" she said. "And please give her my thanks."

Kalanthe took it from her and folded it over one arm. Her expression was measured, and Olsa knew it well. She was attempting to determine how much help Olsa would allow.

"I will," she said. "Only let me find you something more suitable for you in return. It's still cold out."

When Olsa left the palace by the main gate, under the scornful eyes of the guards, she was warmly wrapped in a cloak of her own size, but lost and confused within it.

BEFORE. . . . .

We were more than a month at the inn. Erris and Ladros rode north on some finicky errand of history and lore, and took Sir Branthear with them, as she was a scholar of both in her spare time. Also, she was the only other member of our party who was uninjured. We'd been attacked by demons of the Old God's making on the road, and they'd got us almost as good as we got them back. Terriam had a mind-wound, which Ladros said could have happened to anyone, but which Terriam was taking very personally. Uleweya cracked three ribs, and Kalanthe turned her ankle scrambling to aid Terriam in the mud. I was unharmed, but honest enough to admit that I was pleased not to be dragged through the forest. Lucky numbers were well and good, but they didn't do much when more than half your party couldn't ride. So we found a nice place to wait and settled in.

The first week was agony. Terriam was sound of body but had difficulty sleeping, even with the numbing tea that Ladros had left for her. She didn't wake the whole inn with screaming every night, but she certainly woke us; and then there was nothing that would do but for Kalanthe to try some of her own magic to get the knight back to sleep. Uleweya was grouchy about her inactivity, so I mostly left her alone. That meant I spent a lot of time with very little to do in the room I shared with Kalanthe.

Our quarters were simple enough: a hearth, a chest, a small table for the washbasin, and two narrow beds; but it was clean and the walls were newly whitewashed. Had we been with the whole party, we might have been consigned to a smaller room or even the attic; but since there were only two people at the inn who outranked Kalanthe, we had a better billet than usual. It was a blessing in disguise, I supposed, though some disguise: I missed the road and our companions. The unending boredom was making me as restless as Uleweya, though I imagined I was something less of a bear about it.

Tonight, Kalanthe was practicing some sort of magical technique that looked a lot like sleeping while she was sitting up, and I knew I should give her some peace, but my feet itched and I couldn't stay still.

"Why don't you borrow a book from the innkeeper?" she snapped, as I paced the room for the thousandth time. "She has a large enough collection."

"I can't read," I told her. I wasn't ashamed of it. Very few people I knew could read. On the street you were better served by your memory than by a book. I could list the names, addresses, and guild-rank of every craftsperson in Cadria, but I couldn't write them down. It was safer that way, for starters.

"Oh," she said. "I'm sorry, I forgot."

She got up and went to her saddlebags. I had spread my few belongings out across the floor on my half of the room, but Kalanthe's things were all organized, neat as a pin, though I noticed that she'd left yesterday's hose balled up under her bed.

"It's all right," I told her, as she rummaged in her pack. "I'll find something else to do that won't disturb you. I know I've been restless."

"Come and sit here," she said, returning to her bed with the small notebook she carried and one of her charcoal writing sticks. "I can show you the alphabet."

And that was how it started. For two weeks, we sat together, closer than touch, with our heads bent over her papers. She was very impressed by how quickly I picked up the basics of letters and the sounds they made, but I stalled almost immediately whenever I tried to read an actual book.

"It's probably the printing," she said, as she listened to me stumble through a passage about goat farming. The innkeeper had a lot of books, but they were pretty tedious.

"Your handwriting is much easier for me," I admitted. I set the book down and stared into the fire. Fire was so wonderful when it was always around to keep me warm.

"When I learned to read, it was with simpler books than these," she said. "And the writing in them was much clearer. I think you're doing very well."

"Thank you, my lady," I said, and she giggled as she always did when I rubbed her nobility in her face.

It was easy enough to forget it, most of the time, even though her very bearing gave away her birthright. She never spoke down to me, and whenever there was something I didn't know, she explained it without being patronizing. I didn't know how we would fare in a real house or in polite company, but on the road or in this inn, she was happy enough to be my friend, and I was happy to have her.

She never mentioned the rose. I'd stumbled on it in the woods collecting firewood right after she'd shown me what rosebushes looked like. I had wondered briefly why this rose had bloomed when none of the others had, and then I'd picked it to bring back and show her. For whatever reason, though, my courage had failed me. I couldn't just give her the rose and had instead resorted to subterfuge. It made a pretty splash of colour inside her tent, but she never said a word about it, and now I didn't know where I stood.

Tarvy, one of the boys who worked for the Thief Bosses like I did, said that I was only confused about girls because I spent so much time pretending to be a lad. I thought he was wrong. Surely I liked whomever I liked, whether I was wearing trousers or a skirt. Trousers were only safer in the city and more practical for riding in the country. What I wore had nothing to do with what I felt.

And anyway, Kalanthe wore trousers too, when she wasn't wearing armour. Everyone in our party did, except Terriam, who wore leggings and a rather magnificent leather dress. Its bodice was reinforced with steel plates, while the skirt had side slits that reached well above her boots, and laces that could be left open at the front and back for riding.

At the end of the second week of reading lessons, Terriam and Uleweya were well enough to join us in our boredom. Uleweya decreed reading was well and good, but we mustn't let Kalanthe's physical training slide either, so every morning all four of us went out into the courtyard. I would have been perfectly content to watch them hit one another with blunted practice swords, but Terriam insisted that I be taught hand-to-hand combat, as it was unlikely I would ever carry a sword.

"I could just run away from trouble," I told her. She was squaring my shoulders so that my stance was better. It felt very unnatural.

"You can't run away from everything all the time," she said. "Besides, what if there's something or someone you want to help?"

"You're going to teach me all kinds of noble bad habits," I said. Kalanthe, who was watching us while Uleweya went for drinking water, laughed.

Terriam ignored that and proceeded to teach me all kinds of ways to escape the hold of someone bigger and stronger than I was. By the time we moved on to actual fighting, I paired off with Kalanthe while the knights sparred against each other. They moved in deliberate patterns, and I realized that this form of practice was less about hitting the other person and more about making sure your own body remembered the movements absolutely. I could do some of the acrobatics well enough from my own body's memory, but incorporating combat was a challenge. Knighthood took a lot of work.

So did hand-to-hand. I was hopelessly overmatched against Kalanthe, but she took it easy on me and only dumped me in the dirt six or eight times before the innkeeper's wife took pity, and called us all in for lunch.

"Did I bruise you too much?" Kalanthe said, as I concentrated on eating as much bread as I possibly could. I wanted to eat enough to last forever.

"No," I said around a mouthful. "At least I don't think so."

"Don't interrupt her while she's eating, lass," Uleweya said. "She's missed enough meals as it is."

After lunch, when it was time for the reading lesson, Kalanthe made me stretch first. It felt ridiculous, but she promised me that it would help me be less sore tomorrow.

"Is knight training entirely about pain, then?" I asked her.

"It's about getting you ready for pain, I think," she replied. "Of all sorts. Now, shall we find out what sort of goat prospers best in fields of clover?"

I sighed, pretending great reluctance, but sitting next to her was no trial, even if the words on the page were a constant grief to me. By the time it grew too dark to read, my muscles were starting to stiffen.

"It'll be worse in the morning," she said. "But as soon as you start to move again, it'll feel better. And once your body is used to it, you won't notice it at all."

"I hate knights," I told her.

"Sometimes I do too," she said, and put out the candle so that we could go to sleep.

In the morning, I woke very early to blinding stomach cramps and blood everywhere.

"Kalanthe!" I said, as loudly as I could. She slept like the dead and hated mornings even though she always got up as soon as the sun rose. "Kalanthe!"

"What?" she said, rolling over and rubbing her eyes.

"Is it possible that when you hit me yesterday, you broke something inside of my stomach?" I asked.

She was fully awake in an instant and sitting on the side of her bed.

"What?" she said again.

"There's blood," I said. "And my stomach hurts."

She looked at me and then down at the bed. She leaned forward and sniffed delicately, then blew on her fingers and pointed them at the mess. She was doing magic.

"Olsa, it's only your monthly blood," she said, as if that cleared up everything.

"My what?" I asked.

"Your—" she started, and then stopped. "Oh, Olsa. Come on, let's go to the bathhouse. Bring the sheet."

I followed her down the stairs as quietly as I could, and we crept into the bathhouse. The tubs were full, but it was going to be very cold. Kalanthe stuck a hand into one of the largest ones and said a single word. Instantly, there was steam in the air.

"Get in," she said. "Tell me if it's too hot. Sometimes I do too much."

"It's perfect," I said, after I stripped down and did what she told me to. "Now please tell me what is happening."

With her typical bluntness, Kalanthe described what was going on between my legs.

"What I don't understand is why it's taken so long," she said at the end of her explanation. "You're, what, almost seventeen?"

"Sixteen, I think," I said. "I'm not really sure."

"Most of the apprentices got theirs when they were fourteen, myself included," she said.

"Most of the apprentices eat three meals a day with regularity." Uleweya stepped close enough that we could see her. Neither of us had heard her come into the bathhouse. "I'm a light sleeper, and not everyone is as quiet as Olsa when it comes to going down the stairs in a hurry."

Kalanthe flushed.

"You mean I'm playing catch-up?" I asked, returning to Uleweya's original point. "What other surprises do I have in store?"

Kalanthe looked down at her own chest, and her skin flushed even darker. Uleweya laughed. I sighed.

I stayed in the tub while Kalanthe went back up to our room for something she'd forgotten, and Uleweya went to see if the innkeeper's wife had started the breakfast yet. I floated in the hot water, amazed at all the ways in which the world surprised me.

"I got you something," Kalanthe called out as she returned. "It's mine, so it's not new, but now it's yours."

"Why?" I asked.

"It's tradition," she said, waving a hand. "Now open it."

She had wrapped the small package very quickly in one of the rags she used to polish her mail. I handed the rag back to her, careful not to get it wet. Inside was a lovely steel box with inlaid blue stones I hoped to the gods weren't actually sapphires, but probably were. I had never held anything so valuable that I would get to keep. I opened the box.

"Tea?" I said, recognizing the leaves if not the smell.

"Yes," she said. "It keeps the blood from coming. It also keeps you from carrying a child, but honestly I think the first part is more important for a woman of action such as yourself, eh?"

"Do you drink it?" I asked.

"Of course I do," she said. "We all do, except Sir Branthear."

"Why not Sir Branthear?" I asked, closing the box and setting it on the shelf with my drying cloth.

Kalanthe paused and, for the first time since I'd known her, was at a loss for words.

"You don't have to tell me," I said.

"Oh, it's just that I thought you knew. She doesn't keep it a secret," Kalanthe said. "I'm not sure how to say it best."

I waited while she thought her way through it. Hot water made everything better, even waiting.

"When Sir Branthear was born, there was some . . . confusion," she said finally.

"Confusion?" I said.

"Well, it would be rude to say she was born wrong, since she wasn't." Kalanthe said it very quickly, as though she were angry with herself for even thinking it in the first place. "Only when the physician and midwife first saw her, they thought she was male. It wasn't until she was old enough to tell them herself that they realized they had made a mistake, and that she was a woman."

"You mean she—" I stopped, and looked down at my own body. "It's none of my business."

"No," Kalanthe agreed.

I turned it over in my head a few more times and realized that absolutely nothing about my perception of Branthear had changed while I did it. There were several thieves in the Thief's Court who were men or women depending on who was looking at them, and a few others who never put their trousers off after their bodies changed. It made sense that there were knights who were the same way.

"The world is very big," I said at last. Then I grinned at Kalanthe, and she smiled back at me. "I like it."

"Get out of the tub before you prune," she said. "I'll show you how to line your underthings until the tea kicks in."

Kalanthe spent the rest of the morning in her sitting room reading a book on the history of spoke-word magic. She lived in hope that someday Mage Ladros or one of his fellows would come back from the Mage Keep and resume her training, and she didn't want to be too far behind in her studies when they did. Still, she found it difficult to focus on the pages as she turned them. Once, Olsa had been the easiest person in the world to talk to, and Kalanthe had told her all sorts of things. She didn't like that they had become so awkward with each other. It wasn't fair.

She kept wrestling with the book and her own mind until just before lunch when the door opened, and Triana came in. Kalanthe set down the book, about to remark that she wasn't hungry yet, but she saw that Triana carried no tray.

"What is it?" she asked.

"The queen has asked to see you," Triana said. "She wants you to take lunch with her."

Kalanthe looked down at the dress she was wearing and brushed some errant threads off it. While it was suitable for a morning at the court of law followed by reading, it wouldn't do for a royal audience, even if Sir Erris was more comfortable as a knight than as a queen.

"Do your worst, then," Kalanthe said, and put herself entirely at her maid's mercy.

Triana's taste was as impeccable as her sense of decorum, and in short order, Kalanthe found herself back at her dressing table, sitting in her grey undergown while Triana redid her hair. The style was mostly the same, but Triana threaded gold chains through each braid so that Kalanthe's hair glimmered when the light struck it. She painted Kalanthe's eyes with deep red powder and lined them with kohl. At last, Kalanthe stood while Triana tied a new overdress onto her. This one was a more complicated style and was dyed the same deep red as the powder on her eyes.

"Well?" Triana said. "What do you think? I only just finished making it, but I saw the fabric in the market the other day, and you had the budget for it, so I couldn't resist."

The dress didn't just match her eye makeup. It matched her scar too. Kalanthe raised a hand to touch the mark that ran across her cheek and down her neck, but then stopped, afraid of mussing any of Triana's work. Olsa had not been entirely wrong about the full breadth of Triana's responsibilities when it came to making Kalanthe presentable. When she'd moved out of the barracks, she'd lost access to the common laundry and servants that the apprentices shared. However, if Kalanthe had wanted a servant, she could have hired nearly anyone. She'd hired a lady's maid instead, and it was Triana's job to dress her for the king's court, keeping *all* her future prospects in mind.

"They are going to remember who you are and what you've done, my lady," said Triana fiercely. "Even if I have to rub it in their faces for the rest of your life."

The knights could speak for themselves. The Mage didn't need anyone to speak of him at all. And Kalanthe apparently had the undying loyalty of her maid. A thought came to her, like a bolt of lightning, that Olsa had no one to speak for her, unless it was Kalanthe herself. She didn't think she was doing a particularly good job, but before she could consider it further, Triana was pulling on her hem, straightening the laces on her back, and shoving her out the door.

"Remember you saved her life," whispered her maid, as she always did when Kalanthe's nerves flared before a meeting with Sir Erris. "As much as she saved the king's."

As much as Olsa saved mine, Kalanthe added, but only in her own head, where it didn't do anyone any good.

Once she was in the hallway, Kalanthe focused her attention on not tripping over the new gown. Triana always dressed her for the queen regardless of who else was going to be in the audience, and today was no exception. Usually, Erris took luncheon in private, in one of the gardens, or in her receiving room. Since Kalanthe had not been given a location, she knew the meal was to be served in the queen's own chambers. Erris ate there often enough that it didn't raise too many eyebrows, and it gave her the opportunity to eat as a knight, not as a queen. The rooms were also on the other side of the palace from where Kalanthe was quartered, so she wasted no time.

There were plenty of people about at this time of day. In the lower halls, she passed many pages and upper servants, all of whom had a smile or a polite nod for her. In the more formal halls of the palace proper, she passed guards, who ignored her completely, and other nobles, who she rather wished would do the same. Instead, they would look at her coldly and then turn to one another to whisper behind raised fans. The kindest of them would think her an object of pity, a poor little apprentice knight who must marry as soon as possible to pay off her debt. The cruelest of them would say she was a hanger-on, a scavenger of the queen's goodwill, and, worse, no better than she ought to be.

The guards at the bottom of the queen's tower let her pass without word, and Kalanthe relaxed to be beyond the scrutiny of the members of the court. She lifted her skirts to climb the stairs, and when she reached the solar, she knocked on the door.

"Come in, Kalanthe!" Sir Erris's voice was still more suited for a parade ground than for the palace, and it heartened Kalanthe to hear it.

She pushed the door open and was immediately enfolded in a hug, as the queen greeted her.

"Be careful, Erris," said an unexpected voice. "The girl's all done up to see the queen. Don't make a mess of her."

"Sir Branthear!" said Kalanthe, in happy surprise, for there she sat, and the table was set for three. Then she remembered herself and bowed. "Sir Erris."

"Still so formal," said Sir Branthear, her eyes dancing with mirth.

"Don't remind me," said Sir Erris, sitting down again. "It took me months to get her to stop calling me 'highness.'"

If the courtiers in the royal palace doubted Kalanthe's right to a place there, Sir Erris never had. Though Erris was as bound by the law as anyone until Kalanthe's next birthday, she made it abundantly clear that Kalanthe was to be treated with the same respect as was given to the other knights. This, of course, was probably the cause of much of the nobles' resentment, but there was nothing to be done for it now.

"What a striking gown," Branthear said. "It's perfect for your colouring and it fits you astoundingly."

"My lady's maid is very possessive," Kalanthe said.

"I knew she'd do well by you," Erris said. "Her mother is one of my seamstresses and helps keep me in line, so I knew her daughter would do the same for you."

"And she knows her way around chainmail," Kalanthe said. "Or at least she was willing to learn. I think she likes to think of everything as armour anyway."

Every time the queen summoned Kalanthe, she had a fit of nerves that this would be the time when Sir Erris started to treat her differently. Like a subject or a child. It never happened, of course, but Kalanthe couldn't quite dispel that last bit of fear that it would someday. It was, therefore, a relief as always to fall into easy conversation with former companions, as though they were still on the road and their relationships were not overcomplicated by station. Plus, in the palace they had the added advantage of not being pursued by the Old God's demons, which invariably made conversation difficult.

"I heard you spoke for Olsa again this morning," Sir Erris said. She was passing out a tray of sandwiches, and Kalanthe froze halfway to picking one.

"She was arrested at a gem merchant's house," Kalanthe said. "The magistrate sent for me. I don't think she wants to see Olsa punished any more than I do, but she won't stop."

"*Won't?*" said Sir Branthear, who was always too intelligent. Her eyes were on Kalanthe's scar, which stood out vividly against her skin, thanks to the highlight of the dress.

"Either way, she's still working for the Thief Bosses," Kalanthe said. "And they don't seem reluctant to take advantage of her folk-hero status."

"You think they're setting her up?" Sir Erris asked.

"I think they're being reckless with her," Kalanthe said. "And she's letting them because those are the only jobs she can get and she needs to stay in with them who have always fed and housed her, even though they don't care if she hangs any more than they used to."

"And now she has an escape hatch," Branthear said.

"Some escape hatch," Kalanthe said. "We got lucky this time. Who knows how it will go in the future, and I have no other solutions to offer up. I can't afford to take her into my household."

She had only offered that once, willing to add to her own debt if she had to, to keep Olsa safe. It hadn't gone over very well.

"You think I didn't try that?" Sir Erris said. "She wouldn't come."

Kalanthe didn't imagine that Sir Erris's attempt had gone any better than her own. Olsa tended to ignore everyone's rank unless she wanted something, and she certainly didn't want to be made the object of charity.

"I don't know what to do," Kalanthe said. She looked at the sandwiches and wondered what Olsa was having for lunch. She probably wasn't having lunch at all, and Kalanthe hadn't even tried to send her off with anything. "What if the next time, I'm not here?"

There was a long pause, and Branthear and Erris exchanged a look. Then Erris set down her serviette and became much more queenlike than Kalanthe was used to.

"Kalanthe, I've had a letter from your father, and I shared it with Branthear because I wasn't entirely sure what to do," she said. "I hope you don't mind. Your father had asked for my advice. I don't think he meant for me to tell you either, but Branthear and I are in agreement that you deserve as much information as possible."

Kalanthe looked back and forth between them. She couldn't imagine what her father could possibly write to the queen about. And then, of course, she could.

"There's been an offer, Kalanthe," said Sir Erris. Her voice was very quiet and a little sad. "For your hand."

The axe in Kalanthe's hands was dull, but it still rang out cacophonously when she locked hafts with Sir Branthear. The discordant sounds should have set her teeth on edge, but she was in the practice circle and she was quite at home there. Another strike, and Sir Branthear pulled her into a clinch. Without hesitation, Kalanthe dropped her elbow into the older knight's gut. It wouldn't have worked if Branthear had been wearing plate armour, but both of them were practicing in chainmail this morning. Branthear loosened her grip as the air whooshed out of her lungs, and Kalanthe danced free.

"Well done, Ironheart," Branthear said. She was grinning beneath her helmet, and Kalanthe knew the praise was heartfelt.

They didn't call Sir Branthear "Stonehand" for nothing, though, and before long Kalanthe was on her heels again, dodging formidable blows and trying to keep her footing in the mud of the practice circle. At last, the training bell sounded, and both the knight and the apprentice put up their blades.

There was a rousing round of applause from the observation benches. They'd attracted quite an audience. Kalanthe looked over and saw not only Sir Erris and a few other knights, but also several classes of apprentices, who were waiting for their own turns to spar.

"Thank you," she panted, low enough that only Branthear heard her.

"Anytime, my friend," Branthear replied.

The bout had been Sir Branthear's own suggestion, part as a way to ascertain Kalanthe's fitness and part to help her work through her thoughts. They'd been in discussion with the queen for a long time on the previous day, and by the time Kalanthe had gone to bed, not even Triana could cheer her up. Axe fighting required a clear head, and Kalanthe was happy for the distraction.

Sir Branthear made her way over to the knights, while Kalanthe went to get her own things. The bench she'd left them on was surrounded by apprentices, and Kalanthe steeled herself to talk to them.

"Ho, Kalanthe," said a boy by the name of Davorous. "That was impressive."

"Hello, Dav," Kalanthe said. "Thank you."

Immediately, she wondered if he would resent her overfamiliarity with him. They had once vied for top spot in the apprentice classes, until she'd been selected for the Quest. At the time, Davorous had been upset enough to say that the only reason Kalanthe was selected over him was because of her sex.

The truth was that they were evenly matched, except that Dav had no debt hanging over his head and was therefore not as desperate as Kalanthe was.

"Gods, I can't even imagine standing in the same ring as Lady Stonehand," Davorous said. Apparently, he had made peace with himself. "I think she'd just look at me and I'd crack."

"I nearly cracked the first time," Kalanthe admitted. It hadn't been one of her finest moments. Olsa had laughed for almost an hour.

Davorous helped her peel off her gauntlets, and one of the younger girls that Kalanthe didn't know passed her a cup of water. She splashed most of it on her face.

"They ought to just knight you and get it over with, age be damned," Dav declared. There was a murmur of agreement behind him, though they all looked cautiously in the direction of Sir Erris to make sure they weren't being overheard.

"She doesn't want to be a knight ahead of schedule, Dav." This was Lede, a tall girl with a build so willowy it was hard to imagine her in plate armour at all, until you were facing her across the pitch, and then you'd better be able to move. "We don't all get to follow our hearts, like Sir Erris."

Lede's remark was met with silence, as the apprentices shifted around her. Only a few of them were also due for marriage to pay their debt, and everyone in Kalanthe's year who faced such a future was male. It was slightly more dignified for them, if only because the getting of heirs required much less physical effort if you were a boy.

Heirs were the problem Kalanthe feared most. She could handle a marriage, she was pretty sure. She didn't have a lot of close friends, but that was mostly circumstance. She'd always considered herself approachable and easy to talk to. She could keep accounts, and she was sure she'd learn to run a household as quickly as she'd learned to do everything else. But heirs, well, that was another matter.

The apprentices were called off to their own practice and bid Kalanthe farewell. Having nothing else to do, she stayed on the bench watching them as they trained, but before long, her thoughts drifted back to the queen's sitting room. It was a far cry from the mud and sweat of the practice yards, but Kalanthe couldn't get it out of her head.

"Who is he?" she'd asked after the queen told her of the offer. She was so glad she was hearing this from Sir Erris and not from her father.

"Sir Edramore of Lycenia," Sir Erris said.

"Do you know him?" Kalanthe said. The name was unfamiliar to her.

"He's my cousin by marriage," Sir Branthear had said. "I can't say I know him well now, but we were children together."

"So he's older," Kalanthe said.

"Just past thirty," Sir Erris said, her voice very soft. "But, Kalanthe, that's not everything."

"His first wife died in childbed," Sir Branthear said. "She gave birth to a living daughter, their second."

"Two?" Kalanthe felt fear for the first time.

"The girls are five and eight," Erris said.

"I don't know anything about children," Kalanthe said. She had faced down the Old God's altar. She would not give in to panic now, even though it threatened to crash over her in waves.

Sir Erris stood and came around the table. She sank down and took Kalanthe's hands in her own. This wasn't right at all. The queen shouldn't kneel to an apprentice knight.

"Kalanthe, the girls are why he wants you," she said. "You would marry him, but you would stay at court to oversee their knighthoods."

"Edramore stays mostly on his own estates," Branthear said. "He keeps the law there and does a good bit of the farming himself, according to rumour. By all accounts, he's a good man and a good father, but he doesn't like court life at all. He'd want you to take care of his daughters, and aside from that, he'd give you space."

"Space I have," she'd said, spurred to emotion at last. Only, instead of panic, it was fury. She quelled it immediately, and when she spoke again, it was with staid resignation. "*Space* is just another word for loneliness, but I knew what I was getting into."

Erris looked at her with something uncomfortably close to pity.

"No, you didn't," Branthear said.

Branthear was right: Kalanthe had known that women of the station to which she must marry were required to have heirs of the body. She had known how heirs were got. She had known the parts of her heart that wanted knighthood. She had not known the full meaning of her sacrifice, and she had not known that when she was grown, her heart would beat only for other women.

The offer should have come directly to the queen, who served as guardian for all the apprentice knights, not through her father. Yet her father would have been approached if Kalanthe were any other young girl—too young yet to sign a contract without a witness. She saw that Sir Edramore was covering all his bases, leaving no piece of etiquette to question. She admired thoughtfulness, but wasn't sure how she felt about such a careful application of it when it concerned manipulating her own future. Surely, the court would notice, and then the court would talk, and Kalanthe hadn't yet decided how she felt about any of it.

She didn't remember asking to be excused, didn't remember anything until she was at the bottom of the stairs, passing the guards to go back into the main palace. Though it might have appeared she was wandering aimlessly through the corridors, Kalanthe was not at all surprised when she'd ended up standing in front of the Lady Herald's office, and the clerk there had been only too happy to hand over all relevant records she requested without question.

Sir Edramore of Lycenia, it turned out, was everything that Sir Erris said of him. His arable lands were vast—the source of much of his wealth—and his people seemed to like him. According to the anonymous annotations on the papers, some of the court-iers thought he was aloof, but Kalanthe suspected that he was, instead, too practical to care what they thought of him and indifferent to their opinions. There was, in Kalanthe's experience, little that courtiers hated more. As a man, she rather respected him. As a husband, she was unsure. She left the office with no firmer sense of what she wanted, and went back to her rooms.

She'd only been alone for a few moments when Branthear arrived. Kalanthe didn't know if she'd been followed, and frankly she didn't care.

"At least he'd leave you alone in the bedroom," Branthear had said. They'd been sitting in silence for hours at that point, Kalanthe too numb to even pretend to read, and Branthear apparently content to wait her out.

"What makes you think I want to be alone in the bedroom?" she'd fired back.

"I only meant that he wouldn't try to wheedle you into doing something you wouldn't like and then claim it was marriage rights," Branthear said. "What you do in your bedroom is your own business."

"Not if I'm married, it isn't," Kalanthe said.

Branthear had snorted, surely thinking her naïve, but Kalanthe looked at her sharply.

"I won't swear an oath and then overturn it, just because my husband is leagues away," she said. "Besides, I can't stand being the focus of rumour."

"Lady Ironheart, you are too good for this wretched world, I think," Sir Branthear had said, holding up her hands in defeat. Then she had suggested an early ending to their evening of contemplation, followed by axe fighting in the morning, and Kalanthe had agreed to just get some time to herself.

A particularly loud victory whoop pulled Kalanthe's attention back to the present. Lede had got the better of Davorous and spilled the lad on his rump in the mud. She waited for him to concede, then reached down to pull him up. Soon they'd be adults under the law, as she would, only they had no blade hovering above their heads.

Sir Erris, seeming to appear from nowhere, dropped down onto the bench beside her, and grabbed Kalanthe's sleeve so that she couldn't rise and bow.

"The worst part about talking marriage with me, is that my life worked out sickeningly well," she said. "I know it, the king knows it, and they will write ballads about it for generations. I'm sorry, but I want to help you, even if it's just a way to figure out your thoughts."

"I'm supposed to rescue other people," Kalanthe said. "I'm a knight, or I will be as soon as it's my birthday. I'm not supposed to be the one that needs saving."

"The king and I have spoken about doing away with debt-knights," Sir Erris said. "The problem we keep running into is that if only the rich can afford to be knights, then only the rich will *be* knights. Not only will we lose out on talented people like yourself, but it exacerbates the very sort of class difference that already plagues the realm."

"I'm glad you're trying," Kalanthe said. "If only knighthood wasn't so damned expensive."

"Horses don't feed themselves," Sir Erris said ruefully. "And good steel is worth it."

"I know," Kalanthe said. "And I wouldn't change it, even if I could. Think about what I would have missed."

"I do," Sir Erris said quite solemnly. "And so does the king, who would be missing a wife, even if his own health had been restored."

Kalanthe looked at her hands, ever reluctant to admit the part she had played.

"Do you think people are meant to be lessons?" Kalanthe asked, after a moment. "That you're a lesson in how to follow your heart, and Sir Branthear is a lesson in how to be yourself, and I'm a lesson in how to be a human disaster."

"I think people show us what we need to see," Sir Erris said. "The important thing is to remember that they are more than what we think they are, every time. We must look past what we need to see and find the truth of them."

"If you have any other advice, I am ready to hear it," Kalanthe said. "I'm sorry I wasn't yesterday. Even though I knew it was coming, it was still something of a shock."

"That's why I wanted to tell you myself," Sir Erris said. "I thought it might be easier for you to hear."

The two for them sat silent for a few moments, watching the apprentices spar. Sir Branthear moved among them, correcting posture and hand placement, and occasionally swatting lightly at heads that were too turned by her presence.

"I miss the road too, sometimes, you know," Sir Erris said. "Even with how things turned out, there was a simplicity to it. Mind the horses, plan the route, defend the rear. All straightforward, and the company was good."

"I miss Olsa," Kalanthe said quietly. It felt like breaking a promise she hadn't even made yet.

"I know," Sir Erris said.

Branthear traded blows with Lede, who looked so excited by the attention she might split in two. Davorous cheered when she landed the final stroke of the pattern.

"Meet with him," Sir Erris said. "Don't agree to his proposal outright, not until you've met him and the girls. Judge their aptitude for apprenticeship and his for marrying, and then decide."

"Thank you, Sir Erris," Kalanthe said, as the queen got up to go back to her knights.

It was only much later that Kalanthe realized that while the queen had been giving her advice, her friend been giving her instructions on how best to stall.

We had been on the road for six months when, on a quiet night in the eastern wastes that stretch to the world's edge, Sir Uleweya sat down abruptly behind Olsa and took her head between her hands. Her grip immediately gentled once Olsa was caught, and I saw Olsa relax into her hold; wariness I hadn't realized she carried melting from her.

"What are you doing with your hair, lass?" she said.

"I don't know," Olsa said. "It's longer, so I tied it up. I don't have a shiny hat to keep it under."

"Have you always worn it short?" I asked. I'd given thought to short hair myself, on the grounds that it was less likely to catch in my mail. When we'd first started our training, one of our tutors had shown us how to braid long hair into a weapon or how to wrap it under a cap, which made it workable enough.

"Yes," Olsa said. "It helps keep it free of lice."

"You'll have to do something with it now, or cut it off again," Uleweya said. "These tangles will be difficult very quickly."

Olsa would have drawn her knife then and there, but I put my hand on her wrist.

"I could show you how to braid it," I offered.

Uleweya hummed, then shook her head.

"No, Kalanthe, I will do it," she said. "Olsa's hair is more like mine than it is like yours. The braiding is different."

"Olsa?" I asked. She hadn't said anything, so I thought she might still want to cut it and didn't want to be impolite in turning down Uleweya's kindness.

"That would be much appreciated, Sir Knight," Olsa said quietly.

She only talked like that when she was overcome with emotion and was trying to conceal it. It happened irregularly, but often enough that I knew the signs. Uleweya knew them too, having witnessed it before when she'd given Olsa one of her knives.

"Very well, then," she said. Her tone was business as usual, but her eyes betrayed deeper feelings: a camaraderie of sorts, though not the kind that springs up amongst peers. "I'll show you how to do them tonight because it's still short enough to be difficult, and when we redo them, you can try it for yourself. It'll be easier if we do it after you wash your hair, but we don't have time for that now."

"Do I need to redo them every morning?" Olsa said.

"These braids are resilient," Uleweya said. "They don't fray like Kalanthe's."

"I like Kalanthe's braid," Olsa said.

"It's lovely, but it won't work for you or me," Uleweya said. "Don't move, I have to fetch some oil."

I watched while she combed oil into Olsa's hair. Even the way she used a comb was different, though I could see why. If Olsa tried to handle her hair the way I did, the comb would probably get stuck. Then, Uleweya separated Olsa's hair into sections and began to braid. Over the course of the next two hours, the hair was shaped into neat rows that ran diagonally across the top of Olsa's head. Uleweya was patient, even as Olsa began to fidget, and all of our camp chores were mysteriously completed without us.

"When it's longer we'll do them straight backwards so you don't wind up with all your hair behind one ear," Uleweya said. "But for now we can be fancy."

I looked at Uleweya's head. I couldn't usually see the top of it, either because she wore her helmet or because she was so tall, but now I could see her own braids, much thicker than Olsa's, and how they caught at the nape of her neck to become one thick one.

"Can you braid a spiked strap into your braid the way I do?" I asked. It was self-defense in case someone grabbed my hair in a fight. They would get a nasty surprise.

"I can and I do," Uleweya said. "I don't think Olsa needs one yet, though."

"It may be handy in the city," Olsa said. "All this healthy living you keep forcing on me has given me more of a figure than I used to have. I'll be more of a target when I go home."

"There," said Uleweya, finishing the last braid. I needed string to hold mine together, but Olsa's stayed with nothing. "Don't poke at them too much. And let me know if they're too tight. And wrap your head in a scarf when you go to sleep."

"Yes, sir," Olsa said, and Uleweya went back to her tent.

"Do you really think you'll go back to the streets when we get home?" I asked. I rarely questioned the certainty of our success.

"Where else would I go?" she replied.

I was quiet, looking up at the stars. There were so many of them here, without the lights of Cadria to block my view of them. I tried to remember Mage Ladros's lessons about the different kinds of stars, and the stories behind the names of the constellations; but all I could think about was Olsa, alone again once the Quest was done.

"I don't have that much to look forward to when we're done either," I told her.

"I thought you wanted to be a knight," she said.

"I do, more than anything," I said. "I love everything about it, even the hard parts."

"Then what's not to like about your future?" she asked.

"Being a knight is expensive," I told her. "My family couldn't afford it for me, even though I was clearly good at it, and had magic besides. We're not wealthy the way that some nobles are, and so I had to secure a loan. When I'm knighted, I'll have to pay it back."

"How?" Olsa was running a hand absently over her head, poking at the braids despite Uleweya's admonition. I caught hold of it and held her still. Her hand was very warm.

"Marriage, usually," I said. I'd gotten very good at saying it like it didn't wring my heart to think about it. "A wealthy lord will offer for me, and I'll marry him. Sometimes it's a lady, but these marriages are usually for heirs. He'll pay the debt, and I'll be his wife."

"Someone is going to buy you," she said, her voice flat with anger. "And you consented to this?"

"It's not buying and selling," I said, even though it sort of was. Most of the time, I tried not think too much about how the finding of a spouse worked for debt knights. "My own parents had a marriage contract involving money and goods. It's quite common. Mine will just be more formal and more immediate than most, that's all."

"And you won't marry where you love." It wasn't a question.

"No," I said. "I won't."

"Then what's the bloody point of being a knight?" she said.

"I'll still be a knight," I said. That was the one thing that made this whole mess worthwhile. "I'll be the best knight in the realm, for my age."

"Do you have siblings?" she asked. "Are they impoverished until you can pay the debt back?"

"I have an older brother, the heir. And, no, of course not," I said.

She looked at me with a confused expression, and I squeezed her hand. It struck me how strange my world must seem to her, with its rules and customs. I thought her world was complicated, but at least it was what she was used to.

"The terms of the loan say that only I can repay it, and only I can be penalized if the money isn't repaid," I explained. "My brother's finances are independent, as are those of my parents."

"So they'll be fine, no matter what happens to you," she said. There was a bitterness in her voice I didn't like.

"We'll all be fine," I told her. "And I'll have my knighthood, which is what I wanted. I knew what I was getting into."

"Well, there's that," Olsa said.

I let her sit quietly for a few moments, the weight of it bearing down on us under the clear sky.

"I don't know who my father was," she said finally. "My mother never told me. And then she left, and the Thief Bosses took me in. It wasn't out of charity. They taught me too, you see, like you get your lessons at the palace. Only my lessons couldn't be paid for with a loan."

"Do you owe them a lot?" I asked, almost afraid to hear the answer.

"More than I can conveniently carry, that's for certain," she said. "They'd kill me if I left them. Not out of any particular malice, of course, but they do have reputations to maintain."

"Mine's not like that, I swear it," I told her.

"I'm glad," she said. "One of us should be free."

I didn't have the heart to tell her that this was the freest I was ever going to be. Sitting here, in the middle of nowhere, under this sky, with her, was the most myself I was ever going to be either. I had resigned myself to a husband and a husband's bed, but I had already decided that there were parts of me that he was never going to get, and they were the same parts I wanted very badly to give to Olsa.

"Do the stars have names?" she said suddenly. "It seems like everything else does, from the plants to the birds to those ugly little fish you made me eat when we were by the ocean."

"Those were prawns, not fish," I said. "And, yes, the stars have names."

"Will you tell me about them?" she asked.

It would be cold by the time morning came, but now, with the sun only recently set, the ground still held on to the heat of the day. It radiated out of the sandy soil beneath us, through the cloaks we had spread on the ground. Later, we'd have to crawl into our tents and the warmth of our bedrolls, but for now, the cloaks and the sky were enough.

I lay back, and she pillowed her head on my stomach. My tunic had shifted when I moved, and I could feel the press of her braids on my belly. Uleweya was right: her hair was very different from mine. I liked it, though. It felt reassuringly solid.

"The stars are strange guides sometimes, because they move around," I told her. "Not randomly, or they'd be no use at all. But as the world turns, the stars stay in the same place, so it looks like they move. Does that make sense?"

"Yes," she said. "You're good at explaining things."

I thought she was very clever, and that helped a lot, but didn't say as much.

"Well, because of that, you see different stars in different parts of the world," I continued.

"This seems like a very complicated way to get around," she said. "Why not just wait for daylight?"

"You can't really do that at sea," I told her. "Most of our star-knowledge comes from sailors."

"I guess that makes sense," she said.

"Anyway, there's a star that's more or less exactly north." I took hold of her braided head—gently, in case they were pulling at her scalp—and pointed it in the right direction. "It's that bluish one, do you see it?"

"I think so?" she said. "It looks like it's attached to a plough."

"It is," I told her. "I mean, it's part of a group of stars we call the plough."

"Show me another."

So I did. Moving from the northern cluster, I showed her all the stars I knew the names of and told her the stories that matched them. I knew she was committing it to memory. I only ever had to tell her a thing once, and she had it forever. There was something I wanted to tell her very badly.

"Olsa," I said. "Have you ever loved anyone?"

She thought about it for much too long.

"No," she said. "I don't think I have. That wasn't really how I grew up."

She sat up and looked at me, her eyes shining in the dark. "I think I could love someone, though. Some of the people in the Thief's Court, they're too hard and angry to love anyone, even if they're married or have children, but I don't think I'm like that. I think I could love someone."

"I'm glad to hear it," I said. "There's a lot in the world to love."

She lay back down on my stomach, and we talked about the stars until it was too cold to stay outside and look at them.

I'm telling you, it's true!" The voice was finally loud enough to wake her, where before it had only been buzzing around the edge of her awareness. Olsa slept lightly, but determinedly.

"You heard it from a cloth merchant, and you think it's true?" a second voice said. "They gossip worse than anyone."

"A cloth merchant who deals near weekly with the lady's own maid *and* who had to fill an order to outfit the lady for the journey," the first voice insisted. "I'd say that's reliable."

"Poor lass," a third voice chimed in. "She's young to wed. And he's no spring chicken."

"She got her dream first, don't forget it," the first voice said, not without sympathy. "Now Ironheart has to pay, same as anyone."

The name of the mystery woman finally jerked Olsa to total wakefulness. She'd gone back to the narrow garret above the Thief's Court to sleep after leaving the palace, planning to hang around there and wait to make her next move. She'd spent the evening eavesdropping, hoping to hear something useful, and had finally drifted off without hearing anything she liked. Now she waked to something she didn't want to know at all.

The speakers moved on, out of earshot, and Olsa turned their conversation over in her head. Kalanthe must have had a marriage offer. Was that why she was so blank when Olsa had spoken to her those few days ago? Was that the reason for her warnings? No, she decided. Kalanthe had become adept at keeping secrets from her, but Olsa didn't think she'd have been able to keep that one. The offer had come in the afternoon, once Olsa had been on her way. It hardly mattered. Kalanthe would be off and probably married soon to settle her honour, and even if she came back to court, Olsa would only see her if she ended up in front of the magistrate again. And maybe not even then.

Olsa climbed out of the garret and across two rooftops until she was looking down over the east-market. Mostly food and tobacco, the east-market catered to a low class of clientele, and was not a particularly good place for pickpocketing as a result. Still, Olsa liked it. Even when the sight of all the food was torturous, she liked the ebb and flow of the people walking between the market stalls. This was the world as it should be: simple, straightforward, and clearly laid out for easy navigation.

Today, though, there was something of a spectacle. A crowd of people were gathered around one of the few sweet-sellers in the middle of the market, most of them children. From her vantage point, Olsa had no trouble picking Sir Branthear out of the crowd. Dressed for a long trip of some kind, Branthear had stopped for sweets on her way out of town. It was, in Olsa's opinion, one of the knight's odder habits. However, her free hand with the coin virtually guaranteed a veritable army of small informants no matter where she went, so it wasn't entirely for the sweets.

For one fleeting moment, Olsa was tempted to throw herself from the roof, fly to Branthear's side, and beg the knight to let her come along. She didn't care if it was dangerous, and she knew without a doubt that Branthear would welcome her. With Kalanthe going or gone, there was nothing for her in Cadria anymore.

Yet she couldn't jump. Even as her mind plotted the descent, her body wouldn't take it. Her stupid heart wouldn't let her. Kalanthe wasn't the only one with pride.

Olsa watched as Sir Branthear finished distributing her gifts to the crowd and swung herself into the saddle. She rode out of the market as proudly as the king, with a trail of children parading along behind her, singing their thanks.

"Ride safe, Lady Stonehand," Olsa whispered. "Gods grant you a sure path to your goal, whatever it is."

"Talking to yourself now, thief-of-the-realm?" The roof shuddered under new weight as Tarvy slid down beside her.

He'd grown taller in the year she'd been away, but not much wider. His white skin still burned red with exposure and his muddy blond hair was short and patchy. She'd had a twelve-month of good food and exercise, while he'd had the same as always in the city, and never enough of it. Her reward from the king had bought her away from the Bosses, but Tarvy had years to go before he acquired enough to match his debt, so he ran messages for them during the day and did gods knew what for them after it got dark.

"Shut up," she said. "There's nothing wrong with wishing your friends well, even when they can't hear you."

"Ah yes," Tarvy said. "Your magnificent friends. Who do so much for you."

"They've done enough," Olsa said. "You don't know what it was like. If anything, I owe them."

He eyed the scar on her cheek, the one she didn't like to talk about, and then his eyes dropped to the cloak.

"The Bosses want to see you, if you're available," he said finally.

Olsa chewed on her lip. She didn't much fancy going to see them if they were only going to berate her for the botched job at the gem merchant's. She had her dignity, after all.

"Korin said to tell you no hard feelings," Tarvy continued. "That last job would have been impossible for anyone, and they thought you would have the best chance at it, given your . . . friends."

"I'm so pleased to hear that," Olsa said, dripping sarcasm.

She should be angry that the Bosses used her so blatantly, but she also understood from a practical standpoint why they had. Any other thief would have hanged for what she did, for sure. This way posed less risk to the Thief's Court as a whole, because they had no stake in her. It exposed her something terrible, of course, but if she wanted to remain independent, she didn't have much of a choice. It wasn't like she had hirable skills going spare.

"Tell them I'll be along after lunch," she said. Making her own appointments with the Bosses was one of the chief joys of her new life, after the Quest. That and turning Korin down every time he offered to take her back under his wing. Offers came with too many ties.

"They're expecting you," Tarvy replied. He passed her the token that would get her into the court now that it didn't own her, and slid off the roof like butter off a hot rock.

Olsa stayed up a while longer, watching the people in the market. They reminded her that she didn't need much, not really. She didn't need a room in the palace and a maid. She didn't need Kalanthe. She just needed enough for this: regular food and a roof that didn't leak or provide easy access for thieves. She would get it, and then she'd be just fine.

By the time the sun was nearly overhead, she'd had enough of waiting. She climbed down from the roof and went walking around to the door of the Thief's Court. The garret where she slept was, technically, part of it, but it had no direct access to the floor and was thus considered an outbuilding of sorts. The whole block was an interconnected set of apartments, houses, and storerooms, all of which belonged to the Thief Bosses, but most of them were forbidden unless you had the right pass.

The Bosses liked to keep their possessions controlled, and any outsiders even more so. Olsa was profoundly grateful to be one of the latter.

The guards at the door were unfamiliar, which was not unusual. Life expectancy was not spectacular when you guarded a boss, and the door guards were usually the first to fall when the city watch decided to raid the premises. Olsa showed them the token, and they let her through unchallenged.

She submitted to the weapon's search and left her knife with the inner guard. This woman she knew. Hetya Blademinder was probably the most honest person in the entire Thief's Court, if not the whole city. The people who came here tended to be very attached to their weapons, some of which were quite valuable. Hetya made sure that each weapon turned in was returned to the person who'd left it, and her reputation was better than the king's.

Olsa's knife was a gift from Sir Uleweya, one of a set, and Uleweya kept the second of the pair. Olsa hadn't even had an eating knife when she went on the Quest, having never been given one that didn't belong to one of the Bosses. Uleweya declared this unsuitable. She gave Olsa an eating knife and the knife for fighting, and began training Olsa for combat after Terriam had started her on hand-to-hand. The blade was very well-made, but not particularly ornate, which suited Olsa just fine. Hetya stroked it like a child might stroke a kitten.

"I love this knife," she said, her voice as sharp as the blades she minded.

"I know you do, Hetya," Olsa said. "You tell me every time."

"It's always true," Hetya said.

"And, as always, if I die you may have it," Olsa said, smiling.

"Anyone else would kill you for it here," Hetya said. "You see how patient I am, when it comes to quality."

"I live in awe of your very being," Olsa said. It was not entirely a lie. Hetya had one of the most stable jobs in Cadria, and she never went hungry.

"Get on with you," Hetya said, waving her past. "I'll mind this beauty while you talk business."

Olsa went forward. She would have sworn she heard Hetya crooning to the knife, but before she could tell for sure, the chaotic noise of the Thief's Court overtook her in earnest. Even before the last door was opened, she knew without a doubt what waited for her on the other side. Part of her relaxed into the familiarity of it, but most of her remained on high alert. As usual, getting in was easy.

The room was wide, with high windows and several balconies overlooking the main floor. The balconies all served as paths of escape, of course, though there were several more on the floor if, like Olsa, you knew where to look. Taking any of them would mean abandoning the knife, though, and Olsa had no intention of doing that. The floor was covered with people. They played dice or talked or arm-wrestled, and Olsa ignored them too, once she scanned them and saw that they weren't any of the Bosses' hitters.

She walked straight through the middle of the room, to the four chairs where the Bosses held court. Only one of them was full, and Olsa saw that she'd be dealing with Korin, which was what she'd hoped, anyway, based on Tarvy's message.

"Olsa!" Korin said, once she was close enough that he didn't have to shout. "I'm so glad to see you're doing well."

"It was a bit of an adventure," she said, not willing to give him the satisfaction of letting slip how close she'd come to dying. "What is it this time, Korin? Did you want the godsgem itself?"

"Don't be stupid," he said, looking at her seriously. For all his depravity, Korin was surprisingly pious. It's probably why he made her cut so high now. He knew how close she'd come to the gods, and he admired her for it.

"What then?" she asked.

"It's just a little thing, this time," he said. "But you're the only thief for the job."

Olsa sighed but did her best to keep it to herself. Korin only talked like this when he was proposing the impossible.

"Come, Olsa. Sit down and we'll talk." He looked to the side, where one of the serving girls waited. "You, bring us food and something to drink."

Olsa took the offered seat and the offered lunch, not as good as Kalanthe's breakfast, but better than nothing, and settled in to hear Korin's offer. She had a feeling it was going to be a while before she got her knife back from Hetya Blademinder.

This was the most foolish thing she had ever done. More foolish than agreeing to work for Sir Erris in the first place. More foolish than getting caught by the dark-priests Sir Erris had set her to watching. More foolish even than letting Sir Erris drag her all over Cadrium instead of giving her the slip the first time she saw the opportunity. Or the second. Or the third.

But, no, Olsa had seen all that through, and now she would see this through, even though it was beyond idiocy of her to even try. She'd made sure of her usual terms: she wasn't in Korin's pocket anymore—which included a lack of protection. That only made the risk even higher, but she'd rather take it and know she was only owned by herself at the end.

She had to admit, it gave her a bit of a thrill to make the attempt. Korin had probably been betting on that, damn him.

She was suspended from the rigging of one of the riverboats, dressed in black so that she was difficult to see in the mess of shadows that covered the docks at this late hour. Cadria had no proper ocean port, being a few leagues from the sea, but some enterprising royal had dredged the river at some point in history, and so good-sized boats could make it as far as the city with their trade goods, provided they didn't mind the long row upstream to the city walls.

They also had to pay tolls, and it was toll money that was Korin's target tonight. She wasn't stealing anything, but she was causing the distraction and was therefore the most likely member of their party to be caught. Korin had offered her the best cut yet, and she hadn't been able to turn him down, even though she knew it was beyond reckless, even if she'd still had her Kalanthe-shaped safety net in place. She just craved her full independence so badly, and Korin knew it.

This riverboat was empty, its cargo having been unloaded and its crew gone to seek what pleasure they could before heading back to the sea. That was Olsa's single condition. She hadn't come this far to take up casual murder, and Korin had agreed with little prodding. He must really want the money. Also, the captain was in Korin's pocket, which meant Korin would get paid again when the ship's insurance came through.

She carried two baskets with her, their contents sealed against mixing with each other until she was good and ready for it. She saw one flash of light from the shore, and then two in quick succession. That was the signal for her to begin.

She swung carefully to the top of the sail. It was furled, which made her job more difficult, but she coated what canvas she could with both liquids. The smell was awful, but she was used to worse. She was mindful to turn her face away when she breathed, but aside from that, there was nothing to break her focus on her task. Finally, when everything was well and truly covered, she reached into her pocket for her flint and tinder.

She checked her feet in the rigging before she struck. She wanted to be sure she had a quick getaway. When she was sure of herself, she set a spark to the tinder, mentally thanking Sir Terriam for doggedly forcing her to practice the skill, and very, very carefully placed it on one of the lines that held the sail furled.

The resulting sheet of flame was almost instantaneous. From the dock, the outcry was immediate. Men filled the deck of the riverboat desperately trying to quell the flames. Soon enough they realized it was hopeless; they couldn't reach the source of the fire, and the sail would rain flaming ropes and canvas down on them if they stayed aboard. Someone made the decision to cut the hawsers instead, and they pushed the riverboat out into the river, where it was less likely to damage another boat or the city itself.

That was what Olsa had waited for. She was glad the sailors had acted quickly, because her position was rapidly becoming untenable. As soon as the riverboat was clear of the dock, she swung down to the rail on the side of the ship and dove off the side.

The water was shockingly cold, but a sight better than being lit on fire. When she surfaced, she saw the boat in flames between her and shore, and began to swim sideways so that she could find a place to climb back up to safety. It was going to be a very cold walk back to where she'd left her cloak.

The boat was burning quickly, thanks to its own tar and to the potions she'd applied to the sail, and the current was carrying it downstream. Olsa was a good swimmer, but the cold water and the current were against her. She wanted to get well upriver of the docks before she climbed out, but she was tired long before she'd swum as far as she wanted to. She grabbed a ring that stuck out of the stone part of the wharf, where a longboat could tie off. There was a ladder there, but she was worried she was too close to the main action to escape if she climbed it now. She could hear the patter of steps as gawkers and guards alike came to see the cause of the blaze. There was nothing for it but to wait, and hope she didn't freeze before it was safe to climb up. While she waited, she would count all the things she could buy with Korin's payment and keep herself warm imagining all the hearthfires that were in her own future.

When she could stand the cold no longer, she pried her fingers off the ring, and climbed the ladder. The wind, which she hadn't thought that strong before, pierced her wet clothes and made her wish for warmth, even if it was from the ship she'd lit on fire. This was much worse than the rain of her last adventure.

She reached the top of the ladder and paused, listening hard for any of the sounds that would indicate she had company on the wharf. She was just about to haul herself off the ladder when she heard them.

"Did you see anything, sailor?" It was the watch commander. She had gotten down to the water very quickly. Almost too quickly.

"Aye, milady," said the sailor. "There was a person on the riverboat. I saw the dive myself. It could only have been the thief-of-the-realm, don't you think?"

Olsa cursed under her breath with every foul word that she knew. Before the Quest, that would have been somewhat limited, but travelling with knights tended to expand a girl's vocabulary. There had been no sailors on the wharf to see her dive. She had made sure of it *and* she had dived from the far side of the boat. Korin wasn't just using the burning riverboat as a distraction, he was using *her*, and with her inconvenient status and recognizability, the watch would barely have to track her down. She'd be arrested the next time any of them saw her.

A shudder ran through her as the river's cold wracked her muscles. She was going to seize up soon, and she had no chance of making it back to her garret—let alone getting anywhere warmer—thanks to Korin's betrayal. She took another moment to curse herself for not avoiding all the things she had seen coming, put both hands on the top of the ladder, and threw herself onto the wharf.

The watch, which had retreated to solid ground, spotted her immediately, of course. Three of them descended upon her before she could even think about trying her weight on her freezing legs. All she could really do was roll over onto her back and accept her fate as she was pulled up towards a sputtering torch and a familiar face.

"Olsa Rhetsdaughter," said the watch commander in an oddly emotionless tone, "you are under arrest."

Resistance was out of the question. Olsa just held out her hands for the shackles and let them carry her off. It was considered dignified for thieves to walk unaided, but Olsa was tired and furious with everyone, and so when they carried her by her elbows, she let them. It didn't do anything to warm her soaked bones, but she no longer cared. If they left her in the cells overnight like this, she was dead anyway.

And in the morning, she'd be dead for sure. Kalanthe was probably gone, like she had promised, and there would be no one left to speak for Olsa. Sir Branthear had ridden out of town today, no one had heard from Sir Terriam in weeks, and Sir Uleweya was off on some wild adventure in the north. Sir Erris might care about her enough to order a quick execution, but the queen couldn't intercede again.

The watch dumped her in a cell and left her with a lamp to ward off the chill. It did almost nothing, but she huddled around it anyway. She wasn't sure why this was worse than all the times she'd faced death on the Quest. She'd been cold then and wet and miserable and, on more than one occasion, terrified out of her mind. But she'd never been alone. The knights had been there, with sharp steel and sharp wits, and Mage Ladros too, most of the time, with all his mysterious powers and abilities. More important, Kalanthe had always been there, close enough to touch. Close enough that when it was the most important, Olsa could get to her. And now she had nothing but her soaked clothing and this pitiful lamp. She almost wished for one of the Old God's demons. At least they gave off heat.

She tried to wring as much water as she could from her tunic, going so far as to peel it off and sit, half naked on the floor of her cell, before putting it back on. It didn't do a lot of good. She curled up in a ball, shielding the small heat that remained in her belly and holding it close. Despite her discomfort, exhaustion began to overpower her, and she felt her limbs loosen towards sleep. There wasn't any point in fighting to stay awake, so she left herself drift.

Her memories were warm. Days spent on horseback, riding next to Kalanthe, as the apprentice knight pointed out new plants and told her the proper names of birds. Evenings spent with heads together, reading, or just talking if the light was too weak for them to see the ink. Nights spent, well, *warm* amongst other things. Much warmer than she was now. And free of the fear and anxiety that plagued them all for so much of their journeying.

Olsa had no fear now, only certainty of what was to come when the sun rose. She did wish to be warm, though, truly warm one more time before the end. Maybe it would be a lovely day.

Before she could fall asleep entirely and ignore her problems until morning, she felt a tickle along the bottoms of her feet. She hadn't been wearing shoes when she went into the river, of course, and she thought that her bare feet were rubbing against the straw that lined the floor of her cell. It was the usual damp, moldy stuff, made the worse by her lying on it while she was soaked, and she didn't want it touching her any more than it had to. She shifted her feet, trying to settle so that the straw wouldn't bother her, but the feeling increased, even though she'd moved clear of the straw.

The tickle extended up her ankles and shins, leaving a different feeling in its wake: warmth. By the time it reached her thighs, she was fully in its grip. She knew better than to resist, though. This was magic. And even if it was the Old God Himself, she would tolerate the spell for the warmth it was giving her. The tickle passed through her belly and chest, and settled behind her eyes. It wasn't the soft, subtle sort of magic Kalanthe worked. That was hardly detectable. No, this was the barely containable magic of a great mage, one of those who was so used to working big spells that when they tried to do little ones, they occasionally made their subjects explode. Olsa stayed very, very still.

At last, the tickle was gone. She was warm and her clothes were dry, and it was safe to sit up. Or, at least, as safe as it was going to be.

Olsa sat up and shook the straw off her tunic. She didn't stand. She'd wait for instructions. She did turn her face to where she knew he'd be standing, though. That much was polite.

"Olsa," said Mage Ladros, as if they were meeting in the market at high-sun. "I'm so glad I found you. There's something I need you to do."

BEFORE. . . . .

I thought the thunderstorm might be a little bit over the top. It wasn't enough that we were immured in a bleak castle perched on the edge of a cliff while the waves crashed against the rocks below us. It wasn't enough that we were beset by yet more of the Old God's demons. It wasn't enough that some new dark power was messing around in Terriam's never-quite-healed brain while we waited for Ladros to come up with a solution. No, it had to be a thunderstorm as well.

Kalanthe and I had been banished to our room after what meagre supper our hostess—a baroness—had offered, and I was happy to go. Magic still made me jumpy, unless Kalanthe herself was the one doing it. She was subtle and quiet about it. Ladros tended to be anything but, and if the creature we'd battled in the forest on our way here—the one that had somehow snared Sir Terriam to the baroness's brother's beck and call—was any indication, our mage was going to need all the flash he could get. I was glad to be out of his way.

We were safe enough in our room. We had a large pile of wood, both of our packs carried ample rations, and Kalanthe was skilled enough at arms to fight off whatever might come through the doorway. She shook her head when I said as much, as though she'd doubted her own skill, but I'd been watching her pretty closely in the months we'd been on the road. She was definitely improving. The knights barely checked their swings when they sparred with her now.

Kalanthe stripped off her leather jerkin and boots, but crawled into her bed wearing the rest of her clothes. We'd got inside before the rain started, so we were both dry. I only had the two sets anyway, and no sleeping clothes to speak of, but I knew she was sleeping mostly dressed so she'd be ready for a quick awakening. I lined up my boots next to my bed so I'd be able to find them in a hurry if I needed to and wrapped my scarf around my head. I crawled beneath my own blankets.

I thought I would fall asleep quickly enough. Even with the storm and the general gloom of the castle, I was exhausted from the ride to get here. Erris believed the resident baroness might hold some sort of clue for her, and apparently she was not the only one. We'd seen evidence of the Old God's servants in the forest—in addition to the one we'd tangled with—and it had been a nervous ride to the castle gate. Only when we were inside did we realize what had befallen Terriam, and then it was too late.

There was an enormous clap of thunder that felt like it might be right above our heads, and Kalanthe shot up in bed before the lightning had finished its brilliant flash. I sat up more slowly, still more annoyed that I'd been awakened than truly afraid, but if something was upsetting Kalanthe, then it was probably worth knowing about.

"Are you afraid of thunderstorms, Kalanthe?" I asked her, trying to keep my voice as light as possible.

"No," she said. "Of course not."

Her voice shook while she spoke. I heard her fumbling about with something beside her bed, and then she struck a match and lit the candle. In the light, her face had an unhealthy pallor. She got up, dragging her blankets behind her, and went to settle by the fire.

"Are you coming?" she said, as though it were to be expected.

I sighed. I still wasn't so used to beds that I was happy to give up sleeping in one, but she looked much better by the firelight, so I swallowed my objections and gathered my blankets.

"What's upsetting you so much?" I asked, settling in beside her.

"This place," she said. "The magic here. Can't you feel it?"

"No," I said. "I mean, I can feel the storm and damp of the stone, and from what we saw at dinner, the baroness is so upset that she's probably curdling whatever milk is left in the dairy, but aside from that, no."

"It's less now," Kalanthe said. "When the Old God was actually here, it was so bad that it drove all the servants away. That's why the baroness is alone, except for her brother. Somehow, she found the strength to stay, even though she knew he might kill her."

I shuddered. This Quest of ours often had a higher cost than I liked, if it could turn siblings against each other. The baroness had been forced to lock up her brother, but not before he'd learned how to infect others, including Terriam, with whatever darkness was eating away at his soul.

"It won't kill Mage Ladros, will it?" I asked.

"I don't know," she said. "I'm not that good at magic yet. I just get feelings about it."

I huddled down into my blankets, while Kalanthe got up and added more logs to the fire.

"What about Sir Terriam?" I asked.

Kalanthe jammed the poker into the embers, and they flared. Sparks flew through the grate and landed on the rug, burning small holes in it before they extinguished themselves.

"What is it?" I said.

"It's the worst sort of magic, what's happening to Sir Terriam," Kalanthe said. Her voice was quiet, but it was the furious kind. "The baroness's brother is controlling her body and her feelings, both. It's not right."

"Many things about this castle are not right," I said. I paused for a moment to form my question. "Magic is still a bit hazy to me, so pardon the question if it's rude, but how is that different from what Mage Ladros does? Or you for that matter?"

"I change physical things," she said. "Temperatures of water, the clarity of glass, that sort. Mage Ladros can brew spells, but they only work if a person drinks them, and they work best if a person drinks them willingly. I don't take control of people and make them do things, feel things. What's happening here is wrong."

"I see," I said. There was something else that bothered her, only I didn't know how to ask.

"It's not just that," she said after a moment. "The baroness's brother is making Sir Terriam feel—"

"Infatuated?" I said. That's certainly what it had looked like to me; a near-desperate glaze in Terriam's eyes every time she spoke of him.

Dinner had been exceedingly uncomfortable as Terriam pressed the baroness for information about her brother, despite their hostess's clear desire not to discuss him. Terriam could be something of a badger when it came to fishing for information—unsubtle and bold—but this went past all of that. It was a relief when Erris locked her in her room after Mage Ladros cast a sleeping spell on her. As Kalanthe said, doing magic on a person against their will was not something done lightly, but Terriam's strange behaviour was weighing on the castle as heavily as the raging storm.

"Yes," Kalanthe said sharply. "Sir Terriam doesn't like men, or women, for that matter. It's common enough with knights that they even have a word for it: shield-wed. That's why it's so terrible. The magic is making her change who she is."

"Oh," I said. I should have let it lie, but for some reason I didn't. I kept talking. "What about you?"

"The magic's not affecting me," she said. "I just feel it happening, and that's why I'm uncomfortable."

"No, I meant, girls," I stumbled through it. "Do you like girls or boys?"

As soon as I said it, I wondered if it was too impertinent a question. I knew what waited for her after her knighthood. Her preferences would have very little to do with it. If she was lucky, she'd at least have feelings that pointed her in the right direction.

"Girls," she said, like it was a weight around her neck. "Not that it matters. I can't have what I want."

"You can until you get married," I said. "I mean, you could after too, but I know you won't."

"It would only come to nothing anyway, and then what?" she said. "It's not that easy, Olsa."

I could have told her that it was, that hundreds of people did it every day, but at the same time, I knew that wasn't Kalanthe's way. She would be loyal, even if it hurt her. The firelight on her face was entrancing, and I saw something in her dark eyes that I hadn't noticed before.

"You mean you like someone and you won't tell them?" I asked. "So much for knightly bravery."

Kalanthe looked at me like she wanted to punch me, which should have been enough to shut me up, but for some reason I could not stop talking. It was as though all the feelings I'd been avoiding suddenly landed on me at once, and I was determined that she suffer alongside me.

"I can read you like a book," I told her.

"That's not saying very much," she snapped.

"Don't be petty, I'm getting better." I paused. "Is it Sir Erris?" I asked, only half surprised and entirely disappointed. "Because I can understand that. She's absolutely—"

Then Kalanthe launched herself at me. Thanks to Terriam's hand-to-hand training, I was already rolling when we collided, but she didn't try to hit me. Instead, she pushed me onto my back, held my hands still on either side of my head, and kissed me, as surely as she breathed.

I was too surprised to take advantage of having her so close to me, which I immediately regretted when she pulled away. She didn't go very far, though, only pulling her head back enough for me to see her eyes gleaming from the light of the fire, and from something else besides.

"You should stop talking," she said. Her voice was low and dark, and I liked it.

"Come and make me," I replied, without thinking the better of it. I grinned what I hoped was an enticing smile, but was quickly out of tricks to get her to kiss me again. I had a feeling that the advice I'd picked up from the people who worked in Cadria's brothels wasn't going to get me very far.

Kalanthe only laughed, that same low sound as her voice, and pressed her lips to mine again. This kiss was gentler, but I felt the heat of it down to my very bones. One kiss became two, then three, and then I stopped counting, each breathless contact stoking a fire in my stomach and a want for ever more of it. Eventually, she pulled away again and rested her forehead against mine. We breathed together, and now that my brain was reconnecting, I realized that Kalanthe didn't know what to do with her hands when she was kissing someone. Fortunately, I knew from watching her spar that she was a quick study and good at improvisation.

"That's about as much as I know," she said. "At least when it comes to two girls. Sorry."

My blood was thrumming, and I hoped hers was too. Confident that it was too dark for her to see me flush—as if I wasn't glowing already—I told her what could come next.

"How can you possibly know that and not know about monthly blood?" she demanded, leaning off me a little, so that I wasn't bearing all her weight.

"I hear things," I said, and hoped she understood that to mean "the hetaerae in the Thief's Court talk shop a lot."

"I like the idea of it," she said. "But I don't think it's a good idea for tonight."

"You don't think the Old God's demons would give us our privacy?" I asked.

She laughed, a glorious laugh that I had never heard before, and kissed me again. I hoped it never got less thrilling.

"Olsa," she said, suddenly serious. "Thank you."

"For what?"

"For . . ." She paused. "I don't know, for being you, I guess."

"I don't have a lot of choice," I pointed out.

"You do, though," she said. "You could have let the street make you hard and untrusting, and you didn't."

"It's more fun this way," I said, though to be totally honest I had never thought about it like that before.

"It is, isn't it," she said.

She reached for her blankets and pulled them overtop of us, so that we were cocooned together in the warmth of them. Then I kissed her until the last of the worry disappeared from her eyes, and she fell asleep.

–II–

ON THE
ROAD AGAIN

In the second beginning, when the world was remade in the ruin of the Old God's nightmare, there were no cities and there were no roads. Humans did not travel far from their rude villages. They stayed in their mud-and-wattle huts, close to their peat-and-dung fires, and they learned how the seven gods' world worked.

They replenished their herds of cattle and sheep. They learned to ride on horseback. They built better harnesses, to yoke oxen to plough their fields. They taught themselves to fire clay and weave papyrus. They learned, and they found that their villages were too small, the horizon too tempting. So they did go out, slowly, and they found other humans when they travelled.

Some had stronger clay, some had stronger houses, some had stronger cows. The humans learned to trade. They learned to smelt better metals and forge better horseshoes. They built boats, first clumsy craft for passage along shallow rivers, and then ships, lean and quick and seaworthy, to bear them on the ocean. They learned different trades: farmer, weaver, smith, merchant-of-all, and the exchange of goods made some of them very rich.

With wealth came trouble, but came progress, too. Walls were built for protection and houses for beauty. Flowers were cultivated, not for eating, but for looking at, and for scent. Stories became song, and even common cooking pots had painted decorations that recorded the history of the new world, short though it was.

Kingdoms rose. Cadrium was not the first, but it was one of the most enduring and one of the most stable. With harbours to facilitate trade, land to facilitate farming, and iron mines to facilitate industry, Cadrium wanted for very little and was not given to conquest. Instead, the kingdom divided itself into provinces and duchies, each ruled by a lady or a lord. Several large freeholds were established for trade, and eventually these grew into larger towns and cities. At first, peace was maintained with a small militia—farmers during the off-seasons—but soon enough a permanent military force arose in the form of mounted knights.

The availability of iron in Cadrium meant that knights were relatively easy to supply, and they were used primarily for internal defense and for security. Admission to the training was open to anyone, though there were rigorous physical requirements and financial matters to take into consideration. Since so many in the kingdom sent their daughters and sons to Cadria to become knights, and since the highest caliber of warriors were all trained together, large conflicts between neighbouring estates were few and far between, save when royal succession was involved. Knights served on their own estates or at court, depending on where their talents and interests lay.

The history books will paint stories in a glossy sheen. Storytellers are more likely to tell you the truth. As peaceful and wondrous as Cadrium was, it was not a kingdom without flaws. Knights who came to Cadria to learn were often bullied for their regional accents and cultural variations, and they often went back to their homes at the end of their training nursing some measure of resentment. As seafaring developed, and trade between the continents became more frequent, questions of homeland and citizenship came under consideration, often with negative connotations to those who were most vulnerable. And that is only the beginning.

In every city, town, and village, there were people the law had forgotten, those who starved because they could not work, or worked themselves to the bone for masters who thought themselves better than the king. There were many who stole and some who murdered, and some who committed crimes that most people don't even know the names of. King Dorrenta did the best he could, as his ancestors had done before him, but the king was just a man, and the queen was just a woman, and neither of them was perfect.

The hardest lesson learned by apprentice knights is that not everyone can be helped. The first lesson is that they should never stop trying.

Kalanthe rode out of Cadria with three of her own horses, plus one on loan from Sir Erris. The first horse, her beloved warmblood mare, had been with her the longest, purchased when Kalanthe had come to court at the age of ten. In the years since, Lightfoot had been a testament to loyalty, training, and the merits of not allowing a ten-year-old to name her own horse. The charger, Arrow, was broad shouldered and plodding—when he wasn't putting in his battle-effort, anyway. She'd bought him just before the Quest with the last of the money in her coffers when her previous stallion had been retired to stud. The packhorse was a palace horse—on loan from Sir Erris—nameless and utilitarian.

The fourth horse, a gift from Sir Edramore, was causing trouble. At first appearance, the gelding was unremarkable. His coat was mud-brown, his demeanor was placid, and his saddle and tack were new, but practically made. Once Kalanthe got a good look at him, however, she became uncomfortable. The gelding had clearly been chosen for its unobtrusiveness, but upon closer examination, it was very clear that the mount was well-bred. Kalanthe knew enough about the market worth of horses to know that while his coat would have turned off the more snobbish buyers, the gelding was still an expensive gift.

Edramore had money, enough to spend on a girl he was rather unorthodoxly courting, and he was smart enough not to rub it in anyone's faces. It both soothed and pricked at Kalanthe's pride. She loaded up the gelding with packs to spare the palace horse, and also so that she could avoid riding him for at least the first day.

She left Cadria alone. Even as an apprentice knight, she was more than entitled to travel by herself, but she planned to meet Branthear that evening at a posting inn. The older knight had gone ahead to take care of some of her own business, but intended to accompany Kalanthe to Edramore's estates. As Edramore's kinswoman, she was well within her rights to do so, and Kalanthe was grateful for the company. Amongst other things, Branthear had a way of talking through matters that always made them seem simpler and more straightforward. For the first several hours, though, Kalanthe had only the horses for company: two trusted; one inconsequential; and one that seemed to be loaded with far more of her baggage than she had actually tied to its flanks.

Arrow and the gelding had more or less come to an arrangement as to the order of precedence in the string line that was tied to the back of Kalanthe's saddle. The gelding never stood a chance. After the Quest, Arrow had broken through the walls of his stall four straight nights until they'd put him next to Lightfoot, and the warhorse was not going to let a mere gelding come between them. So, as Lightfoot walked placidly at Kalanthe's direction, Arrow followed right behind while the gelding gave them as much space as he could, and the palace horse brought up the rear, either unconcerned or unaware of the battle that had been waged for the spot in front of it. How simple, to be a horse, and to know one's place in the wide world so easily.

Even though she would soon be meeting up with Branthear, Kalanthe was lonely. Triana had offered to come, putting on a brave face when she volunteered to make the journey, but Kalanthe had not demanded it of her. Triana was city born, and while she didn't mind the odd jaunt down the river, a trek like the one Kalanthe was undertaking was more than the lady's maid was prepared for. When the time came—if the time came—and Triana was needed at Sir Edramore's estate, she would come in a carriage, and be charged with minding the wagons that bore all of Kalanthe's worldly goods.

Kalanthe knew that what she really missed were her companions from the Quest and the knowledge of purpose that came with it. Riding out alone was not nearly as interesting as riding in company, even though her mission was peaceful and she was not likely to need an armoured charge to get her out of any situations that might arise. And, of course, she missed Olsa.

When they had parted last, Olsa had been angry with her. And, truth be told, Kalanthe had been angry too. She knew that their future was complicated at best, but she still wished they might have parted as friends. Instead, their last conversation had been riddled with resentment, and Kalanthe had all but threatened Olsa with the very hypothetical that was now coming to pass: if Olsa was arrested again, Kalanthe would not be there to save her. And she hadn't even been able to tell Olsa she was leaving, because she had no way of knowing if her message had reached her.

At least this time, she thought bitterly, the rumour mill might do some good. Her departure from Cadria would not go unremarked upon, and everyone would know the reason she had left. Hopefully, word would reach Olsa before she had time to do anything that would land her in trouble with the law again. It was too much to hope that Olsa would see reason and go to Sir Erris for permanent help, but maybe, just maybe, if she knew that Kalanthe wouldn't be coming to extricate her from the clutches of the magistrate's court again, Olsa would be cautious.

Kalanthe's hands tightened on the reins: she was leaving Olsa to her death, and she knew it. And she did not turn around, even as she heard the old taunt—*Iceheart*—whisper in the back of her mind. She had tried. She had done, well, not everything—she'd stopped short of kidnapping, for example—but she had tried everything she could think of that still maintained Olsa's treasured independence, and if it wasn't enough, she would be the one to live with it.

At least the weather was fair. Kalanthe had ridden through enough rain and cold to be thankful for the sunny days when she got them. She'd got an early start, and then been stuck in the bottleneck at the city gate. She could have pulled rank, but chose to wait her turn amongst the crowd leaving the city. Most of them were merchants, headed to the sea, wagons heavy with goods they didn't trust to transport on the river. Once she passed the gate and turned east, she was mostly alone on the road. A few wagons were headed inland too, but even with Lightfoot's walking pace, Kalanthe was faster than they were. By the time the sun was high, she was by herself.

It had been very late summer—almost harvest—when they'd ridden out on the Quest, and they had been gone for an entire year. They hadn't always been travelling, of course, but they had covered a lot of ground during that time. Kalanthe had seen more of the continent than most people saw in a lifetime, and sometimes she felt like she was still picking the dust out of her teeth, even all these months later. Now, it was early spring, and the farmers were turning the fields. She'd been in Cadria for more than half a year, long enough to get used to the rhythms of the city and palace, but hopefully not so long that she lost all her road-sense.

More important, she'd been in Cadria long enough to almost reach her birthday. Soon, she would come of age, and then she would be knighted and old enough that her loan repayments must begin. She had funds for pay for a year, maybe two, if she sold Arrow, but that was a heartbreaking and impractical option. But she would legally be an adult, and while that meant some freedoms, it included a full measure of responsibility. If she hadn't gone on the Quest, she could have started looking for a husband earlier, but the thought of being seventeen and looking for marriage made her cringe.

She laughed, an ugly sound in the spring stillness, and Lightfoot shook her head. Kalanthe reached forward to soothe the horse, and then checked over her shoulder to make sure the other three were all right. Arrow was plodding along, the gelding was still giving him as much space as the rope would allow, and the palace horse walked like it didn't have a care in the world.

There was not a lot better about looking for marriage at eighteen, Kalanthe mused, or, in all probability, at nineteen. At least Edramore seemed to understand her reluctance. Kalanthe would feel better after they had spoken in person, and she learned whether he was really as reasonable and canny as he seemed. In the meantime, she felt very young and inexperienced, despite the fact that songs were written in her honour and her age-mates had viewed her as a grown-up since the king had handed her the reward purse at the conclusion of the Quest.

She thought again about what Sir Erris had said about changing the way debt knights were treated. It was a lot of weight to put on a ten-year-old. There were only two contracts a nobly born minor could sign in Cadrium: the debt knight's contract and a marriage contract, though both required witnesses that were kin. Kalanthe had signed the debt knight's contract with her mother, and she had thought at the time that she knew what she was getting into. As Branthear had pointed out, she really didn't. At the same time, without it, she wouldn't be a knight at all. She knew that Cadrium could not afford to pay for all its knights, and she knew that this was the compromise a Queen of Old had come up with, generations before King Dorrenta had taken the throne. Perhaps Sir Erris was right and it was time to reconsider, but that was far beyond Kalanthe's ken.

Arrow nudged Lightfoot's rump, causing the mare to skip sideways. Kalanthe forced herself to stop daydreaming about problems she couldn't solve, and pay attention to her mounts. She turned in the saddle, and Arrow was in range, so she struck him lightly on the nose with two fingers to remind him of who was in command. She didn't hold with hitting horses in general, but chargers could be vicious and stubborn, and it was always best to keep them in line. He wouldn't be any good to anyone if he turned into a bully.

The gelding hesitated, but then kept walking before its rope drew taut. Kalanthe was going to have to give the horse a name before they all arrived at Sir Edramore's estate. She wouldn't want him to think she was ungrateful, and—ugly or not—the gelding was too fine a horse to go without a name. The palace horse plodded on.

Kalanthe sighed and reached into her saddlebags for some dried meat. She chewed and swallowed, and then drank from the flask that hung from her saddle horn. Soon, she saw a rider in the distance. It was a royal messenger, galloping hard for

Cadria, and the first oncoming traffic of the day. After that, she passed a number of riders and wagons. She didn't stop to speak to any of them, nor they to her. If there had been trouble with the road or important news to pass along, she would have spoken, but there was none, and presumably there was none ahead of her either because no one stopped to tell her. Instead, only polite waves were exchanged, and if the wagons were particularly broad, Kalanthe would get off the road to let them pass more easily.

At last, with the sun behind her, Kalanthe saw smoke in the distance. It wasn't the black smoke of unwanted fire—she'd seen enough of that to know what it looked like—but instead the homey grey of hearthfire and strong chimney. Soon, she could see the rooflines of the little village that was her destination. It was small, she knew—the inn, a smithy, a shop, a couple of houses—and really existed only to support travellers such as herself, but she was happy to see it.

Branthear met her in the courtyard and held Lightfoot's head as Kalanthe swung down. For just a moment, as their hands clasped, Kalanthe could pretend that it was like old times again.

The inn was utilitarian, but it was clean and the narrow cots in the room that Kalanthe and Branthear shared were long enough that she didn't have to sleep curled up. She'd looked into the taproom, where the villagers came to drink at the end of the workday with whatever guests were present, but felt no great desire to eat with strangers. After checking with the innkeeper to be sure it wasn't too much trouble, Kalanthe went back to her room to wait for a supper tray to be sent up. She'd asked for enough food for two, even though Branthear was out, because she knew the knight would be hungry when she came in.

There had been a flash of recognition in the innkeeper's eyes as she confirmed that sending up the tray wouldn't be a problem, but she said nothing more. Kalanthe was glad. If word spread into the tap room that one, let alone two, heroes of the realm were in residence, it was sure to be a rowdy night, and neither she nor Branthear was the type to live it up before several days on the road. The ballads never mentioned practical things like how much uninterrupted sleep knights required when they were on a journey.

It was Branthear's custom to wander around whatever village they were staying in, talking with everyone from the farmers to the smith to the children, about any and all topics. Kalanthe had no idea how Branthear mustered up the will to make the effort, even at the end of the longest day's ride, but she couldn't deny that it was an incredibly useful habit. Branthear learned things that came in handy and made friends and connections across the kingdom. On more than one occasion during the Quest, this had resulted in a dry place to sleep or fodder for the horses when they might have otherwise gone without. Kalanthe wondered if she ought to try it, but the idea of casual conversation so regularly made her blood run cold.

"Don't worry about it," Terriam had told her one evening as they watched Branthear return a runaway kitten to a grateful child. "That's why knights travel in groups, Kalanthe. Everyone has their own contributions to make."

So she waited for dinner and her companion to arrive and sat on the foot of her cot, trying not to rearrange her pack for the tenth time. Most of her things were stacked in the corner of the room and wouldn't be opened until the end of the journey, but her smaller pack, the one where she kept her basic necessities, was open as she rummaged for a hairbrush. If she had to fidget, she might as well fidget productively.

Kalanthe retrieved the brush and went to work. Her hair was long and usually it was dead straight, but she had braided it wet before she set out, so it was a bit curled. She didn't need to oil it the way Olsa and Uleweya did, though she knew her mother did that sometimes. Unlike Kalanthe, her mother had never cut her hair, and it fell past her waist. It was far too long to wash regularly, and the oil helped it stay glossy. Kalanthe's hair was only as long as the middle of her back, and she thought it was a mustier black than her mother's, but Lede and the other girls in her age group had often complimented how shiny it was, so she supposed such things were relative.

She had the few knots worked out in moments and was happy to notice that her hair had not picked up too much road dust while she had ridden. Quickly, she put it into two plaits for sleep. Tomorrow morning, when she woke, she would do the more elaborate braid she used when riding, though she would probably leave out the spiked strap she wore when there was danger. Anyone who tried to grab her hair in a fight would get a nasty surprise, even if they were wearing gauntlets, but habit wasn't reason enough to merit use if she wasn't expecting to be attacked. She had to be frugal, for now, and the strap was difficult to replace.

There was a knock on the door as she was tucking the brush away, and when Kalanthe opened it, she found a girl a few years younger than Olsa carrying a large tray.

"Your dinners, Sir Knight," the girl said. She looked around. "Is the other knight not here?"

"She'll be back," Kalanthe told her. It was on the tip of her tongue to correct her on forms of address, but instead she held the door wide and waved towards the table in the corner.

The girl deposited the tray but left the covers on the food. Kalanthe got a small coin out of her purse and handed it over. It was more than worth it to eat in private, and the tray looked heavy, after all.

"Thank you, Sir Knight," the girl said, with a bit of a curtsey. "I'm Madja, if you need anything else."

"Thank you, Madja," Kalanthe said. "I imagine we'll be setting out early. Do you have a breakfast that can be made portable?"

"Oh, aye," Madja said. "Most of the drovers leave before the sun, and even though it's not in season, my mother always has an option for the early risers. I'll let her know."

At that moment, Branthear came in, and Madja's bubbling conversation was halted without Kalanthe having to come up with an appropriate response to it. Branthear carried a jug of water in each hand. Her brown hair was unbraided, and spilled down her back. She was wearing a dark red tunic over black hose, and she had only her long-knife on her belt. Were it not for her bearing, Kalanthe never would have guessed she was a knight. She smiled at Kalanthe.

"I see you've met Madja," she said, nodding.

Madja curtseyed again and took her leave. Kalanthe thought it was just as well, because Branthear was as likely to invite her to dinner. Usually, Kalanthe would not have minded sharing the food or Branthear's time, but tonight she was nervous and wanted to be left in private in case they ended up talking about personal matters.

"How's the road?" Kalanthe asked. Branthear would have all the news by now.

"It's in good shape," Branthear replied with a smile. "The early rains didn't wash out any of the bridges, and none of the ways are impassable. The farmer I spoke to seemed to think it would be a week of clear skies, though she couldn't be sure how far east that would be true."

Kalanthe laughed and took the covers off the tray of food. It was simple fare—spiced bean soup with chunks of pork, thick flatbread with a pat of butter, a small piece of cheese for each of them—but it was still steaming, and all Kalanthe really wanted was something hot. While Kalanthe set up the table, Branthear filled the kettle with water from one of the jugs and set it in the hearth so that Kalanthe could make her tea.

"Sir Erris sent a reply by royal messenger," Kalanthe said, ladling out soup for each of them and breaking the bread into two pieces. "A pigeon, so it's very official. Sir Edramore already knows we're coming."

"He must have suspected, or he wouldn't have sent you the horse," Branthear pointed out. Earlier, before going on walk-about, she had groomed the gelding while Kalanthe took care of the others.

"It was part of his offer," Kalanthe said. "His steward at court was to see it done if I decided to go see him."

"Even when we were children, Edramore was always thoughtful," Branthear said. "I'm not surprised to see that he has remained so. He would be so much help to the king and queen at court, but I can't blame him for wanting to stay with the girls."

"He wants to stay on his own estates even if they leave," Kalanthe pointed out. "It was part of his proposal. Do you know why?"

"I don't," Branthear said. "It's not grief, I know that much. His first wife has been gone for more than five years, but even before that, he didn't come to Cadria unless it was absolutely necessary."

"I can understand wanting to avoid court," Kalanthe said quietly. "I don't like it much either."

"And yet you'd be posted there if you marry him," Branthear said.

"Yes, but I'd have something to *do*," Kalanthe said. "Right now, there's not a lot for me at court besides training and gossip, and gossip is the worst."

"That's fair enough," Branthear said.

She passed her cheese to Kalanthe and went to get the kettle off its hook. Kalanthe ate the extra cheese and then brewed her tea. It was a quiet ritual she liked at the end of the day. On the road, they had all shared in the making of it, even Mage Ladros. It tasted much better hot and steaming, though it could also be drunk cold. Knights on the road carried a second waterskin of it in case there was a night they couldn't boil water, and getting fresh tea was another thing Kalanthe never took for granted after her time on the Quest.

"Come on, then," Branthear said, when the tea was drunk and the dishes were put outside the door of the room. "We might as well go to bed. We'll cover as much ground as we can in the next few days, if that's all right with you, even if it means no inn."

"Yes, that's fine," Kalanthe said. "I have provisions enough. And I've arranged for breakfast tomorrow too."

"Good girl," Branthear said. She grimaced. "I'm sorry, Kalanthe. I should stop saying that."

"I know that you respect me, Branthear," Kalanthe said. "And I am grateful you're coming with me on this . . . trip."

"I should still mind how I address you," Branthear said. "If only so the rest of the world does."

"Thank you, Sir Knight," Kalanthe said, even though she truly would not have minded if the whole world thought she was a girl forever.

Kalanthe stripped to her smallclothes and slid under the covers. Branthear slept in a light tunic that reached her knees. Terriam, Kalanthe knew from startling personal experience, slept naked. Olsa had slept in her clothes until Sir Erris pointed out she didn't have to. Then she, too, slept naked in her bedroll, but only when she was sharing a tent. By herself in a room, or under the sky with more than one person around, Olsa slept in her undertunic and hose, ready to run at a moment's notice. Kalanthe usually tried pretty hard not to imagine what Olsa was sleeping in at any given moment.

"I'll take care of her, you know," Branthear said, after she turned down the lamp. It was light enough to see the outline of the door if either of them needed to go to the privy, but not bright enough for much else.

"What?" Kalanthe replied.

"Olsa," she said. "I know you were thinking about her. I've been thinking about her too—though, I imagine, a bit differently."

Kalanthe made an indelicate sound and then wished she hadn't. She didn't want to sound ungrateful.

"I'll hire her," Branthear went on. "She's basically qualified to be a squire now, so it won't hurt her pride too much, and I'll take her on gentler roads than Uleweya would. I only wish I'd thought of it sooner, but Erris has kept me pretty busy in and out of Cadria since we all got home, and I didn't realize things were so bad."

Tears sprang to Kalanthe's eyes, and she didn't wipe them away. Olsa deserved this much from her, even if it hurt. Because she didn't want Branthear to take care of her. She wanted to do it herself, even while she knew she could only offer room and board. She wanted Olsa. And she couldn't have her. Branthear's offer, made with genuine kindness and deliberate consideration to preserve what Olsa felt was personal agency, felt like giving her up for good.

"Thank you," she said. Her tears fell, and she was unable to keep the tremor out of her voice.

But Olsa deserved that too. Maybe someday Branthear would tell Olsa about this conversation, about how Kalanthe had wept and then made the right decision. About how much Kalanthe cared, even though there were some things that were just impossible to fix.

BEFORE. . . . .

We were attacked in broad daylight, in the middle of an open field. Needless to say, not one of the Old God's wiser choices, even if it was made by His demons. Mage Ladros had tried to explain that the demons all had the Old God's will and mind by means of a sort of brain-transference magic, but frankly, I found it too confusing to remember when they were charging at us. Also, several of them were on fire.

My job in these situations was to take the lead for our string of packhorses and get them clear of the fighting. It wasn't running away, not quite, and each time we were attacked, I found myself more reluctant to leave my companions, even though I couldn't do very much to help them besides staying out of the way. My bad habits were ever increasing.

The knights—and Kalanthe—would switch to their chargers if they had enough time, but each of them rode mares or geldings that were more than capable of bearing them in an unarmoured fight. In any case, their spare horses wouldn't wander off, not even in the face of all the demons the Old God could muster, because of their training. The packhorses were another matter, and unless I wanted to go without them and all they carried, I held the rope.

I watched as Kalanthe fell in beside Mage Ladros. Her task in these little skirmishes was to guard his back so that he could do magic. She was wearing her light chainmail under a blue tunic and had on a helmet, but her hair was in a single braid down her back. I knew from watching street fights that loose hair was not something you wanted in a conflict, but there was no time for her to do anything else.

Sir Erris was barking orders at the other knights, getting them into a line. There were two—no, three—demons coming towards us, and they were driving ten or so badly armed minions in front of them. The minions were mortal, human, and beyond help. They would charge until they died, because the Old God held their souls. It was ugly work, but at least they always attacked, so it wasn't quite like straight-up murder.

Sir Uleweya gave a great cry and spurred her horse forward. Sir Terriam was right behind her. Sir Branthear and Sir Erris swung out, attempting to flank the charging line. Mage Ladros began hurling fire at the demons, and then the battle was joined too close for him to intervene. He shouted something to Kalanthe, but I couldn't hear over the din. She must have, though, because she nodded, and together they began to move out, flanking in the opposite direction that Sir Erris had gone.

Sir Uleweya, mounted on her charger, reached the line of un-souled minions and simply rode them down. They flailed under her horse's hooves and did not get up. Sir Terriam had her sword out and cut one of them down, nearly in half from shoulder to hip. Axe whistling, Sir Branthear laid in from the side, decapitating two, even as Sir Erris cut down a third and turned to engage the demon.

I screamed. I remembered all too well what had happened the last time one of the knights had gone up against a demon directly, and I didn't want Sir Erris to get hurt. By the time I paused to breathe, Mage Ladros was back in the fray, and the demon in front of Sir Erris was engulfed in that special blue fire of his that the Old God's creatures seemed to hate so much. The fire spread quickly to the other demons, and the knights disengaged, pulling back to reassess the situation.

Through the magical blue haze of flame and smoke, no one saw the last remaining minion stumble clear of the fight and turn straight for Kalanthe. Well, no one except for me. I screamed again, and this time, she did hear me, but it was almost worse. She whipped her head around to look at me, her braid flying as she turned, and even as I pointed back at the shambling man behind her, he reached up and grabbed her hair, to pull her from the saddle.

I kicked the side of my horse, trying to get to her, but the pack-horses were terrified and wouldn't go with me, and I couldn't drop the rope. I watched, horrified, as the man's hand closed around Kalanthe's braid, and then, even as she turned to face him, pulling the braid free, he began to convulse. His mouth open in soundless screaming, he went down, and Kalanthe reached over with her sword and coolly stabbed him through the heart.

She looked at Mage Ladros, who nodded absently as he went to examine the smoldering remains of the demons, and rode towards me, her sword in one hand because she didn't want to get her sheath bloody.

"Olsa, are you all right?" she asked, sliding down to clean her sword off in the grass. She patted Lightfoot on the neck and pressed her forehead against the mare's nose in what, I guess, was a reassuring gesture for the horse. I found myself wishing she'd do it to me because I was very unreassured.

"Am I all right?" I said. "All I had to do was stand here with the horses. You nearly died!"

"What on earth are you talking about?" Kalanthe said. She looked up and realized how upset I was.

My knees were locked and I couldn't have got off the horse if the king ordered me himself, so she came over and put her hand on my thigh. I closed my free hand over hers.

"That last man," I said. "He almost got you out of your saddle, and then you would have had to face him in the grass."

I was very slowly learning about combat, and I knew that most of a knight's training was related to their horses. Uleweya and Terriam weren't bad at close-quarters fighting, but I knew at least four ruffians who would take them down for fighting too pretty. On the ground, with the weight of her armour, Kalanthe was much more exposed than she was on a horse.

"Oh, that," Kalanthe said. "There was never any danger of that."

I gaped at her. She pointed to her braid.

"The spike is braided into it," she said. "And my spike is different from the ones that the others wear."

I knew she kept it in a lead box that weighed a lot, and I knew only she ever opened the box or braided her hair with it, but I didn't know what was so special about that. No one else was ever allowed to touch Uleweya's swords either.

"It's magic?" I guessed. It was the only explanation I could think of.

"It is," she said. She thought for a moment, as though considering how to phrase what she was going to say next. "You know how the human body has a heart that beats blood all through it?"

"Yes," I said. Since I'd come on the Quest, I'd even seen what that looks like, because when you cut off a person's arm, their heart still tries to send blood to their fingers, and that gets very messy very quickly.

"Well," Kalanthe continued, "there's a force that controls that. And your breathing and thinking and digestion too. We don't really have a name for it, just 'life,' but my magic can access it and channel it into the spike."

She took off her helmet. I saw a dark circle on the crown of her head that I knew was the top of the strap. It was plain leather—or at least, plain to look at—until it reached her braid, and then the spikes began.

"It's connected here," she said, tapping the top of her head.

"Connected to what?" I asked.

"Me," she said. "My life, I guess. That's why I can touch it. But if anyone else does, well . . ."

She trailed off, and we both looked at the man she'd killed. Mage Ladros usually lit the dead on fire before we left, but he was still examining the demons with Sir Erris, and hadn't got around to it yet.

I was still high on nerves, even though I'd only watched the battle, so naturally I said the most inappropriate thing imaginable.

"How drunk do you think the mages who discovered that kind of magic were?"

For a moment, Kalanthe looked scandalized, as though none of the realm's high mages would ever so much as look at alcohol, but then she began to laugh.

"When we get back to Cadria, I'll take you to the palace library and you can look at the book I learned it from," she said. "Assuming we get back, of course."

"Oh, we'll get back," I told her. "But the chances of them letting someone like me cross the threshold of the royal library? Lady Ironheart, I think you dream too much."

She laughed again and swung back into her saddle. Once she was settled, she shot a furtive glance at where the other knights were watching Mage Ladros burn the bodies. Then she leaned over and kissed me, Lightfoot pressing against my leg. It was clumsy and fast, not the least because my horse skipped sideways, but I appreciated it anyway.

Then she went off to get her charger and Uleweya's mare from where they were waiting for their mistresses. I rode towards the fire, the packhorses finally calm enough to follow me.

"We're going to have to split up," Sir Erris was saying, just as I arrived. "It's not safe and we're too exposed out here."

"We're mounted knights!" Sir Terriam protested.

"Do you want to spend the next two weeks riding in full armour?" Sir Uleweya asked pointedly.

Sir Terriam was mostly recovered from the blow to her head—at least physically—but she still had headaches and bad days, and Mage Ladros thought she always would. The weight of her armour exacerbated the situation.

"Branthear, Kalanthe, and Terriam will go to the university," Sir Erris declared. "Branthear will direct you, and hopefully if the three of you work together, you'll uncover the information we need from the library."

"What about Mage Ladros?" Sir Branthear asked. "He's better at lore than I am."

"I need him," Sir Erris said. "The Old God's demons will probably keep following me. I seem to be their primary target. Ladros and Uleweya and Olsa and I will cross the desert and see if we can't get a look at this relic."

"What?" I said, having heard primarily "Old God's demons," "primary target," and my own name.

"I'm sorry, Olsa," Sir Erris said. "I know it's dangerous, but there's a decent chance that when we find the relic, we'll have to steal it. Especially if it's the object we're after."

We tried to avoid saying the object's name out loud. It created a separate kind of problem with the Old God, and it also made looking for it much more complicated.

"You'll be very well protected," Sir Uleweya said. "I promise."

It wasn't the most dangerous thing we'd done so far, and yet I wanted to do anything but. I wanted to go to the university. Where there were roofs. And hot food. And Kalanthe.

I sighed. There was no use arguing.

Sir Terriam reached over and squeezed my shoulder. I looked up, ready to fight if she was being patronizing, but instead her eyes were only kind.

"Knights make sacrifices all the time," she said. "And they follow orders."

"I'm not a knight," I pointed out.

"No," she said. "But you spend a lot of time with them. That sort of thing is bound to rub off."

I laughed, feeling better, and Kalanthe came back with the horses. Sir Erris decided we would ride out of smelling range of the fire and then camp for the night. The packs would have to be redistributed, and that was easier work to do in daylight. Kalanthe and I didn't talk very much as we did our tasks. After dinner, when it got dark and everyone except the first watch went to bed, I crawled into her bedroll when she held it open for me, and neither of us let go of the other, all through the night.

H ow did you find me?" Olsa demanded. In lieu of an answer, the Mage tossed her her knife, which she knew for a fact she had left specially hidden in her garret. "How did you find *that*?"

"Magic," said Mage Ladros, drawing out the word and wiggling his fingers.

Olsa considered it as she tried to figure out where she was going to put her knife. She was still in her black thief getup, but they'd taken her belt. The Mage tossed her a bag, inside of which was all the gear she'd left on the wharf. The watch must be more thorough searchers than she thought.

"That's not how magic works," she said, pulling her clothes out of the bag. The mage turned around, and she hurriedly got dressed. "You bought one of those kids that Branthear bribes."

"Employed, Olsa," Mage Ladros said with a long-suffering sigh. "Respectable old goats like me *employ*."

"If you say so." Olsa pulled on her cape and slid the knife into her belt. Now that she was warm, dressed, and probably not going to hang, she decided to press her luck and try to get some answers. "I'm decent. What are you doing here?"

Mage Ladros turned around and looked at her. Being studied was never one of Olsa's favourite things, but Ladros had a way of doing it that made her feel like less like a curiosity and more like a potential ally, so she didn't mind him as much. Everyone knew that Ladros was the most powerful mage in Cadrium, and probably the world, but few people had spent as much time with him as Olsa had. He snored, for one thing. And he was terrified of field mice.

"I need your help," the mage said. "I've made a deal with the magistrate, and she's agreed to let you come with me."

"On what conditions?" Olsa asked. The magistrate didn't give away very much for free.

"On the condition that I take you out of Cadria for a while," the mage said. "Which was fine with me, because that was my plan anyway."

Olsa sighed. Cadria was her home, but at least she would be doing something useful. Probably. That or Mage Ladros needed her to hold a lamp at a specific height for a couple of weeks so he could study a certain kind of shadow. You never could tell with mages sometimes.

"All right," she said. "Where are we going?"

"The Mage Keep," he said. "I'll give you more of the details when we're on the way, but time is of the essence, and unless you like standing around in here, I think we'd best be off."

Olsa took one more look at the moldy straw floor, like she'd forgotten something, even though that was ridiculous, and followed the mage out of the cell. They left the dungeon with none of the guards' customary insults ringing in their ears—travelling with a mage had many benefits—and went up into the courtyard, where Mage Ladros had two sturdy-looking horses and a string of mules waiting for them.

There was no question as to which of the horses was hers. Mage Ladros travelled with a veritable apothecary of substances, common and strange, packed away in various bags and boxes on his saddle, all of which were spelled against intruders. Olsa went to the mount that had only a normal waterskin and plain saddlebags. She stuffed her cape into one of them, as the day was looking to be fine.

"If you're in a hurry, why do you need the mules?" Olsa asked. Mules could walk for longer than horses, but they were slower.

"You weren't my only errand in Cadria, Olsa," he said. "There are a few things in the markets here that I can't get anywhere else, and several of my colleagues had requests as well. Besides, the mules will keep up."

Above them, the grey sky was lightening to pink, and a rooster crowed. They were going to get caught in the crowd at the gate, Olsa thought, until she remembered who she was travelling with.

"Come on, then," Mage Ladros said, and swung up into his saddle. He held the line for the string of mules.

Olsa swung up into her own saddle, only a little clumsy for lack of practice, and realized almost immediately that she was going to have to recondition all her riding muscles. Tomorrow was going to be mildly unpleasant.

Still, she sat up straight and pushed down through her heels, and she could tell the guard at the gate was thinking that her posture was far better on horseback than any street thief's deserved to be. The guard looked at the mage, and back to Olsa, and then recognition bloomed across her face. The guard inclined her head slightly when Mage Ladros rode past and looked up at Olsa with great curiosity. None of them said anything, though. Olsa never knew what to say when someone older than she treated her as a hero, and generally speaking, law enforcement types tended to be resentful when one in their custody turned out to be god-chosen, or whatever the ballads were calling her this week.

They made their way through the streets of Cadria, joining the others who were on the road in the morning on their way to the gate. As she suspected, Mage Ladros used his rank to get them to the front of the line to leave the city, and no one seemed to mind. Before long, they were clear of the crowd and heading north, where lay the Mage Keep and whatever strange purpose Mage Ladros had in mind for her.

The main difference, between travelling with a mage and travelling with a mage and knights, it turned out was the pace. Olsa was pretty sure she could have made better time crawling. Backwards. Still, it was better than prison, so she kept quiet. Mostly.

"Are we clear enough of other people for you to tell me what's going on?" she asked. "Don't get me wrong: I really do appreciate not hanging this morning, but I would like to know what I'm getting into. To, uh, prepare or something."

The Mage Keep was home to any mage who wished to claim it, and was, as such, a great centre of learning. Presumably everyone there was much, much wiser than Olsa, and as a result, she wasn't sure what she could offer.

"It's fairly simple," Mage Ladros said. He reached for his waterskin and took a drink before continuing. "You know we have been protecting the godsgem?"

Olsa nodded. Everyone in the world knew that the godsgem was somewhere in the Mage Keep, being protected by the most powerful of magics. She tried not to think about it as much as she possibly could. The godsgem's music was never far from her mind.

"Well, we figure we've laid just about every magical protection we can on the thing," Mage Ladros said, falling back into the habit of not giving it its name. Olsa vastly preferred this custom. "But we want you to come and look, and make sure we haven't missed anything."

"You want me to double-check your work?" Olsa said. "The work of mages?"

"Mages can be very wise, Olsa," he said. "But sometimes we are not, er, the most practical of people."

Olsa recalled the time, standing in the middle of the desert, when Mage Ladros had stared down a fast-approaching waterspout because he was curious as to its formation. Sir Erris and Sir Uleweya had been shrieking at him to get out of the way, and he'd casually sauntered towards them when he finally started paying attention, instead of running, which would have been much more appropriate. Afterwards, there had been a lengthy conversation about weather study and mortality, and Olsa had learned a great deal about mages in the process that she wasn't entirely sure anyone was supposed to know.

"Right," said Olsa. "Practical."

"We want you to see if there's a non-magical way to steal it," Mage Ladros said. "That's why we need you in particular."

"Because I'm the best thief you know?" she asked.

"Because you're the best thief I trust," Mage Ladros said. That was fair. It was also an excuse reasonable enough to pull her out of the king's own cells without making her feel like anyone was doing her a favour.

There were limits to magecraft, some of them practical and some of them desperately esoteric. Olsa had once asked Kalanthe why she didn't charge her armour the way she imbued her braid with her life current. Kalanthe had smiled wryly, and said that she didn't want to kill her horse. Olsa remembered how the man who grabbed her braid had convulsed so violently before Kalanthe ran him through, and realized that Kalanthe made a good point. She could control the current in her braid. She couldn't be so sure if it was her whole body. Oftentimes, mages *could* do something and had to decide whether or not they *should*.

They spent so much time thinking about it, that someone like Olsa could find a great many cracks if she was paying attention.

Olsa's stomach made a loud noise, and she realized it had been hours since the last time she'd eaten anything. Mage Ladros directed her to the food pack on her saddle. She ate one of the trail ration bars slowly because, while she knew it contained all the food she needed for a meal, it still didn't give her stomach that full feeling she liked so much. Eating slowly helped. So did remembering that it was better than the sticks of dried meat that knights were supposed to subsist on while they were on the move.

They plodded on. The mules couldn't trot or canter, so the horses couldn't either. Olsa felt a little bit like she was going to claw out of her skin, even as she looked around at the early-spring scenery. Mage Ladros wasn't one for casual chatter, and unless she wanted a lecture on something, they were probably done talking for the day. She wanted to fly, to take the horse and go, except she couldn't. Her mount sensed her restlessness and shivered underneath her.

"The horse wants to run," Mage Ladros said. Somehow, he managed not to sound too knowing when he said it, even though Olsa knew her own discontent was written all over her face. "You'd better take him on a bit of one. It'll be good for you anyway, to get you back in practice. I've got the mules. Just be sure to circle back before you go too far."

Olsa did not need to be told twice. She pulled the horse sideways, out of line with the mules, and checked to make sure her saddlebags were tightly secured. Then she set her feet, gripped with her knees, leaned forward, and encouraged the horse into a trot. They kept that pace for about fifty strides, and then Olsa turned her heels in, gently, pushing up to a canter. This was usually her favourite speed, comfortable for her and efficient for the horse, but today she wanted to fly.

She leaned forward, low over the horse's neck, and nudged it faster. Like an arrow from a bow, the gelding leapt into a gallop, and girl and horse went flying over the green spring grass.

It felt, Olsa realized, like freedom. She was probably only crying because of the wind in her eyes.

S ir Terriam met them on the road, their second day out from Cadria. She was as tall and broad shouldered as Olsa remembered, strong from years of bearing heavy armour, though she was wearing her leather dress at the moment. Her head was covered by a hood modified from the northern style, the kind used by seal hunters to cover their eyes and keep the snow-sunlight from blinding them. Terriam wore hers to leave her mouth and nose uncovered.

Of all the knights who had gone on the Quest, Terriam bore the most permanent scars, though they were mostly invisible. Sir Branthear's leg had healed and the long cut on Sir Erris's stomach was usually hidden by her clothing. Kalanthe had only the mark on her cheek, the one that Olsa shared, but when Terriam faced the Old God's demons at the altar, it was as though they had found the hurt spot in her brain, and broken it open again. She would never really heal from that.

"Olsa!" she said, falling into pace beside her after greeting the mage and adding her extra mounts to the mule line. "It's wonderful to see you again. How is the capital? How is Erris? Tell me everything."

As Mage Ladros had explained before they arrived, something about the noise and pressure of so many people living in close quarters made it difficult for Sir Terriam to live in Cadria anymore. Instead, she had semiretired to her own estates north of the city, where she ran a sort of intensive training camp for apprentice knights in their final year.

Though no longer plagued by the screaming nightmares that had lingered after her wounding at the hands of the Old God's demon, that would probably be as recovered as Sir Terriam ever got. She would sometimes be needed as a temporary instructor, but mostly she would be isolated from the main events of the king's new peace. Olsa felt a great swell of pity. Terriam always loved to talk, and it must be incredibly tedious for her to spend so much time living in the middle of nowhere, outside of the world's influence. She could still spar against an opponent, as long as everyone made sure to avoid her head, but no one knew how she would manage in open combat. Olsa didn't know what to say. Everything she thought of was either maudlin, or would make Terriam miss her old life and her old friends too much.

"It's not uncommon with older knights," Terriam said, somehow guessing the reason for Olsa's hesitation in answering. She ruffled Olsa's hair as much as she could when it was so tightly braided. "Though, admittedly, I'd hoped to be older when it happened to me. You take too many blows on the head, and you're bound to shake a few things loose."

Only, Sir Terriam hadn't taken a blow *to* the head, so much as she'd taken one *in* the head. But Olsa was hardly the type to quibble semantics.

"You're really happy here?" she asked.

Terriam thought for a moment.

"It's nice to live at home, to have total control over everything," she said. "I can make sure the curtains are all drawn and whatnot, so I don't have to wear this all the time." She pointed to her hood. "And I can arrange everything with my housekeeper so that when I'm inside, my world is still pretty much the same as it always was."

Olsa hadn't considered that, but she supposed it was true. The lady of the house could make whatever decisions she wanted, and if they all made it easier for her to go on living, then so much the better.

"I enjoy training the apprentices and it turns out I like gardening. Who could have imagined that?" Terriam continued. "I do miss you all from time to time. I imagined that when things settled down, I would have you all out to visit; only things never settled down. So instead I badgered Mage Ladros into letting me protect the two of you on the road. I don't wear heavy armour anymore, which I think just makes me better company. Or perhaps better-smelling company."

The Mage Keep was one of the places that Terriam could still safely go: it was usually quiet, and there was no other place in the world that had more people who were experts in both the Old God's demons and also the blinding, terrible headaches that Terriam got if she pushed herself too hard or if something triggered her.

"I'm glad you're with us, Sir Knight," Olsa said. If nothing else, Terriam was more likely to be conversational than Mage Ladros was, though Olsa would of course be careful not to push her.

"Right," Sir Terriam said. "Now, tell me everything that I have missed."

Olsa launched into a slightly edited version of the events of the winter. There was no need for Terriam to know how hungry and desperate she'd been, for example, and she left out most of the crime and magistrate's court. That made the story a little short, of course, so Olsa rounded it out by outlining King Dorrenta's plan of civic restructuring.

"Olsa," Terriam interrupted, about halfway through a particularly detailed description of sewer redirection in Cadria's poorer neighbourhoods. "This is all absolutely fascinating, I assure you—especially the part about managing human effluent—but what about our friends? What about *you*?"

Olsa paused for a moment and then realized that it was pointless to conceal anything. Terriam would find it all out anyway, and Olsa would rather tell her herself.

"I don't really know," she admitted. "Beyond what I hear in the city, of course. I mean, King Dorrenta pardoned me the first three times I was arrested, but I never saw him or Sir Erris, and Kalanthe spoke for me the three times after that, but our conversations were always short and, uh, short. I have no idea where Uleweya is, and Branthear has been running back and forth across the continent ever since we got back."

"You were arrested?" Terriam said. "You were arrested *six times?*"

"Seven," said Mage Ladros. "She was in the dungeon when I went to get her for this excursion."

"Olsa, what in all the hells were you getting up to?" Terriam demanded.

"It was hard," Olsa said. It was the first time she'd ever said the words out loud, and she felt a strange mix of resentment and relief boiling through her. "Everyone went away, and I went back to the streets because there was nowhere else for me to—"

"Olsa," Terriam started, but Olsa was too upset to be interrupted.

"No, that's not true," she amended. "Erris tried to take me in. The queen, can you imagine? Wanted me in her household. What in the world would I do besides stand around awkwardly and be blamed every time anything went missing? And Kalanthe offered, of course, even though she can't afford anyone else on her staff, but I will *not* be in Kalanthe's employ."

"So you went back to thievery?" Terriam guessed.

"Yes. And I did it on my own terms, this time. No more debts. Only now everyone knows my face, so it was next to impossible to get anything done." Olsa felt like she was on fire.

"I had to take riskier jobs and the Thief Bosses knew it, so they kept setting me up and I kept getting caught. The king couldn't show favouritism, and Kalanthe is off to get married, so I was supposed to hang, except Mage Ladros found me, because *everyone else left me alone.*"

She burst into tears and was too upset to be mortified that she was crying in company.

"Oh, Olsa," Terriam said. She handed over a handkerchief, and Olsa blew her nose. "I'm sorry. I was so caught up in putting my own life back together that I didn't even think about you. And of course you needed us!"

"I don't need anyone," Olsa snapped, even though she knew it wasn't true.

"Well, after all this, you can come home with me, if you like," Terriam said. "I know it's the middle of nowhere, but if I'm going to live in isolation for the rest of my life, it would be handy to have someone on my staff who can travel around and collect information and whatnot for me."

"Really?" Olsa said. The idea that she had marketable skills had never really occurred to her.

"Yes," Terriam said. "I should have offered weeks ago, months ago. I am, I promise, very sorry."

"Thank you," said Olsa. She felt like all of her joints were unlocking at the same time, though her grip on the horse didn't falter. "I'll consider it."

"I neglected to mention before," Mage Ladros said suddenly, "but this is of course a paying job."

"*What?*" Olsa said. This was far too much to deal with, and she knew it showed on her face because it always did, but it was too late now. She'd had her outburst, and now she had to face the consequences. It would probably be for the best if she didn't swear at them for their sense of timing.

"Oh yes," the mage said. "The Mage Keep always pays its contractors. I didn't want you to think I was taking advantage of your situation. I will admit, I didn't check the pay rate before I left, but I will consult the bursar when we arrive and make sure all the arrangements are made."

"I didn't know mages paid money for anything," Olsa admitted.

"We don't talk about it," Mage Ladros said.

"Only people who have money don't talk about it," Olsa said. Knowing something that the mage didn't always made her feel better, and she found some measure of equilibrium again.

"Well, see, now we've all learned something today," Mage Ladros said.

"Where are your lands exactly, Sir Terriam?" Olsa asked. If she was going to live there, or be based there, she should know.

"We've been riding through them since I met up with you," Terriam said, gesturing around her expansively. "And we will be for at least another two hours, the way these mules walk."

"That's a lot of land," Olsa said. "Farming?"

"Herding, mostly," Terriam said. "I'm not much of a farmer, but they tell me the soil here is better suited for growing sheep and goats than anything else."

"I am not an expert," Olsa said, "but I don't think you grow goats that way."

"That's why I have stewards," Terriam said. "Though hopefully I will pick up a few things so that they take me seriously in the villages. I don't want to be the Lady Invalid they all support and cluck their tongues over."

Mage Ladros launched into a discourse on sheep and goat breeding that took the rest of the time crossing Sir Terriam's land to finish. By the end of it, Olsa had learned more than she wanted to know about lambing season and the operation of making sure the goats did not become inbred, but she also felt vaguely comforted by the fact that Terriam seemed to learn just as much.

Olsa had never imagined leaving Cadria permanently, no matter how often she'd suggested to Kalanthe that they simply run away from all of their problems. If pressed, she could not have said why Cadria had such a hold on her, save perhaps that it was the only place she'd ever lived, and she knew the streets and alleyways well enough to escape trouble if she had to. The idea of living with Terriam, at least part of the time, and learning a new life together was strangely appealing, in every way except one: Kalanthe wouldn't be there.

Oh, surely she would visit, even after she got married. And surely Olsa would see her, if she was travelling around at Terriam's behest. But it would never be the same. They would both have separate lives and separate homes.

You do already, she thought viciously. You're already as separated as two people can get. Hanging around her only makes you feel worse.

Olsa blinked rapidly, driving away the forming tears before they could fill her eyes. She was done weeping for Kalanthe Ironheart and the life they could not have. It had been a wonderful dream, the best dream, but it was over now. It was time to move forward, and if Sir Terriam could offer a way to do that without Olsa having to swallow too much of her pride, then so much the better.

The last time Olsa had been on a Quest, she'd had no plans at all for what she would do if she survived it. This time, she would, and that would make everything better

BEFORE. . . . .

The university in the southern desert of Gethal should have been a sort of paradise for an apprentice knight. I had no real schedule. I could spar with the other visiting scholars who were of a military bent in the mornings and read all afternoon in the libraries about magical theory. Sir Branthear and Sir Terriam left me mostly to my own devices, beyond requesting that I focus my time in the library on the topics we were meant to be researching. It was the most freedom I had had since I'd come to Cadria and started studying to be a knight.

I was lonely. I spent hours by myself, and realized that while I thought I had been isolated during my apprenticeship, it had mostly been by choice. I had always been on the periphery of a larger whole that was wont to sweep me up at any given moment—if I would let it. There had been friends there, of a sort, but here I had nothing but books and time. I missed my fellow apprentice knights rather more sharply than I imagined I would, and I missed Olsa so profoundly, it took my breath away.

The university itself was a sight to behold. Its array of buildings perched on a sea cliff, overlooking the southern ocean on the edge of the southern desert. It had four great towers where scholars studied the sky and the stars and the weather, and several smaller buildings where more earthly topics were discussed. There were dormitories for the students— judging by the conversations I overheard, not a lot of work got done in there anyway—and also for visitors, which was where we stayed. In the centre of all of it stood the great library, its wide windows and soaring arches a monument to those who came here to learn.

While Sir Branthear and Sir Terriam spoke with scholars themselves, hoping to learn something anecdotal from those who had dedicated their lives to the study of the godsgem, I pored over endless volumes on the same subject and tried to determine fact from fiction. Several of the books were written in old, disused languages I didn't know, but once an archivist told me what language it was, I could tweak my translation spells and read most of the text. Translation spells were by no means perfect, of course; language is too messy for magic to sort out, but I got the general idea, even if sometimes a synonym or idiom threw me off course for a couple of hours while I figured it out.

In the evenings, we compared notes and waited—endlessly— for Sir Erris's party to catch up with us after their errand in the desert was complete. More often than not, I found myself looking out the window at the sea, watching the gulls dive from the cliffs, catching fish and warm air currents in equal measure while they played.

"Well, I hope Erris is having better luck," Terriam said one night about two weeks into our stay. "Because none of the pompous windbags we've been talking to are telling us anything worthwhile."

"Really?" I said. "There's so much on the subject in the library, I thought for sure one of them would know something."

"They all know *everything*, Kalanthe," Terriam said. "That's the problem."

I was confused, so I didn't say anything. Eventually Sir Branthear took pity on me.

"What Terriam means is that the scholars here all have their own pet theories," Branthear said. "And they would rather spend all their time arguing about why their theory is correct than do literally anything else, as far as I can tell."

"I think the books I'm reading are doing much the same thing," I said. "And I'm afraid to skip any of the passages, no matter how inane they seem, in case that's the passage I need."

"And to think," Terriam said, "we picked our tasks based on things we thought we'd be good at."

"I'm good at hitting things too," Branthear said. "Can we please take tomorrow off and just do that? I know we can't really spare the time, but if I don't take a break from these scholars, I might hit them instead."

Terriam agreed with her, and the next morning found the three of us up before dawn, leading our chargers out of the stables to a flat area outside the university walls. Sparring in armour can be loud, after all, and we wanted these people to like us. Even though we tried to be inconspicuous, it wasn't long before we attracted a crowd. They didn't seem angry that we'd woken them up, so we just continued our work.

"Let's give them a good show," Terriam said. "Kalanthe, may I borrow your axe?"

I handed it over and held Arrow's reins tightly as I stood beside his shoulder. An axe fight was exciting even for me, and I didn't want Arrow to wander off and make me miss any of it.

There were several cries from the audience when Branthear squared her mount and charged at Terriam, waving her brutal axe above her head. Terriam wasn't Branthear's equal with the weapon, but she could match her well enough in a training bout, and the two knights traded blows with such seeming ferocity that I took a step back out of instinct. They strove against each other for five full minutes, and then broke apart with no signal—habit was more than enough to account for it. Our audience cheered, and both of the knights put their visors up and waved magnanimously.

Terriam and Branthear rode back to the gate and I followed, leading Arrow rather than remounting him. A girl with a blue headscarf detached herself from the crowd and came up to me. I had seen her in the library: she was often deep in her studies by the time I arrived each day, and I assumed she stayed at her books long into the evening.

"Excuse me, Sir Knight," she said.

She was shorter than I was, and though her hair was wrapped up under the scarf, I assumed from the warm golden brown of her skin that it was dark like mine. She had the look of someone who had spent a great deal of time outside, though how she managed that while she was studying I couldn't guess. She wore a delicately embroidered dark-blue dress that covered her from her neck to her wrists and ankles. Her eyes were brown and looked sharply at everything. I didn't imagine there was very much that she missed.

"I'm not a knight, Scholar," I replied. "Just an apprentice."

"I am not a scholar," she said. There was a bright humour in her eyes. "Just a student."

"I suppose that makes us suited to conversation," I said. "Did you have a question about the fight?"

"I did," the student said. "How do they train the horses to be so calm when there are so many blades around and so much noise?"

She spoke softly, as most people did when they were standing next to a knight's charger, but I could tell her usual speaking tone wasn't much more strident. Her accent was different from most of the others who studied here, and certainly all those who taught. I also sensed a sort of defensiveness and knew that she had fought to be here, fought to stay.

"The same as they train the knights, I suppose," I said. "I mean, we work with our horses for the bulk of our training, so you and your mount learn at the same time, and when you get a new horse, you practice with it just as much. Also, most warhorses are bred of warhorses, so bloodline may play its part."

"I hadn't considered that horses and knights had such a true partnership," she said.

"We're a bit like a turtle on its back without them," I admitted. It was no coincidence that our pace lagged behind the others, and I was only wearing chainmail today.

She gave me a long look, and I wondered what I was being measured for. Whatever she was looking for, she must have found it, because she kept talking.

"The scholars gossip worse than old men," she said. "I know you're here looking for information about the godsgem. I'm not a scholar, as I said, but I'm not ignorant either, and I think I might be able to help you, if you're willing to consider a non-conventional information source."

I noticed she chose to say "non-conventional" rather than "unconventional."

"What's your name?" I asked.

"Giran y'Koda," she said. The name was old, one of those languages I'd been translating. I only recognized the form, not the word itself. Names lasted the longest out of the old languages once spoken in Cadrium, even though now we all spoke the same tongue. Her name meant she was from somewhere specific, instead of a trade name or an epithet like the other knights and I had.

"My name is Kalanthe," I told her. "When can I bring the knights to you?"

"After the breakfast hour," Giran said. "I'll be in the library. You'll find me under a stack of books, in the study area."

"I know it," I told her. "I have spent most of the last few days there myself."

We parted ways so that I could take Arrow back to the stable. Terriam was gone when I arrived, but Branthear was still brushing her charger's flanks.

"I may have found us a source," I said. "Where's Sir Terriam?"

"She was invited to breakfast with the sailing masters, for some reason," Branthear said. "And she didn't want to refuse. But I can come with you, if you like. Who is your source?"

"A student who was watching the axe fight," I said. "She didn't seem like a windbag."

"I like her already," Branthear said.

We finished tending to the horses as the breakfast hour slid by. Branthear had hot rolls she must have charmed out of some assistant cook, and she shared them with me so that we wouldn't have to come late into the dining hall. When we were done, I led her into the library and scanned the study area for Giran's blue headscarf. When I spotted her, I tapped Sir Branthear on the shoulder and led the way across the room to the reading tables. I sat down across from Giran, and she looked up and smiled. She was surrounded by volumes and scrolls, but hadn't yet uncapped her inkwell, so I didn't think we would be interrupting her work if I spoke to her.

"Hello," I said, as quietly as I could, for the benefit of the students around us. "This is Sir Branthear, one of my companions. Do you mind if she asks you some questions?"

"I am happy to help," said Giran. "Though I hope Kalanthe has warned you that I am not yet an accredited scholar."

"Well, thank goodness for that," Branthear said, as easy as ever. "That's part of the reason we want to talk to you."

"My mother and father are traders, so they have been to Cadria before, but I never have," Giran said. "My background means the other students like to think I don't know anything, and the scholars are happy to encourage them in the name of friendly competition, even if it's anything but. For the first few years, I fought them, but then I realized I wasn't gaining anything in return, so now I do mostly self-directed study. They still dismiss me, but they'll have to accredit me when I pass."

"I'm happy to tell you about Cadria, if you like," I said. "Or any other part of Cadrium, for that matter. Our travels have taken us all over the continent." I had learned from overheard conversations that trading information was a common enough way to work together, and I had already told her about the horse. The truth was, if she could help us find the godsgem, I was willing to tell her just about anything.

"I would appreciate that," said Giran. "Now, I know you're seeking information about the godsgem. What would you like to know?"

"Anything you know about it," Sir Branthear said. "Specifically, if you might have any ideas about where it is."

Giran laughed, making a bit more noise than was customary even in this part of the library, and then quickly silenced herself.

"I'm sorry, Sir Knight," she said. "I don't mean to mock you. But all the scholars in this building, and those next to it, don't know that, and you think I might?"

"I didn't ask if you *knew*, lass," Branthear said. "I just wondered if you had any new ideas."

"I've seen the books you read," I said. "They're all about the godsgem. Surely you must have some theory on the matter."

"Besides," Branthear said, "I've spent several days talking to accredited scholars. They are not as helpful as you might think."

"I'm a scarf-wearer girl from a family who lives in tents," Giran said. Her accent shifted to harder sounds, and her whole face and bearing stiffened with it. "I think I understand exactly how helpful the other scholars can be. Give me a moment to think about it."

Branthear gestured, indicating that she should take all the time she needed. I wondered why Giran wore the scarf when she knew what others thought of her for wearing it. Head coverings served a practical function in the desert—and not in the same way the one Olsa wore to sleep did—keeping sand out of your eyes and mouth, and keeping the sun off the back of your neck. Several knights in my training year wore them when they were at home, but not in the city as there was no need. I hadn't seen anyone other than Giran wearing one at the university, even though I had to admit, it was still pretty dusty here. I liked the feel of light fabric on my skin and the way the scarf would conceal my face from strangers, and wished that I could wear one, but it was not my culture, so it wasn't a choice I had. Maybe the scarf reminded her of her home, her roots. Maybe she just liked to be obstinate. In either case, I admired her for it.

"All right, so the general consensus is that the new gods hid the godsgem after they used it." Like most people, Giran avoided talking about the Old God directly. "Why they hid it is a matter of debate, and not really necessary for us to consider right now."

She rifled through a few loose papers—her own notes—and then got up and went into the stacks to find a book. A moment later, she returned with it and began to turn the pages. Her fingers glowed—sense-magic, I realized. Giran could find pages in a book by touch. It was a useful skill for a student to have. I wondered if it only worked in books she had already read.

"Yes," she replied when I asked the question. "It would be marvelous to find anything, at any time, but I like this because it helps me remember the order of the information I learned. I think if it was the other way, my mind would be all jumbled."

Giran's whole hand flared with light. She had found what she was looking for.

"There are so many thoughts about where it's hidden," Giran said. "I'm sure my teachers have told you in great detail where they think it is, in any case."

Branthear nodded.

"So, what I'll tell you is something they won't," Giran continued. "It's a theory that's so unsubstantiated that no one will stake their credibility on it, the sort where if you take it seriously, no one takes *you* seriously."

Sir Branthear leaned forward. I felt my heart speed up, like I was riding into battle or like Olsa was . . . but this was not the time or the place to be thinking about that.

"Here," she said, indicating a paragraph and passing it over to Branthear. Branthear read it quickly and passed the book to me.

The newly inked words on the page were clear enough, written in a steady hand—presumably Giran's—in the margins. What interested me was the original text, written in one of the dead languages of Cadrium by a scholar long since dead. I did my spell quietly, light flaring just as Giran's had, and she nodded approvingly as my own translation appeared, hovering over the page. I squinted, moving a few of the words around to account for sentence structure. Giran readied a quill, which I appreciated.

"'You will not find the godsgem, nor will it find you.'" I read the words I had just translated. It was easier for me to remember things if I heard them out loud. "'Rather, it will meet you upon the road. If you find the godsgem and it is standing still, or if the godsgem finds you and you are standing still, leave it where it lies, for it is not real and its power will only deceive. The true godsgem will meet you on the way.'"

I looked up. "On the way where?"

"I have no idea," said Giran. "The original writings are from Albor y'Zarat, a desert woman like me, so no one takes her seriously. Yours is a good translation. It's very close to mine, though I did it the long way."

"I had read yours already," I admitted. "It helped to guide my thoughts while I did the spell, I'm sure."

Giran smiled, nodding at the compliment, and we lapsed into a thoughtful silence for a moment. I felt like I was right on the edge of something, but I didn't know how to make Sir Branthear understand what I was feeling.

"Kalanthe?" said Branthear. "You have an odd look."

"I know this won't make any sense," I said. "But . . . it feels right?"

"Was that a question?" Branthear said.

"No," I said. "It's just strange and I can't explain it. But magic has a feel to it, and this feels . . . right."

"That's what I thought," Giran said. "My magic isn't strong enough for very much beyond page-finding, but I can usually tell when someone is on the right track. It's something about the feel of the work. At home, my father plans entire seasons of work around my mother's touch-magic. Here, they say it's intuition and laugh."

"I'm starting to think that scholarship isn't as thoughtful as I'd heard," I said.

"They're very good at some things," Giran said. "You just have to be sure you don't think you're good at everything, and sometimes they forget that."

She paused and looked at Branthear, who was already planning the next steps our Quest would take once Sir Erris joined us.

"The godsgem," Giran said to me so quietly I had to lean in to hear her. She smelled like old books. "You don't just want it in theory. You want it for a purpose."

I nodded, unable to say as much out loud, even though I hadn't taken an oath to keep it a secret. I could tell Giran's mind was working quickly now.

"Well, when you find it and use it to save the world, or whatever," she said. "If you find it the way I told you to, can you let me know so that I can publish about it? Imagine the looks on their faces."

This time, it was I who laughed too loudly for the library, though I quieted myself just as quickly as Giran had. It was nice, from time to time, to remember that the world spun on, even as our Quest grew more and more desperate.

"I will," I promised. "Good luck in your studies."

"Good luck in your . . . whatever," Giran said. "I get the feeling we all need it."

Sir Branthear thanked her as well, and then the two of us left the library. We had to find Terriam and come up with a new plan. If finding the godsgem was going to involve magic and destiny instead of rational thought and tracking, then our jobs had all just got a lot harder.

Lycenia was one of the largest provinces in Cadrium, and was located a few days east of the city. Mostly arable farmland, Lycenia butted up against the eastern wastes, which were largely unpopulated due to the paucity of fresh water in the region. Kalanthe had been to the wastes before, of course, while on the Quest, but they had gone there by a circuitous route, following folktales and hedge-stories, and then journeyed north to the coast, so she had never been to Sir Edramore's home.

Sir Branthear had, but not for several years. Still, she was able to point out several of the more notable landmarks as they rode along. Their pace was easy. They had stayed the night before in an inn that was a step up from their usual, because Kalanthe wanted a proper bath. It wasn't just Edramore she had to impress, of course, but his entire household, and she wouldn't do that if she showed up late at night with half the dust in east Cadrium lodged under her fingernails. So she and Branthear had stopped early for the night, taken the time to make themselves present-able, and now they were nearly arrived.

Kalanthe was wearing her chainmail, but no helmet. She had left most of her hair loose down her back, but had put several braids across the crown of her head to keep it from blowing in her eyes as she rode. She wore a deep red tunic that Triana had embroidered in gold to set off her brown skin, and hose of the same colour. Her boots had been polished to a gleaming shine and came up past her knees. She carried a royal shield because she was still not permitted to carry her own colours and wore her signet rings openly on her right hand. She was mounted on Lightfoot, having decided against Arrow, fearing that arriving on a charger would have been too much of a statement, and she couldn't bring herself to ride the gelding, though she had finally named it Constance because it was the most reliable animal she had ever seen.

Beside her, Sir Branthear rode in full armour, mounted on her charger, because as a knight she was entitled to make all the statements she liked. Together, they rode through the village that was on the outskirts of Edramore's main estate and tried to ignore all the day labourers and children who stared at them.

The main estate itself was unfortified, though it was surrounded by a low stone wall. The grounds comprised several outbuildings and one very large house. All the structures, even the one Kalanthe suspected of being the chicken coop, were made of stone that gleamed under a new spring coat of whitewash. The outbuildings had thatched roofs, while the main house had red roof tiles. It was orderly, functional, and almost excruciatingly homelike.

They had been spotted, as had been their intent, so by the time Branthear led the way through the gate, where they left their spare mounts and the packhorses, and into the courtyard that the house and outbuildings looked onto, the entire household was mustered to meet them. Kalanthe's fingers tightened momentarily on Lightfoot's rein. There were so many of them. She knew, academically, that it took a tremendous number of people to keep this sort of estate running smoothly, but she hadn't exactly expected to meet them all at once.

She took several deep breaths, hoping it was not too noticeable, as she and Branthear drew close to the steps in front of the house. Standing on them was a smaller group of people, and suddenly Kalanthe forgot that there was anyone else in the courtyard at all.

Sir Edramore was a tall man, whose bearing indicated that he had trained wearing armour, even if his build betrayed that it had been some years since he had worn any. His white skin was more than a little sunburned, and he had dark-brown, almost black, hair. He had a high forehead and a distinct nose, and he was smiling as though that were his natural state. Beside him stood two girls, his daughters, and Kalanthe realized that their mother must have had skin like Olsa's. The older one had thick, wavy hair that she wore neatly braided. The younger one had the tightly curled cloud Kalanthe recognized from before Olsa learned to do her own braids.

She absolutely had to stop thinking about Olsa.

A groom stepped forward to take her horse and Branthear's, and Kalanthe swung down. Then she turned to face her fate.

"Cousin," said Sir Edramore, coming down the stairs to clasp hands with Sir Branthear, who was closer to him anyway. "It is wonderful to see you again."

"Likewise," Branthear agreed. She turned slightly and indicated Kalanthe. "If I may, allow me to introduce apprentice knight Lady Kalanthe Ironheart."

Kalanthe took a few steps forward and met Sir Edramore's gaze. His expression was entirely neutral, not measuring or wondering in any way. She inclined her head.

"My lord," she said. "It is my honour to meet you."

"And mine as well, Lady Ironheart," he replied. He leaned into her title in such a way that she knew he took her seriously, not as a child or a supplicant. Whatever spirit his offer had been made in, it was as good and kindly meant as she might have hoped. "My daughters, Lady Knights," he continued, gesturing to the girls who still stood at the top of the stairs. They came to him and looked up at Kalanthe with curious expressions.

"My name is Elenia," said the older of the two. "Thank you for coming to see us, my ladies."

"Carster," whispered the younger one before she disappeared behind her father's cape. Kalanthe entirely sympathized with her.

"It is my pleasure," Kalanthe said. She was decently sure that Triana had packed something for her to give the girls, but at the moment she could not for the life of her remember what it was. Hopefully when she unpacked it would make itself apparent.

"Welcome, welcome," Sir Edramore said. He was using a louder voice, one that carried through the whole courtyard. Anyone who listened would know how their lord felt about the visiting knights. "Please, I know the road was long. Come inside. We have much to discuss."

The rooms that Kalanthe and Branthear were shown to were in the northern wing of the house. The family apartments, Kalanthe surmised, were in the southern wing. A large room connected the two wings and served as the place where Edramore held court and hosted any large social gatherings, like the dinner they would attend that evening. Behind that were the kitchens and the various utilitarian rooms that were needed to keep a household this size running smoothly. Lunch was to be taken with the family, the housekeeper said, as she showed them to their rooms, in order to get everyone acquainted.

Since she was mostly clean, Kalanthe spent only a few minutes in her dressing room. She shook the dust out of her tunic and tucked away the few loose hairs that the wind had liberated. She would be made over for the dinner tonight, surely, in any case. She just had to get through lunch first.

When she went back into her sitting room, a young woman stood there. She was dressed neatly in the livery worn by the household, though Kalanthe did not recognize her from the earlier assembly in the yard.

"Lady Ironheart," the girl said with a quick curtsey. "I'm Ayera, and I'm to be your lady's maid while you're with us."

"It's nice to meet you," Kalanthe said. "Could I trouble you to help me find something in my bags? I am sure I have a gift for the girls, and I would like to give it to them at luncheon."

"Or course," said Ayera, and began to unpack.

She took the time to hang up anything that needing hanging and held a dress back to be aired out for dinner. "With my lady's permission?" Eventually, in the bottom of the case where Kalanthe carried her gloves and spare cape, Ayera found the package Triana had included.

"Thank you so much," Kalanthe said. There was a knock on the door, and Kalanthe answered it herself, since Ayera was still busy. It was Branthear and a footman, come to take them to lunch.

"I'll just finish here and see you again later, my lady," said Ayera. She shook out one of Kalanthe's tunics and wrinkled her nose contemplatively.

Kalanthe left her to it and followed Branthear into the corridor.

"Are you all right?" Branthear said quietly while the footman pretended to be quite unaware that they were speaking.

"Yes," Kalanthe said. "It's just quite a bit to get used to."

"I'd forgotten the effect of this place when Edramore brings down the full weight of the Lord of the Manor," Branthear said. The footman smirked. "But he means well."

"I know," said Kalanthe. "And the rooms are lovely. I am sure I'll settle in."

"What's that?" Branthear said, indicating the package that Kalanthe held.

"It's for the girls," Kalanthe said. "I wanted to give them something, and Triana took care of it for me."

"You don't know what it is?"

"I'm sure it's shatteringly appropriate," Kalanthe said. "Triana is very good at her job."

The footman led them through the great room, where tables were being arranged already for the evening's entertainments, and into the family apartments. There was a smaller dining room here, and Edramore and his daughters were already waiting for them. Kalanthe was glad to see that places had been set for the girls. This was, after all, going to affect them too, and they deserved to be present and not stashed away in the nursery.

"My ladies," said Sir Edramore. Then he caught sight of the package in Kalanthe's hands. "Ah, but what is this?"

"It's a gift, my lord," said Kalanthe. "For your daughters."

Elenia bounced over immediately, with Carster trailing at a safe distance. Still, Kalanthe noted that the girls unwrapped the package together. Inside were two hoops and two sticks, a common enough toy, but one that Kalanthe knew from experience could often do with replacing. Also, Triana had decorated the sticks with brightly coloured ribbon in Kalanthe's family colours, which was a stretch, but still well within the realms of legal heraldry.

"Thank you, Lady Ironheart," said Elenia on cue. Carster tried to say something, but her voice finally failed her. Kalanthe smiled in what she hoped was a reassuring way, and the girls dashed off to the corner, to test the hoops, but before they could really get into it, a door opened, and a footman came in with a large tray.

"Girls, please come back to the table," Sir Edramore said, handing Kalanthe into a chair. Branthear seated herself. "We don't want to trip anyone and break the lady's thoughtful gift."

Carster detoured on her way back to her chair to pass by where Kalanthe was seated. She pulled on Kalanthe's tunic, and when Kalanthe leaned over, she whispered, "Thank you," into her ear, before dashing off to take her seat. Kalanthe smiled and turned her attention to her plate.

hile they ate, they mostly talked about the weather and the state of the roads. It was customary, Kalanthe knew, but it was still a little frustrating. Elenia apparently shared her opinions, because the girl asked several questions about the Quest that Kalanthe was only too happy to answer, slightly edited for content of course, and then conversation shifted to the more personal.

Branthear asked several questions about the estate, and Edramore seemed pleased to talk about his home. Kalanthe liked that he was so obviously comfortable with the day-to-day affairs of his house. Some lords cared only for profits and prestige, but Edramore was clearly not of that sort. It was, Kalanthe realized, entirely possible that he knew the names of every single one of his people, and possibly every single one of his *sheep* the way he talked about them.

At last, the dessert was eaten and the plates were cleared away. The girls went off with their nurse—only slightly under protest—and Branthear manufactured an excuse to get out of the room, leaving Edramore and Kalanthe alone.

"My lady, shall we walk?" Edramore said, getting up from the table and extending a hand.

Kalanthe took the arm he offered, and they walked out together. They did not go through the great room again, but rather through a back passageway, and then out a door into what must be the family's private gardens. They were extensive and beautifully maintained. Kalanthe was instantly enamoured with them and happy to follow Sir Edramore as he led her down to a bench that sat beside a quiet pool. They sat together, listening to the wind in the flowering trees and the bubble of a fountain that must be close by, and Edramore appeared to gather his thoughts.

"I apologize, Lady Kalanthe, if any of this causes you discomfort. There isn't a lot of grace in marriage negotiations, and I can only assure that I mean no insult," he said.

"Thank you, my lord," Kalanthe replied. "I will admit, it is very strange."

"It had better be Edramore," he said. "And I will call you Kalanthe, if you don't mind?"

"Of course," she said, though she could not bring herself to tack "Edramore" on the end of it.

"Very well," he said. "I am glad that my daughters seem to like you. Elenia likes almost everyone, but Castriar—that's Carster's real name, by the way—is a bit more difficult to win over."

"Where did Carster come from?" Kalanthe asked, even though it was the least practical of the questions currently floating around in her mind. She couldn't quite say the *r* the same way Edramore did and resolved to practice. A difference in accent was no reason to mispronounce a name.

"That's how she said it when she was learning to talk," Edramore explained. "She might get around to changing it someday, but in the meantime, Carster has more or less stuck."

Kalanthe's own brother had been unable to pronounce his name—or hers—when he was small, so she knew how this sort of thing went.

"In any case," Edramore continued, "I'm very glad you came. It's one thing to receive a proposal and an entirely different thing to back it up. I wanted you to come and visit so that you could see what you might be getting into, and so that we could speak in person."

"Sir Erris—the queen, I mean—said much the same thing, when I asked for her advice," Kalanthe admitted.

"I can tell you are thoughtful," Edramore said. "Not everyone would ask for advice in your case."

He was deliberately not pointing out her age, which Kalanthe appreciated.

"As you can see," he continued, "the estate is what I outlined. We can look at the ledgers if you wish, or my stewards can interview with you, and you can get a better idea of how the place is run. There are a few bridges we need to shore up after the spring flooding, but aside from that, everything is fairly sound. I'll be happy to show you around in the next few days."

"That would be nice," Kalanthe murmured. Why couldn't she talk like a normal person? Oddly, she perceived that he was also nervous about something, though he was dealing with it much better than she was. She cleared her throat. "I would enjoy seeing your estate, Edramore." She didn't even choke on it. "The parts that I have seen so far have been lovely."

"Your manners are impeccable, Kalanthe," Edramore said, "and so I will no longer dance around the real reason I wanted you to come out here and talk to me in person."

She looked at him expectantly. There was a worry line in the middle of his forehead.

"You will wonder, of course, why I do not go to court," Edramore said. "And you will wonder why I am so eager to marry someone whose practicality and sense of duty mirrors my own, regardless of her age."

"I will confess, I have been curious," Kalanthe said.

"The answer to both questions is the same," Edramore said. "But slightly complicated by a portion of personal history. I beg your indulgence while I explain."

"Of course, my l—Edramore," Kalanthe said. His formality made it difficult not to respond in kind.

Kalanthe watched while he took a few moments to gather his thoughts again and then, to avoid staring, looked out over the gardens. They were gorgeous, even though the flowers had not yet fully bloomed. She could smell a variety of complementary scents on the breeze and could tell by what flowers she could see that considerable thought had gone into both seasonal and colour arrangement when they were planted. Yet they were all slightly wild, as though maintained by someone who was not a professional gardener. In a flash, Kalanthe knew that Edramore had done the work, or at least a lot of it, himself. These gardens were another example of the care he took in every aspect of his life.

"Several years ago, before I married, but after I had inherited my mother's title, I began to experience sporadic headaches," Edramore began. "No more than once a month, but they were debilitating. I found that wearing armour made them worse, as did being in company, so I left Cadria and came home. For a time, that seemed to help, but eventually the headaches became more frequent."

A frog hopped into the pond, and Kalanthe looked back at Edramore's face. It was open and honest. Whatever he was telling her was of great importance to him.

"I consulted every healer I could find and eventually employed a mage to come from the Mage Keep to examine me." That would have been very, very expensive, and spoke to the pain Edramore had endured. "And in the meantime, because life does not stop, I got married."

Kalanthe wanted to ask what she was like, if he had loved her. It would be much fairer if they both understood what love was before entering a marriage without it. She held her tongue. There would be time for that later.

"The mage examined me, consulted some of her books and her colleagues, and then was finally able to give me a diagnosis," Edramore paused. "I suppose that, as a knight, you have a rough idea of human physiology?"

Kalanthe nodded. The truth was that she had one time seen a human brain after Branthear had smashed open the skull of a minion who was attacking them, but this hardly seemed like the time to mention that or any of the other things she had seen for that matter.

"Blood moves through a person's brain the way it moves though the rest of their body," Edramore said. "It moves through mine too, except that there is a blockage in part of my brain where the blood passes too slowly. That pressure buildup is what causes my headaches."

"The mage couldn't dissolve it?" Kalanthe asked. Healer-mages had remarkable power.

"She could, but she was unsure how much of my brain she might dissolve along with it," Edramore said. "The blockage is made from the same tissue as the rest of my brain. There's just too much of it in the wrong place, so it was difficult for the mage to target. She practiced on some of my own cows and was not enthusiastic about the results, so I didn't press the issue."

"Could she do anything at all?" Kalanthe said, though she knew in her heart what the answer to that question was already.

"No," Sir Edramore said. "She could lessen the pain of the headaches and she could make it so that I could tolerate more light, but she couldn't cure me."

For a long moment, neither of them said anything.

"There is a spot in my brain, Kalanthe," Edramore continued. He took her hands and looked straight into her eyes. "At any moment, perhaps my next breath, perhaps in twenty years, the spot will become too much. The blood vessels around the mass will burst, and I will die instantly."

Kalanthe stared at him, painfully aware of each breath she was drawing, each breath he was *wasting* trying to make her understand. Again, somehow, he smiled.

"You are wondering how I live?" he asked.

"Yes," she breathed.

"I think about it sometimes," he said. "I wonder if I have been selfish. I certainly never imagined that my wife would die, when I imagine my own death so much. I certainly should have remarried for my daughters, only I wanted them to remember me, so I spent so much time with them."

"I can't imagine that anyone would find fault with that," Kalanthe said.

"It is very strange, sometimes," Edramore said. "To always wonder. I try not to think about it, lest the knowledge crush me, but it's always close at hand."

"There is a mass in your brain that will kill you," Kalanthe said softly. It was a schoolroom habit she hadn't completely shaken yet. If she repeated the lesson out loud, she always remembered it. "There will be no warning, and your daughters will be alone."

"Quite," Edramore said. "Until the king appoints them a guardian who will oversee my estate until Elenia is old enough to inherit."

"And so you want a wife whom you can trust," Kalanthe said. "And you think that we could strike a bargain?"

"No, Kalanthe," he said gently. "Though I will not deny that the idea of being the hero one last time and helping you in your situation is appealing to someone who didn't get to be a hero very often."

"Then why?" she asked.

"You went on a Quest and saved the knight who is now the queen," Edramore said. "In the stories and songs, they speak of your goodness, your dutiful nature. Those are the sort of songs I wish people had sung about me, but I like to imagine that if you go into the village pub, the fieldworkers will tell you that I am good and thoughtful and kind too. I want you to marry me because I think we are the same. I will leave you a great deal of responsibility, and you will rise up to meet it."

Kalanthe knew that it was true. If he left her so much as a kitten, she would take care of it.

"My girls will have a guardian, and my people will have a lady," Edramore said. "It's strange to say it, but I'm not just looking for a wife, Kalanthe. I am deliberately picking the woman I want to be my widow."

BEFORE. . . . .

If there was one thing that deserts were good for, it was thinking. I thought about how hot it was. I thought about how much I missed Kalanthe. I thought about how much I hated sand. I thought about how much I liked the boots that Sir Uleweya had bought for me, months ago when we were only newly embarked on the Quest. My own poor shoes had nearly worn through, and I'd resigned myself to going barefoot into whatever dangers Sir Erris had in mind, when Sir Uleweya presented them to me.

"They'll hurt for the first few days," she'd said, guessing rightly that I had never owned a new pair of anything before, much less boots that were so fine. "But once you've broken them in, you'll be all right."

I had only just finished breaking in my rear on the horse's saddle, so I was less than keen on starting all over again, but I knew I had to do it. The human body, I learned, can get accustomed to almost about anything if you break it in properly. I didn't find it a particularly reassuring thought.

And now here we were in the southern desert, the last check mark on Sir Erris's list, unless she planned to take us by water to some continent beyond Cadrium's shores. We had already done a great tour of the continent. I'd learned to read in the west, how to braid my hair in the east, and how Kalanthe breathed while she was kissing me on the northern coast. Now we were good and south, and I had sand absolutely everywhere with nothing to show for it but a pair of now thoroughly broken-in boots.

Sir Uleweya and I were camped in a small oasis that wasn't on any map, waiting for Sir Erris and Mage Ladros to get back. They had gone into the dunes a bit, to see if they could find the cult we were after. Rumour had it that there was a group of zealots out there somewhere who had a relic that might be the godsgem or, at least, might have some sort of power. They weren't even true southerners, as a point of fact, but interlopers who were living under some sort of bastardization of southern customs. The locals didn't like them very much—rightly so, in my mind—and were all too happy to tell Sir Erris anything she wanted to know about them, on the off chance that she was going to eradicate them. Sir Erris had nothing so drastic in mind, she said, though it was possible that they would disperse after she disproved their relic.

Sir Uleweya lit a fire and put on the teakettle to boil. In the heat of the day, fire was ludicrous, but we still needed it to cook, and I knew that once the sun went down, we'd need it for heat too.

"Did you know how much of your knighthood you'd spend waiting around for something to happen when you started your apprenticeship?" I asked her.

"No." She laughed. "I thought it was all going to be glory, like everyone does."

"Would you still have done it?" I asked.

"I think so," Sir Uleweya said. "The waiting's not so bad, really."

That wasn't exactly what I'd meant, but I let it pass. I noticed she was putting out more food than the two of us needed, and was therefore not entirely surprised when, about half an hour later, Mage Ladros and Sir Erris rode into camp. Sir Uleweya's long-sight was very reliable.

"How did it go?" asked Sir Uleweya, once Erris and Ladros had finished with their horses and joined us around the campfire.

"They've definitely got something," said Sir Erris. "It's not the godsgem, but it's definitely something."

"I don't like it," Mage Ladros said. "I don't mind non-mage folk having items of power, but that thing—whatever it is— feels dangerous."

"I agree," said Sir Erris. "That's why we came back for you two."

The long-sighted knight and the thief. It wasn't hard for me to guess what they were after, but I had learned by now that it was better to put everything on the table when you were involved in group work.

"You want me to steal it?" I asked.

"I would appreciate a closer look at it," Mage Ladros said. "As I said, I don't mind people having things. It just makes me nervous when they use them."

"Is that safe?" I asked. I wasn't as well educated as some, but I knew that touching artefacts with power often involved some kind of blowback.

"I'll shield you," said the Mage, and I knew that he would.

"We'll ride out in the morning," Sir Erris said. "It should be simple enough to get you close. Then Uleweya can find it, and you can infiltrate the camp and take care of it."

"I don't think we'll have to wait for morning." Sir Uleweya was looking hard in the direction that Sir Erris had arrived from. Her eyes were pure flame. "I think some of them have followed you home."

"How many?" Sir Erris said, wearily getting to her feet.

"A score?" Sir Uleweya guessed. "They're kicking up a lot of dust, and even I have trouble looking into the sun."

"Can you tell if they have the object with them?" Mage Ladros asked. He had gone to his packs to get his battle magic ready.

"If it glows green, then yes," Uleweya reported. "I imagine we've got about ten minutes before they get here."

With ten minutes to prep, no angry mob stood a chance against Sir Erris, Sir Uleweya, and Mage Ladros, but there was me and all of the camp gear to take into account, and that complicated things. Eventually, Mage Ladros just led the horses behind a dune, cast an enchanted sleep on them, and hid them with an illusion.

I was another matter. I couldn't just hide because they needed me to nab the artefact. Sir Erris gave me her mace, the only weapon I was even moderately good with, despite Sir Terriam's efforts with the knife, and boosted me up into one of the spindly trees that grew around the oasis's waterhole. I'd have to jump down, but it was nothing for someone who'd been jumping off rooftops in Cadria for most of her life.

I watched Sir Uleweya draw her two swords and swing them around to warm up her muscles. The bright iron whistled as it cut through the air. Sir Erris drew her own sword and readied her shield. Neither of them was expert enough at fighting in sand to take their chargers, so they would do this fight on foot. Normally, this would have put them at a slight disadvantage, but Mage Ladros had laid down a few surprises of his own to even the odds.

The wind picked up, which often happened around sunset in the desert, but after a few seconds, I realized it was blowing in the wrong direction.

"They've got a mage!" Ladros said. "I'll keep a watch for them."

We heard the zealots before they came around the last corner and ran clear of the dunes. Stealth is well and good, I supposed, but if you're about to attack two of the best knights in the realm, you probably want to yell a bit before you do it.

The first five or so ran right into Mage Ladros's first surprise: a wall of fire that burned out of nothing along the sand. Two of them didn't stop in time and ploughed right into it. They screamed as the magefire engulfed them, burning much faster than regular fire ever could, and then fell to the ground and were still. The other three waited a heartbeat, and when the flames died down a bit, jumped over them. They came face-to-face with Sir Uleweya, her swords bright as they threw back reflections of the dying magefire, and didn't long survive the encounter.

I lost track of the exact body count after that. Mage Ladros sprung more fire and miniature sandstorms on the attackers, slowing them down enough for Erris and Uleweya to deal with them. At last, when the numbers were a more manageable ten to two, he turned his attention to their mage.

She was standing on top of the dune, several yards away from the actual battle. I could see that her hands held something bright and green. I knew, somehow, in my very heart that, though it was not the godsgem she clasped, it was something she should not be allowed to keep. When she held it up, the wind blew faster and faster around the oasis. The water in the pond rippled, then heaved, and then rose up in a giant waterspout. Mage Ladros stared, clearly as surprised as any of us were, because we all knew the pond wasn't that deep.

"Stop admiring her handiwork, and get rid of it!" shouted Sir Erris, dispatching the last of her attackers.

Mage Ladros snapped into action. He held his hands out, calling in the wind or whatever it was, until his hands glowed blue in the orange light of the sunset desert. Then, as calmly as if he were merely taking the water's temperature, he stuck one hand into the pond. I felt the ground rumble, even from my perch in the tree. Mage Ladros had a tendency to make things look effortless, but the very earth betrayed his exertion this time. It made sense, after a fact: messing with the weather was a serious business. Kalanthe couldn't yet do it and had told me she didn't know if she'd ever be able to. And here was Mage Ladros, carrying on like it was nothing. He blew on his half-submerged hand, and the blue light flew away from him, up into the waterspout.

For two breaths, the magics combined. Then Mage Ladros's power overwhelmed the unknown mage's, and the waterspout flew apart. Because he was, at heart, a show-off, Mage Ladros held out his hands again, stopping the water from flying off, and returning all of it to the pond where it had come from in the first place. Sir Erris sighed.

From the top of the tree, I saw my chance. The destruction of her spell had stunned the mage. She'd fallen forward and rolled down the dune, much closer to our encampment than I think she'd ever meant to come. I stood on the branch that bore my weight and tested it a few times to see how much of a push-off it could take. Then I leapt, careful not to brain myself with Sir Erris's mace when I landed.

The unknown mage was lying facedown in the sand. She'd

probably have a mouthful of it when she woke up because she wasn't wearing a headscarf—of all the southern customs to not appropriate. One of her arms was pinned beneath her. The other was stretched out above her head, and I could see that her fingers were clasped around a green rock. I was within arm's reach of her. All I had to do was lean over and pick it up, but every instinct I had screamed at me, telling me the stone was a poison, even for a mage.

Instead of reaching for the stone, I kicked it free of her hand with one booted foot. It skittered across the sand and then came to a rest. It looked so unassuming there, just a rock in a desert full of rocks, even if it was green and I had just seen it break several of the laws of nature with that waterspout. If something so little could do so much in the hands of the wrong person, surely in the hands of the *right* person it wouldn't be so bad. There were several neighbourhoods in Cadria that could do with a fresh water source. The two feelings—potential and disgust—warred within me.

The woman moaned, waking up, even as I hesitated. She made enough noise that Sir Erris heard her and began to run towards us. Mage Ladros, sitting by the pond, was clearly more exhausted than he ever let on, because it took him a few seconds to get to his feet and follow her.

I remembered myself, finally, and swung the mace high. The mage woke up just as I brought it crashing down, and her scream pierced the air as I smashed the false godsgem to smithereens against the desert sand. The mage lunged just as Erris tackled her, and Mage Ladros cast some sort of binding spell to hold her in place. He looked at me and then at the shards beneath my borrowed mace.

"How did you know?" He was still breathing hard.

"I just did," I told him.

He turned away and went back to the pool to lie in the shade. Erris carried the bound mage down beside him, but I couldn't leave just yet. I had to be sure.

Now that it was broken, the colour draining out of it like blood into the sand, I could see that it was just a painted rock.

They did not make better time after Terriam joined the party, on account of the mules, but Olsa felt that the miles went faster. Terriam, always happy to talk, filled the hours with conversation that was friendly and well-meaning and, if only by accident, occasionally informative. It reminded Olsa of the camaraderie they had all shared on the Quest, even when things were going badly and there was danger around every corner. She hadn't felt that way since she'd returned home.

They rode north for a week, the weather turning slowly back to winter as they went. When they stopped at a village that still had snow on the ground, Terriam disappeared to the market for a few hours and returned with cold-weather gear in Olsa's size. She handed over the package with no ceremony at all and announced that Olsa's new boots would be ready the following morning.

Any protest Olsa might have made vanished as soon as she saw the gear that Terriam had picked. She had no love for being cold, after all, and freezing would serve no purpose. The heavy woollen hose fit her perfectly, and while the thick tunic that matched them was a little long, it was perfect across the shoulders. There was also an extra cape, several pairs of stockings, replacement smallclothes, fur-lined leather gloves, and a fur hat that looked absolutely ridiculous but was amazingly warm, and therefore worth it.

"Thank you, Sir Terriam," she said, once she had returned to the inn's common room.

"Consider it a down payment," Terriam said. "Or, if you prefer, a bribe against finding employment elsewhere when we're done at the Mage Keep."

Olsa laughed and dug into her dinner. Like most inns, this inn's food was nothing too exciting but it was warm, and riding in the cold always made Olsa extra hungry. After they finished eating, they were recognized as heroes of the realm and would have spent the rest of the evening telling stories of their own glory had Mage Ladros not caused a distraction.

For more than an hour, he made lights dance on the ceiling, caused strange noises to emanate from people's hats, "found" lost objects in people's ears, and generally carried on like a court jester instead of the most powerful mage in all the realm. It was a reminder of what a mage could do. Everyone knew the doom and destiny parts of magecraft, but sometimes it was nice to be reminded that such a powerful force could be used merely for its own sake, for prettiness and humour on an early-spring night when the still-present snow curtailed any outdoor diversions.

"You take all my fun, old man," Sir Terriam said, as they climbed stairs after the bar had closed.

"Consider it payment in full for having had to listen to you yammer on for the past week," Mage Ladros said, without a hint of apology in his voice.

To be honest, Olsa was grateful the mage had intervened. Not only did it spare her from having to listen to stories about Kalanthe, it had also made him smile for the first time in a few days. Their pace on the road was chafing him too, yet he couldn't leave the mules, and whatever it was he was worried about only got worse with each new day. He was, though she knew he would deny it if she asked him, desperate to get back to the Mage Keep. She suspected it had something to do with the godsgem or, more specifically, the spells that were protecting it.

In the morning, they picked up Olsa's winter boots and rode on.

This was a well-ordered part of Cadrium, even if it was currently under snow. Olsa had not come this way on the Quest—it was the first time she'd ever travelled on this road—but everyone knew that the way between the city of Cadria and the Mage Keep was the best-maintained road in the whole kingdom. The road was wide enough that two wagons could pass abreast of each other, and there were mile markers to serve for direction, even when the landscape was obscured by snow. More important, there were inns. They weren't fancy or exciting, but they were all well built and well stocked and that made for an easy journey.

It was, Olsa realized, downright infuriating. She would have given almost anything for an attack by those poor shambling minions of the Old God or any of His demons. Even regular bandits would relieve the boredom. Yet, of course, nothing so exciting happened. She felt a little guilty for even thinking it. She still wasn't any good in a fight, Mage Ladros clearly had enough on his mind without worrying about defense, and no one knew how Terriam would hold up under the strain. Still, she would like a *little* excitement. Instead, they travelled the same distance every day, passing identical mile markers while their mounts plodded along, and then stayed the night in a roadside inn whose floor plan matched the one from the night before so closely, Olsa felt on occasion that they were travelling in circles.

"I know it's disconcerting," said Terriam on the ninth evening. They had put the horses in the stables and were climbing the stairs to their rooms. Olsa had gone to the wrong door and stood stupidly in front of it, wondering why her key didn't work. "The mages have to be so far away for safety or something, and so the old royals did their best to make the road as passable as they could."

"Would it have killed them to show some imagination?" Olsa asked.

"Probably," Sir Terriam said, and laughed.

The truth was, the mages did have to be so far away, for safety, privacy, security, and a host of other things besides. They chose the isolated north because it wasn't farmable land, and they picked someplace far away from Cadria to give the appearance of political neutrality. No one in their right mind would attack the Mage Keep, but conquerors and tyrants were rarely *in* their right minds, so the mages picked a place that they could fortify as well as isolate.

On the twelfth night after they set out from Cadria, they arrived at an inn and found that someone was waiting for them. The innkeeper said as much when they checked in, but they had their horses to mind, so they had to go out to the stable and make sure their mounts were fed and watered and brushed, and Olsa thought she was going to crawl out of her skin with curiosity. When they finally made it into the common room, the innkeeper directed them to a table where a young woman was already sitting.

Even though she was inside and the fireplace was roaring, she was still wearing her scarf. No, Olsa realized when she took a closer look, this wasn't something a person would wear to keep her ears warm. This was the style of scarf worn in the southern desert, mostly to keep sand off a person's face, but also for other reasons that no one had ever gotten around to explaining to her.

"Giran?" said Sir Terriam.

"Well met, Sir Knight, Mage Ladros," the woman said. She rose and bowed slightly, and then took her seat again. "Please, join me."

"We didn't meet, but both Sir Branthear and the Lady Ironheart spoke highly of you, and I saw you on several occasions," Terriam said. "It's wonderful to see you again, but what on earth are you doing so far up here?"

"I invited her," Mage Ladros said. "Weeks ago. When there was no reply, I assumed you weren't coming."

"I apologize, Mage Ladros," she said. "My reply must have gone astray. I came north as quickly as I could, but just missed crossing paths with you when you turned west to go to Cadria. I decided to go on, but then I realized that if you had sent for me, it might be best to arrive with you."

"I feel like I am missing half of this conversation," Olsa said.

"My apologies, Olsa," Terriam said. "This is Scholar Giran y'Koda. She is the one we met when we went to the university, who was so helpful. Giran, this is Olsa, one of our companions."

"It is my honour," Giran said. "But it is Accredited Scholar now, Sir Knight. They had to admit that the study of my countrywoman was valid after your Quest was successful. Lady Ironheart sent word to ensure that my accreditation was confirmed."

"Congratulations," said Mage Ladros, bowing.

"Yes, cheers." Sir Terriam held up her glass.

Olsa, who still felt out of the loop, waited for someone to keep talking.

"In any case," Mage Ladros said, "I invited Accredited Scholar Giran to come to the Mage Keep because her arguments may help sway my colleagues."

"Why are your colleagues arguing?" Olsa said. "Wait, why aren't *your* arguments swaying your colleagues?"

"It's complicated," Mage Ladros said. "You know I hate keeping secrets for secrets' sake, but there is too much at risk for me to discuss the details outside of a secure location. You're a clever girl, though, so I'm sure you can figure out much of what I am not saying."

Olsa harrumphed but accepted his declaration. It must have something to do with the godsgem. And this scholar—Accredited Scholar—Olsa remembered Kalanthe saying something about meeting her at the university when Olsa had been off in the desert with Sir Erris. Giran worked with old texts about how to find the godsgem, and one of her own ancestors or something had a theory about it, but everyone ignored her because her pastoral background meant she wasn't a scholar's idea of what a Scholar should be. Olsa had a great deal of sympathy for that.

But they didn't need to find the godsgem. They needed to protect it. She started to ask a question just as the servingman came over with a tray of food, but then realized that this was exactly the sort of public place that Mage Ladros was talking about when he was talking about things being insecure. Olsa sighed and filled her plate. At least they were only two days away.

"How is Lady Ironheart?" Giran asked as they ate.

Olsa nearly choked on a mouthful of bread and refused to look anywhere but her plate.

"She is well," Sir Terriam said. "She is almost old enough to be knighted, and I have heard that soon she'll be getting married."

"She has written to me about that," Giran said. "I had hoped that perhaps another solution had presented itself."

"No," said Sir Terriam, carefully avoiding any number of large, invisible animals that had just paraded across the table, "though from all accounts the lord who has asked for her hand is an excellent match for her in most ways."

"I had hoped to see her," Giran admitted. "But if I give you a letter for her, will you pass it along in the event that I do not?"

"Of course," said Sir Terriam easily, and then, mercifully, she changed the subject.

Olsa finished her dinner as quickly as she could, uncomfortable with the feelings that were rising in her chest. Men were one thing, an inevitability that Kalanthe's station and financial situation couldn't escape, but this girl? Who she had met the moment Olsa turned away for an instant?

Memory surfaced, of a night in an inn after their two questing parties had been reunited, and Olsa found she was fighting off a blush. No, of course Kalanthe hadn't strayed. She never would, and Olsa felt badly for even thinking it of her.

When she looked up, it was into Terriam's understanding gaze. Olsa swallowed her mouthful of food and determinedly forced her way back into polite conversation.

. . . . **AFTER** . . . .

In the end, it was nearly impossible not to like Giran. She was clever and thoughtful, a combination Olsa regarded with high esteem, and she never made Olsa feel like she was uneducated, even though she was. Her insightful commentary, added to Terriam's endless chatter, made the last two days of their journey north pleasant, despite the weather.

Though Mage Ladros assured them that, any day now, the warm winds would come out of the west, carrying spring with them, the weather remained decidedly chilly. In her new clothes and boots, Olsa was comfortable enough, but Giran was downright miserable. Olsa remembered being cold in the desert, at night, when the sun went down, but even that was no match for the dampness of melting snow, and she did what she could to make Giran more comfortable.

Giran's riding clothes and saddle were unlike anything Olsa had ever seen. Since she still wore a dress that covered her to her ankles, Giran didn't ride astride like the rest of them did. Her delicate mare was instead saddled with a sort of swooping seat that allowed Giran to ride with both of her legs on the same side of the horse. Olsa thought that couldn't possibly be maneuverable, but when Sir Terriam voiced similar doubts, Giran demonstrated otherwise, leading her mare through a series of what could really only be called horse acrobatics.

"How do you get her to do that?" Terriam had said, her professional curiosity now good and piqued.

"Training," Giran said. "My parents trade horses like this, so everyone in my family knows how to do it. I have less practice than my siblings because of school, of course, but still."

"Could you teach a charger, do you think?" Terriam looked critically at her graceless old stallion.

"If he's amenable to it," Giran said. "Some horses just don't adapt to the style."

"I might come and visit your family when this is done," Terriam said. "If they would be all right with that, of course. There might be something to say for war-horses that are smart about where they put their feet."

"I'll let them know," Giran said. "I'm sure they'd be interested. Traders are always on the lookout for sources of income."

Terriam grinned at her.

As they rode along, the conversation became sparser, and Giran wrapped a heavy scarf across her face. She was still wearing her regular scarf, but overtop of it she wore a hat like Olsa's and then over *that* she'd wrapped the second scarf. She wore fur mittens, not gloves, and a heavy coat overtop her dress. She was bundled so tightly that Olsa was surprised she could breathe, and yet she was still shivering.

"It's the damp, more than anything," she said, when Olsa asked if she was all right. "I'm not used to it, is all."

"Do you mind a bit of magic, Giran?" Mage Ladros asked.

"Not if it's going to keep me warm," Giran replied.

"Then here," he said. He reached into one of his saddlebags and came up with what appeared to be a large egg. "Crack this over your head."

Giran looked at him for a moment like he might be making fun of her, but then carefully took the egg in her mittened hand and lifted it above her head. With one swift movement, she cracked the shell over her hat, and Olsa half expected to see egg yolk dripping down. Instead, a yellow glow suffused Giran's head, and then she laughed.

"That tickles," she said.

"Well." Mage Ladros turned a bit pink. "Nothing's perfect."

"How come we don't use those all the time?" Olsa demanded.

"Because feeling cold is your body's way of warning you to be careful," Mage Ladros said. "What if you had one of those and were so warm you decided to go for a walk in a blizzard? You'd be fine for a couple of miles, but you'd still get sick from exposure and die if you didn't find shelter."

"So it's an illusion?" Giran said. "I only think I'm warm?"

"No, you're really warm," Mage Ladros said. "But on the inside. The spell doesn't change the air or the air's effect on your skin. It's safe enough for you because we're with you, and because if you took that scarf off your face you wouldn't get frostbite anyway. But humans have a tendency to push themselves further than they should, and magic that helps them do it has to be treated with the appropriate care."

"That makes perfect common sense," Olsa said.

"You'd be surprised how much mages are willing to ignore because it makes perfect common sense," Mage Ladros said darkly. "Come on, let's see if we can push the mules a little bit. I want to be home as soon as we possibly can."

The mules couldn't really be pushed, but it was making the mage feel better, so they all continued. They stayed one more night on the road, in the last inn before the Mage Keep or, Olsa supposed, the first inn if you were coming from the other direction. Giran and Olsa shared a room because the innkeeper took one look at the amount of clothing that Giran was wearing and declared that the best hearth in the inn was in the room with two beds. Giran thanked her, and they all went upstairs to unbundle themselves for dinner.

Olsa changed quickly. It was warm enough inside that her regular clothes would do. She sat down to wait for Giran, then saw that she was halfway through unwinding her headscarf.

"Did you want me to go?" Olsa said, averting her eyes once she realized what she was looking at.

"Oh no, Olsa. It's fine," Giran said. "It's all right if people see me."

Giran's hair was longer than Kalanthe's and was very dark too. It wasn't as shiny, though. Olsa ran a hand across the top of her head, reflexively checking her braids. The rows were still neat and they would hold for a while longer. She would wash them tonight, since the inn had the proper facilities and she had picked up some dust along the road.

"Why do you wear it?" Olsa asked. "If that's an acceptable question to ask, I mean."

"I don't mind," Giran said. She ran her fingers through her hair and then wound it up in a loose knot at the nape of her neck before putting her scarf back on. "Practically, we wear them because it keeps sand off us. You've spent time in the southern desert, so I am sure you can understand that part."

Olsa grimaced. It had been months, and sometimes her skin still felt gritty.

"But we also wear them to remember," Giran said.

"Remember what?" Olsa asked.

"Everything, I suppose," Giran said. "Our families and our history. Where we're from and where we're going. The new gods made the desert livable after the Old God had burned the land to ruin it, and we live there, so we remember."

"I like that," Olsa said. "It's nice to always have part of your home with you."

"Indeed," Giran said. "Not everyone sees it that way, of course. There are many, even in the desert itself, who see the scarf as a sign of country ignorance, but we know better."

"Thank you," Olsa said.

Giran smiled, put the final pins into her headscarf, and led the way down to the common room where Terriam and Mage Ladros were already waiting with dinner.

"Is there anything we should be aware of, when we get to the Mage Keep?" Terriam said, passing around the cheese. "I know you don't want to say too much in public, but I don't like walking in with my eyes closed."

"The Mage Keep is, I imagine, a great deal like Giran's university," Mage Ladros said. "Mages are wise and hardworking, and generally they don't go out of their way to be spiteful or hateful, but they are also very involved in their own ideas."

"What does that mean?" Olsa asked.

"It means that once they think of something, they are disinclined to change their minds," Giran said. "Even when there is overwhelming proof."

"But that's stupid," Olsa said.

"Oh yes," Mage Ladros said. "Many of the mages are quite stupid. And perhaps I'm stupid too, thinking that they will listen to reason. But that's why I brought all of you."

"And the mules," Olsa pointed out. Mage Ladros had seemed very dour lately, and she was hoping she could make him smile.

"The mules are also integral to my plan," he said. He did smile faintly. "Or I would have left them behind days ago. Sometimes my colleagues answer well to bribery, so I've fulfilled as many of their requests as I can."

Olsa's faith in the mages was sinking fast.

"Don't look so glum," Ladros said. "The one thing mages can't stand is looking foolish. It offends their dignity. If we can convince them that they're being fools, then we might have a chance to change some minds."

Olsa finished her dinner in silence, not feeling particularly optimistic. If Mage Ladros couldn't convince them, how in the world was she going to? Assuming they would even listen to her in the first place. It also annoyed her a great deal that such powerful people could be so petty and shortsighted. If she were a mage, she thought, she would use her magic to do useful things, like feed the children who starved in Cadria, for a start.

They retired after dinner, all of them anxious for an early start the following morning. Olsa washed her braids while Giran watched, peppering her with questions about technique and texture. After months of practice under Sir Uleweya's tutelage, Olsa was actually pretty good at it, though she kept it simple.

They left in the morning, as the sun was rising, and rode without stopping all day. By mid-afternoon, Olsa could tell they must be getting close: Mage Ladros had stopped scanning the horizon in front of them like he was willing the city to move closer. Sure enough, a few moments later, they crested a low hill, and there—still some miles away, but visible in its gleaming white glory—was the Mage Keep.

The city was round, with a high wall and uniformly spaced white towers placed around it. Inside the walls, Olsa could see what looked like two main ring roads, as well as two broad avenues that bisected them and the whole city. There were probably smaller streets and alleys, but they weren't visible at this distance, because the buildings obscured them. In the centre of the Keep there was a large white, flat circle, and Olsa couldn't even begin to *guess* what that might be. She could tell the Mage Keep was a planned city. No natural human habitation grew like that. Someone had decided where every part of the Mage Keep was going to go, and then someone else—a lot of someone elses, probably—had built it as directed.

The tower nearest to them was emitting oily blue smoke that marred the otherwise pristine appearance of the city.

"What is that?" Sir Terriam asked.

"It's customary when a mage dies in the city to burn—well, it's magic, but the result is blue smoke at the gate tower," Mage Ladros said. His voice was endlessly sad.

"I'm sorry," Giran said.

"That's a lot of smoke for one mage," Olsa said, and then immediately wondered if that might have been rude, but Mage Ladros only turned to her and nodded.

"Yes," he said. "I've been gone for almost a month. I would guess the death toll is at least ten by now."

Then he put his heels to his horse's flank, and led them the last few miles in total silence.

BEFORE. . . . .

You know, I've been thinking," Olsa said, leaning back on her elbows with a wicked grin on her face. It was all I could do not to knee her in the head, but she liked to play and, so help me, I liked to let her, so I didn't.

"Oh?" I said, inordinately proud that it had only taken one attempt to get the word out.

"Why do you think that some people get sense-magic and some get plain magic?" She wasn't going to move again until I started talking.

"No one knows, really," I confessed. "There's an outdated theory that both magics run in family lines, but there's never been any proof and no one's ever given a solid reason why one family would get one type and another family gets the oth-ther."

I stuttered when she leaned back in. Now it was a contest to see how long I could maintain rational discourse about magical theory and class prejudice. I always lost. I didn't mind.

The only thing about the whole arrangement that made me uncomfortable was my unwillingness to return the favour. For reasons I could not articulate, I just couldn't bring myself to do it. Olsa had told me time and again that she didn't mind, that she would rather have me how I was comfortable, but it still made me feel like I wasn't holding up my side of the bargain.

"It's not a bargain," she'd said, the first time I'd tried—and failed—to explain myself. "I promise you, it's more than that, and I'm more than fine."

I usually believed her, but somewhere between the lines of "don't stop" and "enough, enough," I always had a moment when I felt like she deserved more from me.

I was gasping when she pulled back again, magical theory far from my mind, and my arm over my mouth in an attempt to stay quiet. For the first time in several weeks, we were staying in a real inn with the rather unlikely name of The Gilded Vole. Amongst other things, the Vole had real beds and real walls and we were taking advantage of that, but we weren't sure how much sound the walls would muffle. I watched, a bit hazy, as she wiped her mouth on the sheet and then crawled up my body to kiss my nose. I giggled at the ridiculous intimacy of that, and she slid off my chest to snuggle in against my side and tangle her legs with mine.

"You know," I said, once my breathing had mostly returned to normal, "I always think about asking where you learned that. Do I want to know?"

Olsa shrugged against my chest.

"There are people in the Thief's Court who talk a lot," she said. "And a while ago, there was a lad I knew who was curious too, so we decided to see if what they said was true."

It didn't bother me, I was pleased to note. Not that she'd learned all this with someone else, nor that she'd learned it at all. I thought about what was whispered in the dormitories between my age-mates and realized it was probably much healthier to work with real information.

"I wish I were more like you, Olsa," I said. It was hardly the first time, and so I knew what her reply would be before she said it.

"I like you like this," she said. She ran her fingers through my hair. I think she liked the length of it. I wondered what her hair would be like if she grew it out as much as I did. I liked the idea of her with braids to match Sir Uleweya's. "Weird and repressed and open to suggestion."

I breathed a laugh. I honestly didn't seek out compliments intentionally, but I did like to hear them.

"No," I said. "I mean that you like lads and lasses both. It would be much easier if I liked lads and lasses both."

She stiffened. I knew that she was getting used to thinking of me as *hers*, and when I alluded to the future, she always turned possessive.

"The kids I ran around with always said I was confused because I dressed as both a girl and a boy," she said. "But I don't think that's how it works. I like who I like, regardless of what I'm wearing."

"Of course you do," I said. I looked down at the top of her head, and then buried my fingers into her braids. "There's a word for it that the scholars use, you know."

She pulled her head up abruptly and looked straight into my eyes.

"I didn't know that," she said, her voice a bit harsh. "How could I possibly know that?"

"I'm sorry," I said. "I forget sometimes that we know different things."

"That's one way of putting it," she said. She was still pulling away, and I didn't want her to go.

"No, Olsa. That's not what I meant," I said. "You know so many things that I don't. Do you think I could survive if I were plunked into your life tomorrow? But I bet you'd do fine in mine."

"Until someone asked me what the scholar word for something was!" she said, but she'd stopped moving.

"When that happens, you just say you've been studying so much lately that you'll have to consult your notes," I told her. She snickered and let me pull her close enough that I could kiss her properly for a bit.

"What is it?" she asked, when we'd come up for air. Her hand ghosted up from my hip.

"What's what?" I asked, always a bit spacey after her tongue had been in my mouth.

"The word," she said. "The scholar word for lads and lasses both."

"Oh," I said, and forced myself to concentrate for a minute.

Olsa was smiling, which meant she knew exactly how difficult she was making it for me to think by what she was doing with her hand. I closed my eyes and called up the vocabulary lists we'd learned, and then the supplementary lists we added.

"Bisexual," I said finally.

"Well, I understand the sex part." Olsa's grin was a little crooked.

"*Bi* means 'two' in the old scholar tongue," I said. "From back before the language in Cadrium shifted to incorporate individuals who don't have a particular gender. It's commonly understood nowadays that someone who is bisexual will be attracted to all—"

I gathered the lesson was over.

Later, when she was finally sleeping, I slid out of bed to open the window. The moon was full, so when I pulled the curtains to the side, pale white light bathed the room. I liked the look of Olsa in moonlight. It wasn't a carnal thought, though she was very attractive, but rather something else I couldn't quite put my finger on. The moonlight washed out my skin, making me paler than my usual brown. I knew my hair stayed midnight dark, and I imagined the effect was a bit ghostly. The moon only high-lighted Olsa's dark-brown skin, though, and looking at her was like looking at the night sky; I thought it might go on forever.

I unlatched the window and pulled it open. A gentle gust of night air blew past me into the room. It reminded me that the real world existed outside, and despite what we whispered to each other and what scholar words might have for us, I knew that, unlike the night sky, we were doomed to an ending.

If only I knew the *sort* of ending, I thought, it would be easier. If we were going to die on this Quest, then there was no reason to change. If anything, I should wake her up right now and go again. I would weave us so close that when the end came, we died together. I wasn't afraid of dying, but I knew that Olsa was. If I could be with her, then maybe she wouldn't be so afraid.

If we lived—if we were going to live—then what I should do was push her away. I should start right now. I should climb into my own bed and never see her naked again. I should stop trying to make her laugh and stop letting her get under my skin. I should do a great many things, but I didn't want to do any of them, even as my brain would not stop populating the list.

I wanted both. I wanted to live and I wanted to keep Olsa. I had no idea how to make that happen, and it was slowly crushing my heart. Or, maybe, it was crushing hers.

Because she had my heart, all of it, in her keeping. I had given it to her without realizing it, weeks ago. Sometime between a rose on my bedroll and that awful night in that baroness's castle, my heart had stopped being mine and started being hers. I didn't mind, and I was happy for her to have it, but I worried that meant she had given me her heart in return, and I knew that I was a poor keeper for it because I would only break it.

My heart was useless for me, so it did no harm for her to keep it. I knew I wouldn't use it when I married, and if she had it, then perhaps I would always remember the time when I had been happy and alive. But Olsa could give her heart again.

She wasn't like me, cold and sealed off, the way I was, the way I made myself be. If I owed her anything, it was her heart back, so that she could have a life after my fate claimed me, and I could no longer be hers the way she wanted.

I had no idea how to do it, though. I mean, I could cut her out of my life entirely, or as entirely as I could given that we were on a Quest together and spent a lot of time in each other's company, but I knew that would be impractical. How could I still have this—by which I meant this moon-dappled room and this girl who trusted me enough to sleep naked in my presence—without promising her something I could never, ever deliver. I had given her a part of me, and now that I couldn't give her the rest, I wondered if I had made a terrible mistake.

The breeze gusted around me again, cool against my belly. The moon was so bright it blotted out the stars above us, a different kind of nighttime beauty than I was used to. Nothing, I supposed, was only ever one way, but you couldn't have stars and a full moon at the same time, because one obliterated the other. We were still in the desert, so it got cold at night. I should probably close the window before I went back to bed; I just needed to decide which bed I was going back to first.

I heard a rustle as Olsa rolled over, and her hand landed in the place where I had been. She woke—or stirred, rather; I'm not sure how conscious she was—and I knew I should go back to her before I woke her with my absence. I closed the window and pulled the curtains shut, plunging the room into darkness.

It took a moment for my eyes to adjust in order for me to make it safely across the room without tripping on anything.

"Kalanthe," she said, her voice musty with sleep, "I can hear you thinking all the way across the room. Come back to bed."

I shouldn't. I should make the hard choice—the right choice—and end this right now. We were travelling with the greatest knights of a generation. Of course we would be successful. Of course we would survive.

"Kalanthe?" she said, more awake now than she had been before.

And just like that, I was moving. I knew it was hopeless. More hopeless than a Quest to face the Old God and all His demons, but I could not resist. I crossed the room, slid into bed, and took her in my arms again.

–III–

THE MAGE KEEP

BEFORE & AFTER . . . .

T here is a city where magic holds sway. Though it is near lands traditionally held by the Crown, it has neither lady nor lord. It pays tribute to the Queens and Kings of Cadrium because it chooses to and because it is always a good idea to be neighbourly. Its white walls gleam in the sun and weep with the summer rains, though that is more the accomplishment of clever architecture and careful maintenance than true magic. Its rooflines shine bright green from copper, every tile hammered down with the deliberation that comes from good planning, and its sewers are so well engineered that their existence is invisible to all but the most discerning.

It is not the sort of city where people come to live, though of course many do reside there. To come to the Keep is to come to learn, and even those in service—the merchants and the chimney sweeps—are students in their turn. Magic is cheap but the study of it is not, and all who come to the Keep must pay their way. The master mages might serve the wealthy and powerful at the courts of kings, but once upon a time, they scaled fish in the scullery and mucked out the stalls like their own teachers before them. If nothing else, it is a useful way to teach diligence and empathy, without which magic is merely brute force.

At the centre of the Mage Keep is the wide, round lawn where magic began. The grass that grows there is evergreen, even in the winter. Most lessons are taught in that circle because it does not rain or snow anywhere inside of it, and the air is always pleasantly cooled by the softest of breezes. It is magic that does it, of course, and one of the most complicated spells in the entire world.

Of all the tasks to be assigned in the maintenance of the Mage Keep, the weather spell is the most honoured and the most feared. Students would rather wash the marble walls or carry coal to the myriad hearths and fireplaces or peel the multitudes of potatoes necessary to feed everyone who came to the tables than be trusted with the spells that controlled the weather. It was a mark of prowess and ultimate talent to hold back the rain and the clouds and the cold, but it destroyed most of the mages who tried it.

Mage Ladros had held the weather over the lawn for six months before he was granted his mastery. They say he did not eat or sleep the entire time. They say his feet grew moss and his hair reached his knees by the time his service was up. They say the lines upon his forehead, etched in the concentration of holding so many delicate spells for so long, became permanent furrows there, aging him before his time. They say it was a punishment for outshining his masters. They say it was a reward for his brilliance. They say a great many things.

What is true is that almost anyone can cast a spell. The masters describe it to their pupils as picking up a rock and throwing it into the river. Eventually your back will tire from bending over and selecting the perfect rock, and eventually your arm will tire from throwing, but both actions are natural, fluid. Most people have magic, if they can to learn to use it. Most people don't bother: it is almost always easier to pick the rock up with your hand than with your mind.

Holding a spell is different, and that is what they teach at the Mage Keep. Students learn to call power into themselves and channel it, how to navigate the very edge of the deep ocean where the gods play with powers unfathomable. How to pick up that rock and carry it for leagues, bearing the weight of it upon their fragile human forms. Almost anyone can, with sufficient study and practice, *make* a thunderstorm. Controlling it, even to the slightest degree, kills most of those who try.

However Mage Ladros held the weather over the grassy lawn in the centre of the Mage Keep does not matter. What matters is that he did it, and survived it, and was able to go out into the world afterwards. Several of his predecessors had survived, but had been driven out of their minds by the details of the spell, the possibilities and potentials of every breath of wind and ray of sunshine, but Ladros walked free, and no one got in his way, inside the walls of the Mage Keep or otherwise.

When the Old God's servant laid an evil spell upon King Dorrenta, forcing him to carry more weight than his superficial magical training had prepared him for, Sir Erris Quicksword turned to Mage Ladros for aid. Dorrenta had only a little power, and Erris had significantly more, but Ladros eclipsed them both, so he answered the desperate plea for help, and went out into the world again. When he returned to the Mage Keep, he carried with him something of terrible power that no magic alone could protect: the godsgem of old. The Mage Council deliberated for weeks and months while Ladros held the godsgem as he had held the weather. Their solution was imperfect, dangerous, but so was the spell that Mage Ladros held.

In the Mage Keep, magic does not hold the stones to the mortar in the walls nor the cobbles to the ground nor the tiles to the roofs. It does not cook the food or milk the goats or kennel the dogs. It does not rule the mages or their students, yet in the Mage Keep, almost everything that walks or breathes or *is* is under magic's control.

The Mage Keep is the safest city in the world, and it is also the most perilous.

Kalanthe had very few memories of the formal dinner that night. She was seated next to Sir Edramore, with Sir Branthear on her right. Elenia and Carster sat at the high table as well. The lower tables were jovial, but not overly boisterous or openly curious as to Kalanthe's presence, which she appreciated. Everyone in the household had a place at the table, and there was plenty of food and conversation to go around, even if the formal seating arrangements—like so many ducks in a row—excluded Kalanthe from most of the latter. Instead, she talked with Edramore himself and pretended that he hadn't just offered her the entire world in return for what was, in her consideration, a relatively small mercy.

The fare was simple, a far cry from what the king served at welcome banquets, but Kalanthe appreciated it. As far as she could tell, everything they ate was from Edramore's own fields and forests. There were stuffed pheasants, cut into small pieces for eating with one's fingers, and then roasted venison with gravy and a variety of root vegetables to be eaten on trenchers of bread. Then came a course of soft cheeses and tiny apples so sour that Kalanthe's eyes watered the first time she tried one. After that, a soup with spiced lentils, and at the very end, a light pastry that was stuffed with nuts and soaked in honey.

Throughout the meal, Edramore introduced her to the various people who helped run his estates, from the steward, who was sitting next to Branthear, to the boys and girls who kept watch over the hunters' dogs. Kalanthe realized that her earlier guess had been correct: he did in fact know all their names. She wasn't sure if she was going to be able to keep them straight after a single night, but everyone who greeted her was gracious enough that she didn't think they would hold it against her if she asked to be reminded of their name the next time they met.

The evening ended early—most of Edramore's people were farmers after all—and Branthear walked with Kalanthe back to their rooms only a few hours after sunset. Kalanthe hesitated only briefly before inviting the older knight into her sitting room.

"Do you need anything, my lady?" Ayera was waiting for her.

"No, thank you," Kalanthe said. "I can undress myself."

"I'll see you in the morning, then, my lady," Ayera said, and nodded to Sir Branthear. "Sir Knight."

When Ayera left them alone, Kalanthe waved Branthear towards one of the chairs, and then activated the anti-listening spell she'd showed Olsa what felt like a lifetime ago. Edramore hadn't requested she keep what she'd learned to herself—a sign that showed he trusted her to keep the right counsel—and she needed Branthear's help.

As quickly as she could, she outlined the situation. She paced in front of the fireplace while she spoke, too anxious to sit. Mercifully, Branthear did not interrupt her while she was speaking, though it was clear she had questions. When Kalanthe finished, she sat down in the other chair by the fire and waited for Branthear to finish mulling over what she had learned.

"Well," Branthear said after a long pause. "That certainly explains more than it doesn't."

"I agree," Kalanthe said. "He's told me he doesn't want an answer for a week—he would like to show me the whole estate and see how I get on with the girls—but I can tell he really means it in good faith. He thinks I would be a good choice."

Branthear huffed. "Of course you would be," she said. "For exactly the reasons he outlined. Remember when we all first met and Terriam used to tease you for being so honourable? This is exactly what she meant."

"Is it so bad?" Kalanthe asked. "To be like me?"

"No, lovely," Branthear said. She closed her eyes and leaned back against the top of the chair. Kalanthe suddenly remembered that they had both ridden a very long way to get here. "It's only that not many people are like you, and so everyone always waits for the other shoe to drop, such as it is."

Kalanthe stared into the fire. It was vaguely musty in the room, and the fire was only just starting to take the edge off the damp. Edramore must not get many guests.

"I'm going to give him the week," Kalanthe said. "It seems like the least I can do. Will you stay?"

"I think that's the best idea," Branthear said. "And of course I will. I wasn't just couriering you here to make Erris feel better about your safety. I'm here for you, Kalanthe. As your friend and for advice if you need me."

"Thank you, Sir Branthear," Kalanthe said.

"But I really need to get some sleep if I'm to be any use at all," Branthear continued. She stood up and stretched her arms above her head. She hadn't worn chainmail to dinner, choosing a dress instead, and so her shoulders popped rather alarmingly. "Ah, growing old," she said. "Well, I suppose it beats the alternative."

"Yes," Kalanthe said, thinking of what it would be like to live knowing that every breath might be your last. "I suppose it does."

"I'll see you in the morning, Lady Ironheart," Branthear said, and took her leave.

Kalanthe stayed by the fire for a while longer, staring into the flames and thinking. She could be happy here, she thought, until it was time to take the girls to court so they could learn to be knights. And it wasn't that far of a journey from here to Cadrium, with safe roads between. She knew what her decision had to be, knew it for several reasons, but she couldn't help but feel that it was cruel of her to do it. To marry a man, wait for him to die, and then take over his life seemed callous. It had occurred to her, of course, that once Edramore was dead, she would be free to follow her own heart again, provided the girls were safe and cared for, but surely if she was his widow she owed him more respect than that.

This was why she needed the week, she realized. It was much too much to process in a single night, even on a full stomach and with the counsel of a friend. She should get some rest.

She stood up and turned down the lamps in the sitting room. The fire in her bedroom was lit too and had warmed the space to a cozy heat. She stripped off her dress, taking care to lay it over the chair so it wouldn't wrinkle, and then shucked off her underdress and shift. These also went over the chair. She missed Triana, but knew that they would see each other again soon enough. She wasn't wearing any face paint because she lacked the confidence in her own skills to apply it, but she still splashed her face in the washbasin before kicking off her stockings and crawling into bed. Like everything else that was part of Sir Edramore's little world, the bed was comfortable and homey, and it took her almost no time at all to fall asleep.

For the next week, Sir Edramore showed Kalanthe every part of his estate. She saw the bridges being restored and the fields being ploughed. She visited the schoolhouses he had set up in the outlying villages, for the children who couldn't walk to the main house every day to take their lessons with Elenia and Carster. She walked the trails with his hunters and witnessed the birth of no fewer than six goats. She sparred with the guards and anyone who wanted to learn self-defence, and then with

239

Sir Branthear herself. Carster took her to collect eggs in the morning, and Elenia dragged her into the dairy in the evenings when the cows were getting their second milking. It was all so bucolic she thought she might cry.

She loved it. Every fence post, every bucket, every brick, every tile. It was everything she had ever dreamed of defending, and never thought she would actually have. Often, knowing what they did about her future, her age-mates assumed that Kalanthe wasn't interested in home except as a matter of necessity, but they were wrong. She only wanted that home to be something she loved, because she knew it wouldn't be with some*one* she loved. Here, in this determinedly built paradise, she had found something that was almost—almost—both.

"It really is like a little kingdom," she said to Branthear one night. "My parents run an estate, but it's not like this."

"Lycenia is incredibly well managed," Branthear agreed. "But if there was flooding or if the rains didn't fall, it would be just as hard up as anywhere else."

"That's true," said Kalanthe, thinking of the bridges. "It's just—"

"It's just that when you see a place like this, you wonder why the whole world isn't the same way. I understand. When I first went out into the world, I was always surprised at how bad parts of it are, considering I knew there were places like this," Branthear said. "That's why we're knights, you know. To keep working."

Kalanthe conceded the point and grew no closer to making a decision. She was coming to care about the girls a great deal. They had both spoken to her about their dreams of being knights, asking questions both practical and esoteric about her training. Carster, for example, had wished to know if it was possible to get a very small horse so that she could start right away, while Elenia had expressed some distaste at the idea of sharing a privy. Kalanthe felt that they would both grow up to be excellent knights—should they still wish to in a few years when it was time to make the final decision—knights she would be happy to sponsor and to teach.

As for their father, Kalanthe was forced to admit that Edramore was exactly the sort of man she, of all people, should marry. He was kind and practical, he already had heirs, and he had no interest in bedding her. It would have been perfect, except that Kalanthe wanted to be bedded by someone. And also, she didn't want him to die. Though she knew he would, whether she married him or not, she felt as though her acceptance of his proposal would be some sort of call to an unseen executioner. It was silly, and Branthear said as much when she told the older knight why she was still undecided, but she couldn't shake the feeling. Taking over the estate was one thing. Taking over a life was something else.

On the eighth morning, Kalanthe was woken very early by a knock on her bedroom door, followed by the entry of the housekeeper. She was awake instantly, because she was expecting

Ayera, and not until sunrise. It was fully dark outside. The sky hadn't even started to turn grey yet.

"My lady, you must come," the housekeeper said.

Kalanthe was wearing a long white sleeping gown—luxurious beyond her usual wear—and she didn't have time to get dressed. The fire was down and the lamps were still low, so it was cold and she could barely see. She stumbled towards her wardrobe, looking for the robe Ayera had given her to wear when she went to the bathhouse, and wrapped it around herself when she found it.

Without another word, the housekeeper led her out into the hallway. Ayera was there, pale and wakeful, but didn't say anything. The housekeeper indicated that she should wake Sir Branthear, and then pulled on Kalanthe's elbow, leading her forward.

Halfway through the great room, Kalanthe's sleep-muddled brain caught up with her, and she realized what must have happened. As they approached the family apartments, she heard the sound of weeping, which only confirmed it.

Sir Edramore of Lycenia had finally died.

The housekeeper—Norenti, Kalanthe's brain provided—paused at the door of what must be Sir Edramore's sleeping quarters, her hand raised to knock. She shook her head, tears in her eyes.

"My lord always gets up before the dawn," she said, her voice low. "So his valet was awake, waiting to hear the bell, only the bell never rung."

She took a deep breath, steeling herself, and then opened the door, drawing Kalanthe behind her.

The room wasn't large or ostentatious, just a wide four-poster bed, a dressing table, and two chairs before the hearth. Someone had kindled the fire, but the lamps were shuttered, so it wasn't very bright. The valet stood next to a clothespress, weeping openly, and the housekeeper flew to his side to console him. Alone, Kalanthe turned to look at the bed.

Sir Edramore had clearly died in his sleep. As a point of fact, he looked like he was sleeping still. It was calming, in an odd way. A fitting—though early—end for a calm life.

Norenti came back to stand with Kalanthe, having sent the valet on some errand.

"He always said it would be best if he went like this," she said. "Imagine if he'd been out in the fields, or with those poor girls? No, this is best."

"I'm so sorry," Kalanthe said, finding her voice at last. "He was a good man, and I could tell his people loved him."

"He was one of the best," Norenti said. She straightened. "I've sent Digonne to seal my lord's study. There are some papers there that must be secured, and you should see them before anyone else does. This is the key."

She passed Kalanthe a brass key. Kalanthe gave some thought to protesting this trust, but there was something in Norenti's eyes that made her stay quiet.

"Will you take me to see the girls, please?" Kalanthe said. "Unless you think it will be too confusing for them?"

"Of course," said Norenti. "That was my plan, in any case."

They went back into the hallway and past several doors until they reached the nursery. Inside, the fire blazed and the lamps were all turned up, so Kalanthe could see very clearly. The nursery was much bigger than Edramore's room. It had two beds and a large hearth, several trunks that Kalanthe guessed were full of toys, and two wardrobes. There was a door to the side, which led to the nurse's room, and several tables, including one where the girls ate their meals. Kalanthe could easily imagine growing up in this room, though she could only barely imagine what its two occupants were feeling right now.

Carster was sitting dry-eyed on her bed, hugging her knees and swaying slightly, while Elenia was wrapped up in her nurse's arms on the hearthrug, both of them crying. When she saw Kalanthe, Carster flew off the bed, and Kalanthe caught her without really thinking about it.

"My father is dead," Carster said, her voice flat. Behind her, Elenia's weeping intensified.

"I know, little one," Kalanthe said. "I'm so sorry."

She carried the girl across to where her sister and the nurse were, and set her down. Elenia pulled away from the nursemaid and came to hug Kalanthe as well.

"He told me that this would happen," she said sadly. "Father always keeps his promises."

"He wanted you to be ready, I suppose," Kalanthe said. "Though I don't imagine anyone is ever ready for this."

Elenia buried her head in Kalanthe's shoulder, and Carster watched them both. The nurse pulled herself together and went to fetch shawls for both girls, muttering about early-morning chills.

"What did he look like?" Carster asked. "You saw him, didn't you? What did he look like?"

Kalanthe paused, and she knew that Norenti and the nurse were both frozen behind her.

"He looked like he was sleeping," Kalanthe admitted. She paused again, considering. "You could come and see him with me, if you like, and maybe say good-bye? He'll be cold, though. It will be very sad."

Elenia looked vaguely repulsed at the idea, but Carster looked up at Kalanthe, her eyes blazing.

"I want to say good-bye!" she insisted, and then nothing would do but for Elenia to come too.

Kalanthe picked up Carster again and took Elenia's hand. She hoped she wasn't about to make a mistake, but Norenti was nodding as she passed her, and Kalanthe walked back down the corridor. The door to Edramore's bedroom was ajar, and when they went in, they saw the valet had returned and was laying out Edramore's funeral clothes. He looked at the girls, surprised.

"If they don't see him, they will wonder all their lives," she said, and the valet nodded.

He held out his hands, and Elenia went to him. He led her beside the bed and turned up the lamp, just a fraction, so that she could see. Tears streamed down her face, but she made no noise as she leaned forward and kissed her father's cheek. She held her hair back with one hand, as though she were afraid to tickle him. Then it was Carster's turn. Kalanthe set her down, and the little girl did exactly as her sister had done, though her face was still dry and the valet had to lift her up so she could reach.

Then they all returned to the nursery, where Branthear was waiting. On the table, there was a tray of tea and bread with honey. Norenti was pouring cups for everyone, and the nurse was preparing plates. Carster took one look and finally burst into tears, throwing herself back into bed. Kalanthe started to go to her, but the nurse got there first, cradling the little girl and whispering nonsense into her ear.

"Honey was Father's favourite," Elenia said. "He said it was a clever way to sneak in sweets at breakfast."

Nobody was very hungry after that, but they did all drink their tea. It was warm and comforting, and by the time they were finished, the sun had started rising and the sounds of a household waking up for the day could be heard.

"Come, girls," said Norenti. "We are going down to the kitchen. You are sad, of course, but so is everyone, and staying alone in your rooms won't help. It's better to cry together, eh?"

Both girls looked dubious, but they let their nurse dress them anyway. Elenia's hair was tied back in a single braid, while Carster's curls were simply tucked under a kerchief. Kalanthe hadn't even checked her own appearance once she put the robe on. She hoped she looked appropriate, but didn't want to check and appear vain while the others were watching. At last, the girls were ready. They nodded to Kalanthe one more time and then dutifully followed nurse and housekeeper out of the room. Branthear made to follow them, but Kalanthe held up the brass key in one hand. Branthear raised an eyebrow.

"The office," Kalanthe said. "His office. Norenti said there were some things I should read, and she had the valet seal it off until I could get there. I might as well go now."

"Lead on, then," Branthear said, and off they went.

Sir Edramore's office was attached to his rooms but had a doorway from the hall, so they didn't have to walk through the funerary preparations again. Kalanthe slid the key into the lock and turned it, and the door opened without so much as a creak.

The room was lined with bookshelves and lit by scholar-style brass lamps, built specially to reflect light to make them brighter. The fire was high, and the desk was polished. It was an almost unseemly cheerful room, and Branthear shut the door behind them. Kalanthe walked around the desk and sat down in the chair, supposing that if she had a key to the room, she was also allowed to sit here. Branthear hovered near the bookshelves, reading titles on the spines.

The desk was well ordered. Neatly trimmed quills were lined up next to a pretty inkbottle. A decorated quill-knife box sat next to the blotter, and Kalanthe surmised that if she opened the box, the knife would match. Most people would have kept the set in a drawer, unless it was a gift, and Kalanthe found herself wondering who it was from. Edramore's seal was also displayed, and a quick examination of the top drawer turned up his sealing wax, sand, and several scraps of paper he had previously used for blotters. There were a few letters stacked in one corner of the desk, and in front of where Kalanthe sat, there were four pieces of heavy parchment.

The first was a legal document, written in Edramore's hand. It said that he was of sound mind to make decisions, and then outlined his medical condition and the preparations he had made to follow his death. There was no mention of her by name, but there were several references to a guardian, and Kalanthe supposed that would have been her position had things gone differently. The document was signed by Edramore and witnessed by a healer, a mage, and a magistrate—a royal magistrate. It was dated around the time he had made his proposal to Kalanthe.

The next two were letters for the girls. They hadn't been put in envelopes yet, and Kalanthe read the first bit of Elenia's by accident before she realized what it was. As soon as she was aware of what she was reading, she hastily put the letters aside, leaning up to stack them with the others. She quickly examined those envelopes. There was a letter for the king, one for the local magistrate, one for the valet, and one for several other household members. There was also a very thick packet of notes that Kalanthe guessed was Edramore's legal will.

She sighed. So much planning to make sure his loved ones would be taken care of, and her hesitation had ruined everything. She leaned back in the chair and picked up the final piece of paper.

She must have made a sound of alarm because Sir Branthear turned away from the bookshelves and came over to see what was going on.

"Kalanthe?" she said.

"It's the marriage contract," Kalanthe said after a moment.

Branthear sighed and sat down in the chair on the other side of the desk. Her shoulders rounded in a slump, and her fists were balled up in her lap. Leaving everything else aside, that was sign enough that today was not the day to spar with the knight called Lady Stonehand.

"I'm sorry, Kalanthe," she said. "I know you had your doubts and they were reasonable ones for all I made fun of you sometimes. I admire you tremendously, you know, for what you've done and what you're going to do. I wanted this to work out for you so much because I thought you deserved it, and that's why I kept pushing. I'm sorry it was all for—"

"He signed it," Kalanthe said, her voice so low she thought she might have to repeat herself, except Branthear straightened immediately and leaned forward. The other knight was wide-awake now, and had pushed all grief to the side. Kalanthe could almost hear the gears turning in her brain, and she hated herself a little bit for the ones turning in her brain too.

"What?" she said.

"It's signed," Kalanthe repeated. "It's not dated and witnessed, and obviously I haven't signed it yet, but he did. He signed it."

If Kalanthe added her name to the paper and found a witness, the marriage would be legal, and everything that had been Sir Edramore's in life would be hers, as his widow, in his death.

There was a quick knock, the door opened, and Norenti came in with a different breakfast. Kalanthe could tell as soon as she looked that Norenti knew exactly what the contract said. Norenti set down the tray, put a piece of bread on a plate with some cheese and fruit, and handed it to Kalanthe.

"Good," she said. "I see you've found the pens."

After Kalanthe's party reunited with mine on the southern coast, Sir Erris found us a ship heading north and persuaded the captain to take us to the Holy City. It took some fast talking, and a not insignificant amount of money, because the piers at the Holy City were all ruined, and besides that, no one went there unless they couldn't possibly avoid it. It was ruined and haunted by goodness only knew what, and by all accounts, had long ago been stripped of anything of value. That was why Sir Erris and Mage Ladros had been forced to follow old stories as they sought the godsgem instead of harder evidence. Yes, the new gods had lived in the Holy City once and made houses of gleaming stone, but the Old God had lived there too, and His altar was best left unseen.

Naturally, that was exactly where we were headed.

In spite of the urgency of our errand, I enjoyed our time at sea. I could go about the deck, as long as I stayed clear of the sailors. I enjoyed looking out at the water. Kalanthe often joined me, though she was less steady on her feet the first few days.

"Sea legs like you were born to them," an old sailor on watch said to me, after I helped Kalanthe up the ladder to the forecastle. Her face was weathered and tanned, but her eyes were bright. Clearly, she enjoyed the ocean even more than I did. "Maybe you were meant to be on the ocean with all of us."

She gestured widely, and I wondered who exactly she was including in "us." In any case, I took her approval of me as permission to ask her questions, about everything from how the ship worked to the places she'd been, and she was more than happy to answer me.

"Well, we mostly sail along the south coast, now," she said. "The captain doesn't like cold, and I can't say I do either, but I suppose if the cargo was worth it, she might sing a different tune, and we'd all dance to it if we wanted to be paid."

I could understand that well enough.

"How far south have you been?" I asked. I knew from hearing merchants talk that there was at least one other continent in that direction. I'd had a fair amount of practice looking at maps in the time we had been on the road, and now that I could read them I found I liked it. The wide expanse of space no longer scared me as it had done when I first left Cadria. I had learned to fill in the gaps.

"When I was a young lass, we sailed all the way to the other continent a fair few times," she said. Kalanthe leaned a bit closer to listen, though she didn't loosen her grip on the railing. "Lands down there, they call it a jungle. The air steams, it's so humid and hot, but flowers like you would not believe bloom all over the place. Some of them were the size of my head."

I looked at her skeptically, trying to decide how much of her descriptions I was willing to believe.

"It's the greenest land I've ever seen," she said. "Grass is well enough, I suppose, but something about all those trees and vines. And there are cities too. Great stone buildings rising right out of the jungle, like steps to the very sky."

"That sounds like some complicated engineering," Kalanthe said. From her tone of voice, I could tell she was aware that it was possible and was trying to wrap her mind around it.

"I know it sounds far-fetched," she said. "But I swear it's true. We don't build anything like it up here. Even the lighthouse at the Port of Cadria looks like a little hut compared to those cities in the south."

The lighthouse at Cadria, the one that marked the river to the main city, even though Cadria itself was miles upriver, could be seen far out to sea when the weather was clear.

"It sounds wonderful," said Kalanthe, "but I'm glad we're headed north. I don't mind adventures and seeing new places, but we've been on the road for a while now, and I'd like to rest a bit at home before I travelled anywhere like that."

"That's the best part of living on a ship," the sailor said. "You take your home with you wherever you go."

The sailor looked back out at the sea, and Kalanthe and I moved down the railing a bit so we wouldn't disturb her with idle chatter.

"Do you think it's real?" I asked. I wanted it to be. I wanted a great big world full of mysterious, unbelievable, beautiful things. "All those things she talked about?"

"I think it's mostly real," she said. "I believe she's been to the southern continent and seen all those things, but stories have a habit of growing."

"So maybe the flowers are only as big as *my* head?" I asked.

Kalanthe laughed. She had been so serious when I'd met her and then had opened up on the road, only to close down again over the last few days. I knew she wasn't afraid of the Quest, but I wondered if she might be afraid of what came after. I was prepared to fight for her, of course, but I wasn't entirely sure she'd let me. She could be incredibly obstinate when honour and nobility were on the line, and as much as that was one of the reasons I loved her, it also made reasoning with her a challenge rather frequently.

I leaned out over the side of the ship, and felt Kalanthe's hand grip the back of my tunic, even though I was more firmly set on my feet than she was.

"Be careful!" she said.

I ignored her. "Look!" I said. "Kalanthe, just find your balance, and look!"

She was afraid, I realized. My brave nearly-a-knight who faced her death as calmly as she faced her breakfast was afraid of falling overboard. I put my arm around her.

"Come on," I said. "Slowly, and together."

Finally, she leaned forward, and saw what I wanted her to see.

We were just behind the bow of the ship, running north with a good breeze behind us. The ship leapt from wave to wave, moving forward at a fair clip, certainly faster than any horse. The sun was bright, which meant the water was the brightest blue, except where the shadow of the ship fell on it. Alongside the front of the ship were two or three bright pink creatures with sleek bodies and pointed faces, skipping along the surface of the water with us.

I stood up straight, bringing Kalanthe with me, and ran to the other side of the deck.

"They're over here too!" I called out, and then came back to her.

"They're playing," she said, leaning out on her own now to watch them.

"I wonder what they are," I said. "I've never heard of fish like that."

"They're dolphins," she said. "And they aren't fish, exactly. They breathe air like you and me."

"Well, I certainly can't swim like that!" I said, and we laughed together as we watched the animals cavort along the side of the ship.

"You've seen our friends, I gather?" said the old sailor. Someone had come to relieve her from her watch, and she was headed below to her bunk.

"They're marvellous," said Kalanthe.

"It's good luck to see dolphins," the sailor said, and then lurched down the ladder and went belowdecks.

"Well, we certainly need all the luck we can get," I said.

It wouldn't be so bad, I thought, going back to my old life when all of this was done. I would have my memories to keep me company, even if all of my companions remembered that they were women of the world and very far above me. I didn't expect them to pay me any mind after we went our separate ways. It would hurt, of course, I knew that, but it was how things went. And I'd seen dolphins and heard stories of the south, told by someone who had seen the far continent herself. There weren't many on the streets in Cadria who could claim that.

I would miss Kalanthe, though. The thought ran through me like pure fire, and I could hardly bear it. I didn't want to see her wed to a lord because of some stupid debt. I didn't want her to have to bear children because of her stupid station. I wanted her to stay with me, even if everyone else abandoned us, and we had to run away to sea to find our fortunes. I knew she wanted to be a knight, and I knew that came with rules and responsibilities, but surely there was room for me somewhere in all that mess.

It was possible, I thought, that Kalanthe had learned her knight-lessons too well. Branthear and Uleweya both spoke casually of their own conquests—I'd seen a few of Branthear's mornings-after with my own eyes, at various inns along our way—and from the colour Erris turned whenever anyone mentioned the king, I knew her thoughts about him weren't entirely ladylike. Terriam had no interest in that sort of thing, of course, and I really didn't want to know that much about Mage Ladros, but when it came to Kalanthe's convictions, she seemed to be made of, well, iron.

Ironheart, the other apprentice-knights had called her. I felt like I was starting to understand why. Once she was committed to a thing, she was for it, and she was committed to every part of being a knight, which meant being committed to every oath she would ever swear, for the rest of her entire life. She might love me, but I knew she wouldn't forswear herself for me, if she had made a promise to someone else.

Only, love was a sort of promise too. The words were different, but surely the bond was no less strong. I felt it weighing on my heart, not always in the bad way, mind you, and I imagined she must too. Which meant she felt both of her obligations pulling at her, all the time. I wanted her to be free to choose, but I wanted her to choose *me*, and I didn't see how that was going to happen unless there was some sort of miracle.

I leaned over the rail again, looking at the dolphins. We were headed for the Holy City. I knew Sir Erris was hoping for a miracle before she faced the Old God, and I was pretty sure Mage Ladros was too. Maybe I would hope for one as well. Nothing so titanic as saving the world, not for me, but if the new gods saw fit to toss a small, personal miracle my way, well, I would be grateful to them for it for the rest of my days.

I looked back at Kalanthe. She was still smiling as she watched the dolphins play. Her face was almost golden in the sunlight, and the wind had worked several large locks of her hair out of the single braid she'd tied it back in this morning. She was the most beautiful thing I'd ever seen, I realized, in this moment and in a hundred others. I wanted to remember her like this, if I had to lose her. I didn't want to lose her at all.

I leaned into her, and she looked down at me. Then, because I was a thief, I stole a kiss.

They entered the Mage Keep in a rather subdued manner. The gates opened with no fanfare, and the mageguards admitted them after only a short look at Mage Ladros's face. They left the mules in the courtyard, Ladros giving instructions as to what was to be done with them to a groom, while the rest of the party stood by awkwardly. The air was very smoky, and Olsa's eyes kept watering.

They followed one of the mageguards into the city. She was on foot, so they led their horses as they followed her. Terriam had both her gelding and her charger because she had no place yet to leave them. They walked up the wide avenue that bisected the Mage Keep on the north–south axis. There was almost no one in the streets, despite the fact that it was barely the supper hour; Olsa's skin crawled as they passed nondescript white building after nondescript white building.

Eventually, they came to the centre of the city. Here was the large white circle that Olsa had seen from a distance. Up close, she saw that it was actually a snow-covered glade. In the middle of it stood a mage, his eyes so focused on whatever spell he was working that he didn't notice their arrival at all. Ladros looked at him for a long moment, heartbreak in his eyes, and then turned away to follow their guide up the short steps and into a squat little tower.

"Ladros!" cried someone, before Olsa's eyes had quite adjusted to being inside. "Thank the new gods, you have returned."

"How long has he been out there?" Ladros asked, and Olsa knew he meant the mage in the snowy glade. The other mage's expression darkened.

"Only since luncheon," he said. "Come, there is much we need to discuss."

The mage led them into a large room that was ringed with chairs and full of mages. Ladros took a seat in one of them and indicated that Terriam, Giran, and Olsa should sit behind him. There was some murmur at that.

"These are my companions and consultants on a matter of magecraft," Ladros said loudly. The murmuring quieted. "They have earned seats on the floor, rather than up in the gallery."

"We have no interest in hearing more of the same arguments, Ladros." A wiry old man with a long white beard and enormous spectacles had spoken. "None of us care what experts you've managed to produce."

"Speak for yourself." This was a stately woman in deep green robes. "I have watched nearly a dozen people die from these very windows for your pride, Drayyof, and if Ladros has another solution, then I think we should listen."

"Thank you, Mage Helcathia," Mage Ladros said.

He rose to his feet and assumed what Olsa had come to know as his lecturing pose. This time, though, there was no absentmindedness to his countenance. What he was about to say was of the deadliest importance. She sat up straight and paid attention.

"As you know, some six months ago, I returned to the Mage Keep after restoring the health of the king of Cadria," Mage Ladros began. "I had in my possession a gem of spectacular worth."

"Just say godsgem, Ladros," the mage named Drayyof said. "It's not going to kill you."

"It might kill him." Ladros pointed out the window. "And may I inquire as to where you are in the schedule we drew lots for?

Drayyof said nothing more.

"As I was saying," Mage Ladros continued. "This council began to debate how best to keep the gem safe, and I was bidden to fashion some manner of protective spell work to conceal it while the discussions went on. The gem burned through every spell I thought to cast upon it, until I hit upon the idea of meshing the protection spell with the weather spell in the glade."

Instantly, Olsa knew the spell he was talking about and could have kicked herself for missing it earlier. The glade outside this tower was meant to be green and warm at all times of the year. If there was snow it in, something must have happened to the magic. Apparently, as a matter of fact, *Ladros* had happened to the magic. She'd always known he was powerful, but the glade was bound by one of the oldest and most powerful magics in Cadrium, if not the whole world. It must have taken tremendous effort.

"For six months, I held the godsgem in the glade outside this very tower while you continued to talk and you have decided nothing," Ladros said. "Mage Helcathia finally persuaded you to let me go and get these young women"—here he gestured at Giran and Olsa—"while others held the spell." He hesitated. "I am told that ten of them have died since I departed. I beg you, listen to what these people have to say."

There was some shuffling and muttering as Mage Ladros sat back down.

"Why didn't they just throw it into the sea?" Olsa hissed when he was close enough to hear her. "That would have hidden it well enough."

"My compatriots are worried that we might need it again someday," Mage Ladros said. "And therefore they would like to know where it is, even though it keeps trying to go somewhere else."

Olsa stared at him, horrified.

"I told you mages were very stupid, Olsa," he said. "Giran, if you would?"

Clearly used to lecturing publicly—and not always to friendly crowds—Giran stood and waited for the room to quiet. When she finally had everyone's attention, she began to speak.

"My name is Giran y'Koda, and I am an Accredited Scholar from the university in Gethal, in the south of Cadrium. In the course of my studies, I came across many ancient texts relating to the finding and keeping of the g—of the gem," she said, not naming the thing out of respect to the man who laboured outside the window. "One such text was ignored by most of my fellow students and held with some disdain by my teachers."

"Then what use is it to us?" Drayyof said. "Ladros, we don't have time for this."

"You will address your questions to me, Mage Drayyof," Giran said. Her tone was like adamant, and Olsa was pleased to note that Drayyof straightened in his chair like a schoolboy before he realized what he was doing. "The text I speak of was ignored because it was written by a southern woman like myself, only unlike me, she was not even a student at the university. She had none of the qualifications that my teachers did, but instead had the intelligence one acquires over a life lived by paying attention."

"We could use some of that around here, if you ask me," muttered Helcathia. Giran smiled at her.

"Albor y'Zarat's words are clear," Giran said. "I passed them along to Sir Erris Quicksword's companions because I believed they might be useful. She says that the gem will always find the person it seeks, as long as that person is also seeking it."

"That's gibberish," Drayyof protested.

"It makes perfect sense to me," Mage Ladros said. He turned to Giran. "Thank you, Accredited Scholar."

Giran sat down, and Mage Ladros waited again while the room settled.

"Giran's hypothesis was proven correct," Mage Ladros said. "Sir Erris did not find the gem where it had rested since time immemorial. It met her along the way. It does not matter, therefore, if we hide the gem somewhere away from here, with little magical protection on it. If it is needed again, it will find the one who needs it."

Ladros sat down, and the debate began. Olsa soon stopped trying to follow it. If she wanted to watch people yell insults at one another, she could go down to the fish market on a day when the catch had spoiled.

"Why don't you tell them you'll hold it again, and then walk off with it?" Olsa asked, sure that the room was noisy enough she wouldn't be overheard.

"I thought about it," Mage Ladros said. "I couldn't put any spells on the gem—it just burns through them—but we all put a lot of magic on the box. Anyone holding it can't move."

"It's fairly gruesome, really." Apparently, the room wasn't as noisy as Olsa had thought. Mage Helcathia had joined them. "When the first mage died after you left, she stayed standing. We had to break her fingers to pry the box out of her hand and give it to the next bearer."

Olsa shuddered.

"I'm sorry you came all this way just to be yelled at, Scholar Giran," she continued. "If you would like to come with me, I know some of our more sympathetic ears have questions for you."

Giran went.

"Hopefully my bribes will do some good, and those ears will increase in sympathy," Ladros grumbled. "Pigs may fly."

"You don't want me to try stealing the gem just so you can find a way to protect it," Olsa realized suddenly. "You want me to really steal it outright."

"Hush," said Ladros. "But yes. I'm sorry, Olsa, it was all I could think of, and enough of these idiots bought the lie to let you try it."

"Will you be the one holding it?" she asked.

"Yes," he said. "Holding spells is one of my gifts. I have always been good at it, even when I was young. It's not a particularly practical skill, but it has been very useful lately. For whatever reason, I survive it. My plan was to eat something, then relieve that poor fellow in the glade."

"Then go," Sir Terriam said. "I will stay with Olsa."

"I must speak with Helcathia first," he said. "If she can remind the council to let Olsa try our defences, then I will go, but if they need me to speak to them first, I'll have to wait."

"I'll be ready," Olsa said. "Giran can help me prepare, I'm sure. And if she figures out the truth, she won't tell anyone."

Mage Ladros nodded. "Hopefully, I will see you both later." With that, he left them and went to where Helcathia, Giran, and several other mages were conversing. He drew Helcathia aside, leaving Giran on her own with her audience, and after a moment, Helcathia nodded. Then Ladros waved to Olsa and slipped out of the room.

A few moments after he left, there was a mighty clap of thunder, and everything went very dark for a heartbeat. Even though she had expected something startling to happen, Olsa still jumped when everything went dark. Terriam clasped her shoulder. The mages rushed to the windows to look out. Olsa followed and had to stand on a chair to get a decent view.

The glade was still covered in snow, but there were two fresh sets of footprints. One, going in, belonged to Mage Ladros. He now stood in the centre of the glade, holding something in his hands. Olsa could see the strain on him, even from this distance. How he had lasted for six months already was a mystery to her, but she was going to save him if she had to wrestle every idiot mage within these walls to do it. The second set followed the younger mage out of the glade. He was weaving on his feet, and twice he stopped to vomit, but eventually he made his way clear to the tower and stumbled inside. Helcathia dispatched a medic to attend to him.

"Mage Ladros has renewed his hold, granting us more time," she announced. "Now we must turn to the other matter."

All eyes turned to Olsa, who was still standing on a chair looking out the window. So much for everyone taking her seriously.

"My name is Olsa Rhetsdaughter," she said. Let them think whatever they wanted of her. She had been on the Quest. More important, she had never been as wasteful with human life as they were being right now. "I am going to steal the godsgem."

They let Olsa have all the schematics she and Giran could think of when they made their request in the morning. It took several hours for her to realize that the mages were so free with their information because, with the possible exception of Helcathia, they didn't think she'd actually succeed.

"I mean, you did stand on a chair and announce that you were going to steal something," Giran pointed out. "I thought thieves were generally more stealthy."

"There is something to be said for the production," Olsa said.

"Maybe that's why you kept getting arrested?" Terriam said dryly.

"Wait," Giran said sharply. "You're an actual thief?"

"At your service," Olsa said. "Though, to be honest, I am mostly reformed. Probably because of the bad influence of the company I keep."

Terriam laughed, and they all went back to flipping through onion-skin-thin pages of wall diagrams and tower layouts.

They were working in a room that Helcathia had shown them to. At first, Olsa had assumed it was a library, but soon she realized that it must be Mage Ladros's study. She recognized a few of his personal knickknacks scattered about, and the books were all arranged by subject order, in the way that Ladros preferred. It was a nice room, she thought, or it would be if its master wasn't outside being slowly crushed to death by the weight of a spell only he really understood. The windows were wide, so there was plenty of light, and the polished wood kept everything from being gloomy. He even had several comfortable chairs to sit in while they worked, each one strewn with pillows and brightly coloured blankets, in case their knees got cold. Giran was currently ensconced under at least three of them.

As far as Olsa could tell, the actual exit from the city in possession of the godsgem would be the most challenging part. She would have to make it to the outskirts, then flee into the snowy wilderness without a horse—she didn't even know where theirs had been taken and she didn't want to raise suspicion inquiring about it—or very much in the way of luggage. Wearing all her cold-weather gear during a heist wasn't the most comfortable option, but it was the most practical. She'd have to tie her boots around her neck to carry them, though, or they would make too much noise when she walked.

"I don't think there's much point in pretending to flee south and then doubling back," Olsa said, as they pored over a map. "The key will be to get as far away as I possibly can before they realize I have legitimately taken it, not just tested their capabilities."

"So you run north to the ocean and hope you get there before they catch you?" Giran said.

"There are cliffs up there, if my memory serves," Olsa said. They had looked rather forbidding when she'd sailed past them more than a year ago. "I can just run to one of them and throw the blasted thing over. If they catch me afterwards, it won't matter, because I'll never tell them what cliff I was standing on."

"What if they follow your tracks?" Giran said.

"The cliffs are basalt," Terriam told her. "They barely hold on to any snow after a few hours of sunshine. If Olsa can get past the snow line, she might have a chance."

"That still means she has to run for a day with the whole of the Mage Keep behind her," Giran pointed out. "Unless you wanted to cause a distraction after she's left?"

"Well, I plan to free Mage Ladros by then," Terriam said. "Even if I have to take the box from him myself."

Olsa had a momentary flash of annoyance: how like a knight to rush in to the rescue without knowing how said rescue would affect her. Terriam was wearing her hood, as usual, so Olsa couldn't even get a clear look at her face. Sometimes, dealing with nobility was like trying to stop an avalanche.

"All right, well, we've all accepted that the escape plan is only moderately terrible," Olsa said. "Let's go back to the plan to get the silly thing away from Mage Ladros in the first place."

Giran had spent a few hours reading a treatise that Helcathia had got for her on Ladros's spell, but confessed to only understanding the very basics of it.

"I didn't study much in the way of plain magical theory at school," she said apologetically.

"It's all right," Olsa said. She wished, for a fleeting moment, that Kalanthe were here. That would solve any number of her problems.

"It says you can't hold the box," Sir Terriam mused. "Can you touch it?"

"Probably," Olsa said. "They had to get it out of the dead mages' hands, after all. I went out and had a look at Mage Ladros earlier because I wanted to get a look at the box as well. He's holding it from the bottom, so the latch is visible and the hinges are unimpeded."

She didn't mention that looking at Mage Ladros had been incredibly painful. As odd as she found him, he was still her companion from the Quest, and she hated seeing him like that.

"But you can't just pick up the gem," Giran said. "It has to come to you."

"Can I pick it up with a spoon or something, and put it in another bag?" Olsa asked.

Giran looked troubled. "I don't know," she admitted.

"Well, this is just perfect," Olsa said. "The actual plan to steal the thing is mostly hypothetical, and the escape plan is only slightly better. Maybe this *is* why I kept getting arrested."

"It wasn't your fault that you had to do more and more dangerous crimes," Terriam reminded her. "And it's not your fault that these mages have made it next to impossible for you to do your job."

"I'd still feel better if we knew anything for certain."

"I know something for certain," Giran said. They all looked

at her. "If you're meant to carry the gem, there isn't a force on this planet that can stop you."

Olsa was sure that Giran meant that to be reassuring, but instead it only felt like another rock for Olsa to bear, another duty for her to carry out. If this was how Kalanthe felt all the time, staggering about under the weight of her obligations, no wonder she was so quiet and determined. Only, Olsa hadn't had as much practice, so she mostly wanted to run.

There was a knock at the door, and Helcathia came in.

"We're about to serve the evening meal in the main dining room, if you would like to join us," she said.

Olsa looked out the window and realized that the sun had set. Terriam must have turned the lamps up when she wasn't paying attention.

"That's probably a good idea," Terriam said. "Come on, you two. We can work more after we eat."

Olsa didn't think she was going to think of anything else, ever, but she was hungry, so she followed everyone along the corridor and down several flights of stairs to the dining hall. It was full of mages, and she imagined that in better times, they would talk and joke with one another as they ate. Instead, silence reigned, and stares followed them as they found seats where Helcathia told them to.

"Will you be telling us when you attempt to steal the gem?" This from Drayyof, whom Olsa was coming to dislike rather extremely. "I think I might like to watch."

"Of course not," she said, helping herself to the curry and lamb they were having for dinner. "If I told you, then you'd know. The whole point is to surprise you."

"A proper experiment requires witnesses to ensure the variables are maintained properly." This was from a younger-looking mage whose pompous tone indicated that he had no particular interest in the outcome of the argument. He was merely trying to play both sides against each other for his own amusement in the false name of enlightenment.

"A proper crime can't have witnesses," Olsa fired back. "Or it isn't a proper crime."

"Leave it alone, Radki," Drayyof said. "There's no point in conversing with someone like her."

Olsa took the high road and did not point out that he had started the conversation in the first place. Privately, then and there, she decided that she was going to steal the godsgem that very night. There was no point in waiting around for inspiration to strike Giran while Mage Ladros came closer and closer to death in that cursèd glade. The sooner she acted, the better.

It was possible that Sir Terriam had guessed what she was up to, but since both the knight and Giran fell asleep before midnight, Olsa took that as permission to act. She tied the laces of her boots together and strung them around her neck. Then, with only a bit of dismay, she rolled her fur hat and all of her outerwear in an unlit fireplace, using the soot to mask any of the shiny parts that might reflect the light. She put on a second pair of woollen stockings, stuffed Sir Uleweya's knife into the waistband of her hose where her tunic would conceal it, pulled on her heavy coat, and went out into the night.

In the night, the Mage Keep was as silent as a tomb. The streets were empty as the mages stayed inside to work late or sleep. Olsa saw no one as she made her way through the city to the glade where Mage Ladros kept his vigil. There were no regular guards posted here, but Olsa waited a full five minutes before she went into the courtyard anyway. She wouldn't have put it past Drayyof to add something and not tell her about it, just for the chance to humiliate her.

After she was sure she was alone, she began to cross the glade. The weather had been still and cold ever since Mage Ladros had taken up his forced vigil, so she followed the footprints she had made the day before when she went to examine the box. After a few minutes, she stood in front of him. It was almost like he was holding the box out to her. Very slowly, she reached out and undid the latch. The magic didn't fry her, so she reached again and opened the lid. The song of the godsgem filled her mind once again. Oh, how she had missed it.

The trouble with snow, of course, is that it muffles footsteps. Even without the godsgem's music, Olsa would not have heard the careful footsteps of Mage Drayyof as he crept up behind her.

"You selfish cheat!" he shouted, tackling her facedown into the snow. She hit the box as she went down, breaking several spells at once, but he didn't stop to notice.

The box went flying out of Mage Ladros's hands, and he sprang to action in an instant with no sign of stiffness, for all he'd held perfectly still for more than a day.

"Drayyof, stop this at once!" he shouted, trying to pull the mage off Olsa.

Drayyof roared and tightened his hold. Olsa's hands were pinned under her chest. She found something in the snowy grass beneath her, or, maybe, it found her.

Mages filled the glade, attracted by the noise. Terriam, who mustn't have been as asleep as Olsa thought, appeared by Mage Ladros's side and took stock of the situation. She pushed Drayyof over, noticing that Olsa had stopped struggling, and worried that the mage had knocked her unconscious.

"Sir Terriam!" shouted Giran, one end of her scarf blowing in the gentle night wind. "Sir Terriam, the gem isn't in the box!"

"Drayyof!" Terriam roared. With all her strength, she picked the mage up off Olsa, but by then it was too late.

There was a flash of bright green light that blinded everyone for a moment. The snow melted instantly, as springlike weather returned to the glade. Mage Ladros fell to his knees, overwhelmed at last, but not before punching Mage Drayyof squarely in the mouth.

And Olsa Rhetsdaughter, thief of the realm, floated up into the air. She hovered several feet above their heads, her eyes closed and her face serene, with the godsgem held against her breastbone like a prayer.

The Holy City rose above the horizon in the distance, and we sheltered in a hollow making the last of our preparations. Sir Erris had sent the ship back out to open sea without us, and it had taken all our spare horses and most of our packs with it. When we were finished here, if we survived, we were to signal from shore, and the ship would come back for us. Sir Erris had told them they didn't need to wait longer than two days.

Sir Uleweya had gone ahead on foot, to scout with her far-sight, and see if she could give us an idea what waited for us in the city the gods had once called home. Even without sense-magic, I could see the smoke. It burned brown, casting a pall over the whole city. Someone had relit the Old God's altar.

Olsa was hunched up beside me, wrapped in a cape and toying with the knife Sir Uleweya had given her all those months ago. She looked miserable, I imagine we all did, but also determined. I hadn't known what to make of her when we met, but in the year that passed since, we had covered a great deal of ground together—metaphorical and otherwise—and I was glad that I had got to know her.

Sir Branthear was sharpening the blade of her axe, an ear-stretching sound at the best of times and particularly annoying now, but there was really no help for it. One couldn't expect a knight to go into battle with anything less than a perfect weapon. I had already checked my own sword and axe, and they were well enough. Sir Terriam had her sword and shield lying out, and she was smearing the shield with soot so that the gleaming metal would be less visible.

Sir Erris looked at the ruins of the Holy City, and what she was thinking I could not tell. She believed, as I did, that godsgem would find her because she was trying to find it, but I think we both hoped she would find it sooner rather than later.

At last, Sir Uleweya returned.

"There's about fifty of them here," she said, indicating with a stick in the rough map she'd drawn in the dirt for us. "They're in front of the Old God's altar. The good news is that the altar is in the open air, so we can sneak up behind them, this way. There's a culvert that we can fit through, even in armour. We'll have to leave the horses at the city's edge, though."

"They wouldn't leave the rear undefended, surely," Sir Terriam protested.

"No, there are a few demons there," Sir Uleweya admitted. "But for the sake of speed, I think we should trust Mage Ladros to clear that pathway for us. It's easier to defend the altar than to attack it."

"Valid point," said Sir Branthear. "Assuming everyone stays where they are right now."

"We can adjust our tactics as necessary," Sir Erris said. "In the meantime, here are some generalities we can nail down: Olsa, I want you to stay with the horses."

I thought she might protest, but she didn't.

"Kalanthe, you will take your usual place near Mage Ladros," Sir Erris said. "He'll have a lot to deal with, and I'm sure the Old God will have any number of surprises for us, so you will have to be on your guard."

I nodded.

"Terriam and Branthear, after the initial charge, you will concentrate on the rabble," Sir Erris said. "Uleweya and I will worry about holding the altar."

"What about the godsgem?" Terriam asked.

There was a mental component to knight training, as well as the obvious physical one. We were taught to push pain aside in the name of perseverance. We were taught to face our limitations and surpass them. We were taught to sacrifice ourselves if needs must, and to identify those situations quickly and efficiently. We were taught to rely on our bodies and our brains with equal measure, and it went against that very training to leave anything to chance, much less the very focus of our Quest.

"I know this is a lot to take on faith, but I have to assume it will find me when it's ready," Sir Erris said.

Something that had been bothering me for a few days, ever since Giran had told us what she suspected, now surfaced again, and I cleared my throat. They all looked at me.

"I have a stupid question," I said.

"At this point, I will take stupid questions," said Mage Ladros.

"How do we know it's supposed to be Sir Erris that finds the gem?" I asked. "I mean, we know she wants it, and we know she's looking for it, but couldn't any one of us be the one to wield it?"

There was a heavy silence, and Sir Uleweya began to laugh.

"I'm sorry," I said, mortified. "I shouldn't have—" Sir Erris laid a hand on my shoulder.

"It's a good question, Kalanthe," she said. "You're right. We should all think about finding the gem. It could be any of us that meets it and uses it."

"If it does come to you," Mage Ladros said, "you must go before the altar and press it to the Old God's idol there."

"Will that destroy the Old God?" Olsa asked.

"It will destroy the only worldly item through which He can channel His power," Mage Ladros said. "And without His power, He is Nothing."

"We'll probably have to kill all of His sycophants, though," Sir Erris said. I could tell she was thinking specifically of the one who had betrayed her belovèd king. "If any of them survive, they may be able to reconstruct Him again."

"I don't think it would be quite that easy," Mage Ladros said. "But let's not leave anything to chance."

"Well, my ladies," said Sir Erris. "We might as well get dressed."

Getting into armour isn't a particularly slow process, but it is a methodical one. There are pieces that have to go in a certain order, and there are straps that must be tightened in a certain way. With their years of experience, the knights were much more quick about it than I was, and after watching me for a moment, Olsa came over to help. I hadn't realized it, but in the year she'd spent watching us get in and out of our battle gear, she'd learned how to help put it on.

"Don't do anything stupid, Kalanthe," she said, just before she handed me my helmet. "Please. I need you to live, even if it's going to be a disaster."

I didn't know what to say, so I stood there like a tree stump while she kissed me, and reached up to put my helmet on my head. She had to stand on her toes and lean close to reach, and I put my gauntleted hands about her waist to steady her.

"There," she said, when it was done and I released her. "Like a bloody hero of old."

Poor Lightfoot was not pleased to carry me even a little distance in full armour, but she bore up well. We rode closer to the Holy City, and I started to see what Uleweya must have seen.

The Holy City wasn't a city in the usual sense. No one lived there. Occasionally, pilgrims stopped by to leave things at the new gods' altars, but they didn't camp within the city walls. The city was nothing but a collection of eerily preserved empty buildings, paved streets, and the new and Old altars. We entered the city, dismounted, and left Olsa with the horses as we made for the centre of town.

The first attack came before we reached the culvert. Twenty warriors, all in possession of their own souls, rushed us in a blind alley. Quarters were so tight it was nearly impossible to maneuver, and we were almost more danger to ourselves than we were to our attackers. Still, knightly discipline carried the day, and before long, Sir Erris had literally carved a space in their ranks to give herself room to move, and soon after that it was over.

"Branthear!" Sir Terriam exclaimed.

Sir Branthear had been leading the way, and thus had borne the brunt of the rush. It appeared that she had been gored by a pikestaff. She was sitting against a wall with her hand on the wound, trying to hold her blood in place.

"Kalanthe, get Olsa," Sir Erris commanded. "The rest of you, help me carry her into the culvert."

By the time I returned with Olsa in tow, the knights had installed Sir Branthear in the questionable safety of the culvert and removed her leg plating. The wound wasn't as bad as I had originally thought, but she still wouldn't be able to fight anymore.

"Kalanthe," she gasped, and I went to her side. She held up her axe. "Take it."

It was a far better weapon than my own.

"Thank you, Sir Knight," I said, changing her blade for mine.

"You're my sister now," Branthear said, the ghost of a smile on her face. I couldn't bring myself to smile back at her.

"Olsa, stay here and pack the wound," Sir Erris was saying. She handed over a bag of supplies.

Olsa was shaking, surprised, I suppose, that we had fallen on difficulty so soon. But she nodded, took the bag, and went to work.

"Come on, then, the rest of you," Sir Erris said. "Let's finish this."

I had a very strange moment of clarity then. I knew, without a doubt, that I wasn't going to die. I can't say how, but I knew it more certainly than I had ever known anything in my whole life. It made me braver than I should have been, or more reckless, I suppose, and so I strayed a little farther from Mage Ladros's side than I should have as the fight began.

It went more or less exactly as Uleweya had suggested. We came through the back of what had once been the temple and found the way guarded by demons. Mage Ladros set them on fire, and they shrieked, which gave away our position to the rest of the Old God's warriors. I lost track of how many of them charged us. Sir Erris and the others could certainly handle them, poorly trained and ill-equipped as they were, but there were so *many*. I wondered how so many people could fall at the Old God's feet, knowing the horrors He had caused.

A shout caught my attention, and I looked at the altar. Standing in front of it was the broken-mage who had waked the Old God enough to poison the king's magic. She was screaming incoherently at Mage Ladros, too far into her rage to use magic and without another weapon. She began throwing rocks at him, attempting to distract him from doing his work, so I went to his defence.

I couldn't just shield him with my arm because I would have to stand too close to keep fighting, and then he wouldn't be able to see. Furthermore, if the broken-mage did get a spell off, both Ladros and I would be sitting ducks. I was going to have to cut her down and hope that she didn't regain enough clarity to use magic on me before I got to her. I called up the best magical shield I could—they don't move well, and I needed to be mobile—and charged forward.

She saw me as soon as I moved because I had blocked her line of sight to Mage Ladros on purpose. She didn't let up her bombardment at all when she realized she faced me instead of him. With Branthear's great axe and with my shield covered in soot, she probably thought I was a real knight.

Step by step, I went towards her, shrugging off each stone she cast my way. Some of them were paving stones, others the size of my fist. I was impressed that she could lift some of them, let alone throw them, but I suppose desperation gave her strength. For my own part, I was almost overwhelmingly calm. I knew I wasn't going to die, and I knew I would handle whatever she threw at me. I'd never killed an unarmed person before, though clearly she was attacking us and must be stopped, and I wondered if I was about to change myself irrevocably for the sake of king and country.

Then, her strength fading, she bent one last time and threw one more stone—a pebble really—right at my helmeted face. Without any logical explanation at all, I cast my shield aside and reached out to catch it, instead of doing the smart thing and getting out of the way. I heard my training masters berate me for my foolishness, but I heard something else too: the most beautiful song I could possibly imagine, filling my ears and drowning out the sounds of the battle that surrounded me.

"Kalanthe!" shouted Sir Erris, and I caught the godsgem in my gauntleted fist.

S ign it," said Sir Branthear.

"What?" Kalanthe looked up from the bread and cheese, an overwhelmed expression on her face.

"Sign the contract," Branthear said, immovable. "Now."

"I can't!" she protested.

"Kalanthe, you have to," Branthear said

"You just said my arguments against signing were good ones," Kalanthe said. She felt very small.

"I take it back!" Branthear got up from the chair that she had perched on the arm of. She was brandishing one of Sir Edramore's books as she faced Kalanthe down. "Kalanthe, this is everything you could have hoped for. Sign the damned contract."

"But why me?" Kalanthe said. There were tears in her eyes. "There are other people who need something like this just as much as I do, perhaps even more! I don't deserve it."

Branthear swore loudly and sat heavily in the chair. "It's like talking to a brick, sometimes," she said, to no one in particular.

"Are you going to be cruel?" said Norenti. Kalanthe had almost forgotten the housekeeper was still in the room, even though she was standing right next to her.

"What?" Kalanthe said.

"Are you going to be cruel?" Norenti repeated.

"No, of course not," Kalanthe said, appalled.

"Are you going to let this place fall to ruin to serve your own profits?" Norenti uncapped the inkbottle.

"No."

"Are you going to withhold investment from people who might need your money to start a good business?" Norenti demanded.

"No!"

"Are you going to mistreat the girls in their own home?" The housekeeper was relentless.

"Of course I won't!" said Kalanthe.

"Well, Lady Ironheart, I've only known you a week, but you seem to be the decent sort," Norenti said. "I don't doubt that the songs about you are exaggerated, but no one *gets* songs if they don't earn them in the first place. You'll take care of what we've built here, and you'll make sure it prospers. Maybe you think you don't deserve it, but have you ever considered that perhaps we deserve you?"

Kalanthe picked up one of Sir Edramore's quills, dipped it in the inkbottle, and signed her name.

"There," said Norenti. "That wasn't so bad, was it?"

"It's not legal until it's witnessed by kin," Kalanthe said. She felt very strange. "I'm not old enough."

"Give me the quill," Branthear said. Kalanthe was frozen, but Norenti complied. "Erris said something during her wedding about us all being sisters. She'd already been crowned at the time, and that makes it a royal decree. I am certain she will back me up in a court of law."

And Branthear signed her name on the witness line.

"Shall I knight you now and get it over with?" Branthear asked. "As a married woman, you're entitled."

Kalanthe burst into tears. Norenti gave her a hug, then said, "Eat your breakfast, my lady." The demand was unspoken and inarguable; the weight of the "my" the ultimate seal of the housekeeper's approval. "I'll let the household know what's transpired."

"Let me tell the girls?" Kalanthe asked. She looked around for a handkerchief, and Norenti supplied one.

"Of course, but you'd best do it soon," Norenti said. "On a day like this, the rumour mill is bound to move spectacularly fast."

The housekeeper swept out of the room, leaving the two knights alone. Branthear rummaged through the shelves until she found a decanter. She sniffed delicately, and then poured a measure of it into each of two glasses. After a pause, she added a bit more to one glass and passed that one to Kalanthe.

"It will steady your nerves," she promised.

Kalanthe was through arguing for the day, or at least the next few minutes, so she upended the glass. It burned her throat, but she'd had worse, and didn't so much as flinch.

"I supposed we should have toasted first," she said. Branthear gave her just the tiniest bit more. "To Sir Edramore," she said, holding the glass aloft. Branthear mirrored her. "May he be comforted."

They emptied their glasses and sat in respectful silence for a moment. Kalanthe's mind was already spinning quickly. There was much to do, and the first thing on her schedule was finding the girls. She got up and went to the door of the study. A footman was waiting there for her.

"May I help you, my lady?" he asked.

"Do you know where the girls are?" she asked. "The ladies, I mean."

"I believe they're still in the kitchen, my lady," he said. "Shall I fetch them to you?"

"No, lead the way, please," Kalanthe said.

They followed the footman to the kitchen door but didn't cross the threshold into the organized chaos there. Instead, Kalanthe had the footman retrieve the girls, then she took them into the little room where the silver was stored. Not the most comfortable location, perhaps, but it was private.

"Do you know why your father asked me to come here?" Kalanthe asked once the door was closed and they were alone.

Elenia nodded. "Father wanted you to marry him."

"That's right," Kalanthe said. "Do you know how getting married works?"

"You go out into the garden," Carster said, "and a magistrate or a mage comes, and they say the words, and then you have a party."

Kalanthe smiled. "That's most of it, but there's something else too. What makes a marriage legal is the contract. You can have a contract without having the garden or the party."

"Father had a contract," Elenia said shrewdly. "You're our mother now."

"I'm your guardian," Kalanthe said. At least Elenia didn't sound appalled at the idea. "I'll take care of you and help you become knights, and then when you're old enough, you'll inherit your lands and title. There are a lot of rules with the contract that might not make a lot of sense to you."

"Will you tell us when we're older?" Carster said.

"You'll have to, you know," Elenia said. "She's got a whole list of things people have promised to explain when she's older."

"Of course I will," Kalanthe said. "That's actually one of the rules."

The three of them stared at one another for a few minutes, and though she knew it would get easier, Kalanthe had a moment of near-crippling doubt. There was so much she didn't know and didn't know how to do.

"I'm not happy," said Carster. "Is that all right?"

"I'm not very happy either, Carster," Kalanthe admitted. "But that's normal. All we can do is try to work together, until we are happy again. Does that sound like a plan?"

"Yes, Lady Ironheart," they chorused.

"I think you can call me Kalanthe now," she said. "Let's go sit in the garden until someone finds us and tells us what to do."

Two days later, Sir Edramore was laid to rest in the family crypt. He was buried in full armour, next to his first wife. Kalanthe laid fresh flowers from his own garden on both graves, and the girls left him little paper boats they had folded out of scraps of parchment. Branthear left a shield with the family crest, and Sir Edramore's sword was wrapped tightly in oiled cloth and laid in a carved wooden case until the day came when Elenia would carry it.

Kalanthe wrote a great many letters: to her parents, where she tried to explain the tidings as best she could; to her banker, explaining the change in her status; to Triana, asking her to prepare her things; and to Sir Erris, thanking her for her counsel. Rereading it before applying her new seal, Kalanthe thought it was an oddly impersonal letter, given her relationship with the queen. She couldn't think of any way to make it more heartfelt, though, lest her very heart bleed into the words. Instead, she settled for a brief postscript—*If you can, please look out for her*—and set the wax. Sir Erris would understand.

When she wasn't writing letters, she was learning her way around her new estate. She chose to stay in the guest wing for now, annexing Branthear's sitting room to use as an office. She wanted to give the girls their space, and also, she didn't much fancy sleeping in the bed Sir Edramore had died in just yet, even if the mattress had already been replaced. She still spent a lot of time in his office, though, reading his records and learning everything she could from his careful notes. It was like he had left her a road map, and often she found herself crying at the pure thoughtfulness that had been a man's life and death.

The girls remembered how to laugh. Branthear taught them to ride, on ponies, not her charger, though she did carry both of them up on her great horse for a turn around the paddock. Kalanthe looked into getting a training sword made for Elenia and agreed with the blacksmith when she pointed out that if Elenia got one, there would be nothing but for Carster to get one too.

At the end of the week, Norenti had the black curtains taken out of the windows, and the flag with Lady Elenia's colours was flown above the house again. Many of the household staff still wore black armbands, but Sir Edramore had dictated that the living not spend too much time in mourning for the dead, so the windows were opened and fresh flowers filled the house.

Just as Branthear was getting ready to ride for Cadria to fetch Triana and the rest of Kalanthe's things, word came from the fields that a rider had been spotted, making for the main house quickly and not troubling themselves to ride on the road. Kalanthe barely had time to make it to the courtyard when a horse rushed through the gate and reared as the rider pulled on its reins. The horse was lathered with sweat, clearly having been pushed as far as it could go, and Kalanthe knew the rider instantly.

"Sir Uleweya!" she said.

Uleweya had on a short-sleeved tunic that left most of her arms bare, and a pair of linen leggings. Her skin was dark enough to gleam in the sunlight, and her braids streamed behind her as she moved. Somehow, Kalanthe had forgotten how outrageously tall Uleweya was until she was once again standing beside her. Even without her formal armour, she cut an impressive figure.

Branthear came out of the stables, having left her horse behind, and crossed to give Uleweya a bear hug.

"Well met, my friends," Uleweya said. "But I have urgent news."

"Come inside, then," said Kalanthe. "You can have something to drink while you tell us."

They sat in the small dining room behind the great room where Kalanthe had first eaten with Sir Edramore, and Norenti brought the tea tray herself but left them alone after she had set it down.

"Now, tell us," said Kalanthe. "What is going on?"

"I've been on an errand for Mage Ladros," she said, "trying to find unmelting ice."

"That's a myth," Branthear scoffed.

"You can believe what you want," Uleweya said. "The important thing is that I had a magenote on me, in case of emergency."

"What did he say?" Kalanthe asked. If Ladros had needed to send a message by such flammable means, it couldn't be good news.

"The note caught fire pretty quickly so I almost missed it, but before it turned to ash, I was able to see enough to know that I needed to come here and fetch you. We're needed at the Mage Keep as soon as we can get there."

"I can't leave!" Kalanthe protested. "I've just inherited this estate—it's legal but also kind of spurious—and in any case, it would break the girls' hearts to leave them so soon after their father died. Not to mention, it's the middle of planting season!"

Uleweya looked at Branthear. "It's nice to know that some people never change," she said. She turned to look at Kalanthe very directly. "The note said it was the godsgem, Kalanthe. Trouble with the godsgem, and with Olsa."

T he first thing Kalanthe did was send for Norenti and explain, in a slightly edited fashion, what was going on.

"To be fair," Norenti said, "I knew you were a hero when I bullied you into signing that contract. I'll see to the arrangements, but I assume you'll want to tell the girls yourself?"

"Are you sure I can be spared?" Kalanthe had never felt so torn in her entire life. Every part of her screamed to go to Olsa, but she knew she had serious matters here as well.

"We'll manage," said Norenti. "Most estates get by with their lords and ladies in and out all the time, you know."

Kalanthe thanked her, sent Uleweya to Branthear's room to take a nap, and requested that food be sent to her in an hour. Then she faced the girls.

They knew something was up the moment she entered the nursery. The whole house had heard that a rider was inbound, of course, and that Kalanthe had spoken with her privately.

The girls were as ready for battle as Kalanthe might have been.

"You're leaving," said Carster, before Kalanthe could say anything at all. The little girl stood in the middle of the room with her hands on her hips, fury personified.

"I wouldn't go unless it was deadly serious," Kalanthe said. "But, yes, I am."

"Everyone leaves us," Carster said, crumpling suddenly. Kalanthe knew how she felt. She went to the girl and drew her into her arms.

"I promise I'll come back," she said. "I swear it."

"Father always kept his promises," Elenia said. She was sitting in a chair at the lunch table, a poised lady receiving an audience. "Even when he promised he would die."

"I know," Kalanthe said. She straightened, and Carster went to sit with her sister. "And I hope that someday I might be as honourable as he was, but in the meantime, you can trust me to keep my word."

"I'll vouch for her on my honour as a knight. Kalanthe is the best person I know," Branthear said, from behind where Kalanthe stood. "And I'll stay here with you, if that's all right," Branthear continued. "Uleweya will need my horse as a spare, and you can take Lightfoot and that gelding, Kalanthe."

"His name is Constance," Kalanthe murmured, still reeling a bit from what Branthear had said.

"Of course it is," Branthear said. "Will that be all right with you two?"

"Yes, Cousin," said Elenia grandly. "We will accept your company."

Carster whispered something to Elenia, who rose and came over to Kalanthe.

"We would like you to travel with our colours, Lady Ironheart," she said. "It won't take long to fit a sigil onto your shield, or you can take one of ours. I looked it up in one of Father's books, and you're allowed to do it."

"I helped," Carster said proudly.

"She stole the key to Father's office from Norenti and kept watch," Elenia admitted.

Branthear laughed. "Well, at least no one is going to accuse me of being a bad influence on the pair of you. Come, say your good byes now, Lady Ironheart needs to pack."

Both girls hugged her, and Kalanthe thanked them for the shield. When she went to her room to fetch her things, a guard was waiting to meet her, and took the shield off to have the sigil fitted. Uleweya's rest hour was nearly up, so Kalanthe sent orders for her horses and Uleweya's to be saddled and loaded, and then she went to the kitchens to pick up some food for the journey. Norenti was waiting for her with a saddlebag full of provisions.

"Well, my lady," she said, "two weeks ago I don't think you could have mustered a whole household as quickly as you just have."

"I do my best to get things done," Kalanthe said, and then wondered whether that might have sounded pretentious. "I only mean—"

"I know what you mean, my lady," Norenti said. "You're a good lass, and I tease you because it's amusing to watch you squirm."

"You're not the only one who does that, you know," Kalanthe said.

"Is that who you're haring off to rescue?" Norenti asked. "I know you didn't come here for love, and I heard a name attached to all that talk about the gem."

"It's complicated, but, yes," Kalanthe said. "Her name is Olsa."

"You will bring her here in time," Norenti predicted, "and we'll have to teach her how to deliver lambs the same way we taught you."

"Olsa will be a much quicker study," Kalanthe said. She heard the sound of horses being led into the courtyard and took the saddlebag. "Thank you. Don't spoil Branthear too much while I'm gone, or she'll never leave."

"I'll keep that in mind, my lady," Norenti said, and after a quick stop at the privy, Kalanthe was off.

In the courtyard, she attached the food bag to Constance's saddle and mounted Lightfoot. Both of her horses were saddled for riding because they would be switching often for the sake of speed.

She watched Uleweya mount Branthear's horse and take the reins of her own horse to lead it. Kalanthe leaned down to clasp hands with Branthear and looked up to where two little faces were waving in the window. She held up her shield to them, then she turned Lightfoot with her knees, and rode out of the courtyard. She let Uleweya pass her as soon as they were clear, because she was the one who knew where they were going. Kalanthe could get to the Mage Keep on the road, but they didn't have time for that, and were going to cut cross-country instead. Uleweya checked to make sure everything was fastened to her saddle securely, and then took off at a gallop with Kalanthe right behind her.

Uleweya kept their pace because they both knew that Kalanthe was too upset to do it herself. After a year on the road, Kalanthe was far better at calculating how far a horse could go, and how quickly, than most other apprentice knights her age, but she lacked the experience to make cool decisions when her heart was involved, and she knew it. So they rode at a canter after their first bit of speed, even though Kalanthe felt like her very blood was screaming at her to gallop—to fly—if it would get her to Olsa sooner. She knew that would only hurt the horses—she knew it—but she was having trouble listening.

Uleweya decided when they switched horses. Kalanthe found herself wishing she'd spent more time riding the gelding, because breaking in a new saddle was no one's idea of a good time, and an even worse one when the rider was in a hurry, but there was nothing for it. At least Constance was living up to his name. He kept up with the others and didn't shy away from her, even though she had never been up on his back before today. They ate lunch and dinner in the saddle, walking to give the horses a brief respite, but after it got dark, Uleweya called a halt.

"There's a river here," she said. "The horses will need it."

The horse needed a great many things, as a point of fact, not only because of what Kalanthe and Uleweya had put them through today, but because they expected the horses to do the same thing again tomorrow. The banality of camp chores—the washing and the brushing and the polishing tack—calmed Kalanthe's restless mind a bit. She was crying into Lightfoot's saddle blanket for almost a minute before she realized it. Uleweya just looked at her and waited for her to talk.

"We didn't part very well," she said finally. "Olsa and I, I mean. It fell all to pieces and I didn't know how to fix us, so I just left."

"You and I both know that's not what happened," Uleweya said. "And we both know that things are different now."

"I suppose that's true," Kalanthe said. "It doesn't make me feel better, though."

"Did you know that broken-mage hated Sir Erris's mother?" Uleweya said. "That's what drove her to the Old God. She saw how Sir Erris's mother had influence over the old queen, and she guessed that Sir Erris and Prince Dorrenta were keeping secrets from everyone. She wanted more power, so she nearly broke the world open to stop a knight from marrying a prince."

"Is that supposed to make me feel better?" Kalanthe asked. "Because I haven't rewoken a timeless evil to get what I want?"

"Well, that's one way of looking at it." Uleweya smiled. "But what I meant was that Erris and King Dorrenta had a great deal more between them than you and Olsa do, and look how they turned out."

Kalanthe had not considered that.

"Ask me whose turn it is to do the cooking," Uleweya commanded.

"Whose turn is it to do the cooking?" Kalanthe asked, smiling already at the old joke.

"Yours," said Uleweya.

They both laughed while Kalanthe set a pot to boil and filled it with trail rations that would turn into a sort of soup. She also got the kettle for tea and some of the fresh bread the cooks had pressed on her as she was leaving. They would be on travelling bread for the rest of the trip, and that was much less fun to eat.

Uleweya took the dishes to the river to rinse when they were done and rubbed the horses down one last time. Kalanthe got out her bedroll and sat on it. She rebraided her hair into the travelling braid she usually wore when she didn't have to wear a helmet, but hadn't thought to do in the rush of leaving the house.

Above her, the stars burned brightly. When Uleweya returned, Kalanthe went down to the river to wash her face and use the privy. When she got back, Uleweya was banking the fire, ready for sleep.

"I'll set up wards," Kalanthe said. "That way we can both get some sleep."

"Thank you," said Uleweya. "I don't usually mind, but I've covered a lot of ground in the past few days."

Kalanthe didn't like to set wards very often, because it was complicated magic, and for some reason she hadn't figured out yet, it spooked Arrow. But Arrow wasn't here. She got the packet out of her saddlebag and measured out a portion of the herbs. She'd have to be careful, or her mix wouldn't last all the way to the Mage Keep. They were travelling through uninhabited lands, for the most part, but if a year's worth of questing had taught her anything, it was to prepare for as many calamities as she could.

Kalanthe cast the spell and saw the horses shudder as the ward washed over them. She felt it press on her own head for a moment, and then pass through her. Now they would be safe and concealed until the morning, even if they had to go down to the river in the middle of the night to use the privy again.

She checked the horses' hobbles one last time, poked the fire for no particular reason, climbed into her bedroll, and went to sleep.

MORE OR LESS THE EXACT MOMENT OF

I t was a stupid thing to do.

I had packed Branthear's wound as best I could, using my own belt to secure the bandages. I had picked up quite a bit of emergency medical training over the last year, but I knew that all I could hope to do was slow the bleeding until Mage Ladros had time to look at it. If he ever had time to look at it. My knife had dropped on the cobblestones when I took my belt off, but when I picked it up, Branthear held her hands out for it.

"Give me your knife, Olsa," she said.

Her voice was raspy, but it didn't have that horrible croak in it like I'd heard some of the door guards with the last time the watch had raided the Thief's Court and stuck the lot of them full of metal. Those men and women had all died, so I hoped that Branthear's voice meant she would live. I mean, live a bit, anyway. I wanted her to live as many bits as she could. I handed over my knife, and she passed me Kalanthe's axe.

"Go," she said. "They will need everyone who can stand."

I didn't want to stand. I wanted to run. But I knew I couldn't. It wasn't just Kalanthe; it was all of them.

"Are you sure?" I said. "I don't want to leave you alone."

I meant that I didn't want to leave her to *die* alone, and I think she understood that.

"It's all right, Olsa," she said. She was so much braver than I was. "Go."

She didn't have to tell me again. I didn't want to die either, but if I was going to, I wanted to be with Kalanthe when I went. If Branthear didn't mind dying alone, then I was free to go to her, so I set out. I slid out of the culvert where we were hiding and crept up the little hill on which the Old God's altar had been built.

I didn't just rush into the battle, of course. I'd spent enough time with knights to know that was how you got yourself, and possibly others, killed. I paused on the fringes of it to take everything in. The altar stood in the centre of a stone plaza that was about fifty yards across. The paving stones were uneven, the result of years of ivy and other plants growing up through them, and I could tell right away that footing was treacherous, even before it was made slippery with blood. Three columns marked the front of the plaza, though their arches had long since fallen. The Old God's forces were split in two: the group that had presumably been guarding the altar itself, and the larger group that had remained in the street.

I saw Sir Erris and Sir Terriam standing between the pillars, fighting the horde. I saw Sir Uleweya with her back to them, cleaving her way to the altar, like she was clearing a path. They must have run to the pillars as part of their initial charge and were working out from that point. I saw Mage Ladros standing with his back to me, facing Sir Uleweya. He was finished with the Old God's demons and had turned his attention to the Old God Himself, trying to get through whatever magic surrounded the altar. And I saw Kalanthe at the very back of the plaza, *holding the godsgem.*

I had no idea how it had come to pass, but I knew that it couldn't possibly mean anything good. I had to get to her. I had to stop her before she did something heroic and got herself killed without me.

Crossing a battlefield is an awkward thing to do, even if the fighting in concentrated in a part of it where you are not trying to go. At some point, Sir Erris realized I was there, but was far too busy to do anything about it. Uleweya had gone as far as she could, some unseen force was keeping her away from the altar itself. She shouted at Erris to switch places, and Terriam covered them while they moved. It was almost like watching poetry, if poetry was very, very bloody and cut off a lot of people's arms and legs.

Mage Ladros was attacking the altar, but he couldn't seem to break through. A woman I didn't recognize was crumpled at his feet—wait, no, I did recognize her. She was one of the old queen's advisers, the one who had started this whole mess by reviving the Old God in the first place. I hoped that Mage Ladros had killed her. She had caused no end of trouble.

Kalanthe was walking towards the altar slowly, like she was in a dream. I was worried that some of the fighters who had slipped past the knights might kill her, but it seemed like she was invulnerable. Every time one of them charged her, she struck true with Sir Branthear's axe, and they went down. The longer I stared at her, the more I heard a strange music. It was the most beautiful thing I had ever heard, and even though I was slipping through blood and gore, I would have stayed in this place forever if I had been allowed to keep hearing that song.

Sir Erris reached the altar and hammered on the unseen force with her sword. I thought she must have magicked it, because it was glowing brighter with every blow, but none of them seemed to be working. Mage Ladros shouted something at her, and they both struck together but still nothing happened.

At last, I reached Kalanthe's side. She had killed all her attackers, and no more were nearby. I took note of which hand she was holding the godsgem in and grabbed the other one, even though she was still carrying Sir Branthear's axe.

"Kalanthe!" I screamed. "What are you doing! We have to move!"

"It's all right," she said. Her voice was dreamy. I'd never heard her sound this vague before, even when she was just waking up from actual sleep. "Nothing can hurt me here."

"Well, it can certainly hurt us!" I shouted.

"Then go," she said. "Go and be safe, Olsa."

"I'm not leaving you, you great idiot," I told her. "There's no way I am leaving you. Come on, come with me."

I led her back the way I'd come in, walking past all the bodies she'd cut down in the process, until we were on a part of the floor that was clear of them. Maybe once she was farther from the altar I could snap her out of it, and she would rejoin the fight. She followed me easily enough, and though the fighting raged on around us, it couldn't seem to touch her. The music was getting louder. I never wanted it to stop. *I have to make it stop.*

"Kalanthe," I said. "Kalanthe, listen to me. It's supposed to be Erris, remember? Erris is supposed to get the godsgem."

"You can't pick the godsgem up," Kalanthe said. "It has to meet you halfway."

"Now is not the time!" I shouted, but before I could say anything else, several things happened at once.

The old queen's adviser leapt to her feet, wailing at an inhuman volume and moving jerkily, as though she were not in control of her own arms and legs. Mage Ladros stumbled back, and she threw herself at him. He was so startled, and she was so close to him that he had to fight her without magic at all, even though she was clearly possessed by a demon. The minions Sir Terriam and Sir Uleweya were fighting did the same thing, only they had already been standing when they attacked with renewed fury. Sir Terriam went down screaming, clutching her head in what appeared to be absolute agony, as Sir Uleweya tried to protect both herself and the fallen knight.

And at the altar, a great figure rose out of the idol.

"Sir Erris Quicksword," said a terrible voice. It blotted out the music. It blotted out everything. "You have come so far and yet you have nothing."

"I have my companions!" Sir Erris shouted defiantly.

The Old God laughed. It was not a pleasant sound.

"Your friends are dying," He said. "Worship me, Sir Erris, and I will save them."

"I will not!" Erris screamed. It sounded like it cost her everything to defy Him.

"Your king is dying too," the Old God said cruelly. "Every part of his body is tearing slowly apart. He is in agony, Sir Erris, and only you can save him. Worship me, Sir Erris, and I will heal him."

"No!" Erris was weeping now, but she would not give in. She must not give in.

"The world is burning, Sir Erris," said the Old God. "It burns because of your Quest and because of the one who has awoken me. Millions will die, but you can stop it. Worship me, Sir Erris, and you will save the world."

Sir Erris fell to her knees beneath the horrible power of His voice, but she would not yield. She set the point of her sword between two paving stones and used it to push herself back up to her feet.

"I will never," she said. "Not for anything you can offer. Because everything you offer is a lie!"

"Then burn, Sir Erris," said the Old God. "But watch your companions die first."

There was a moment before He struck when everything was quiet. My mind, which had been filled with battle and then the music and then the horror of the Old God waking, was clear. I looked into Kalanthe's eyes, and I knew that her mind was clear too. Erris needed a moment, and Kalanthe was going to give it to her, even if it got us both killed. I nodded, because this was something that was worth it and because, this way, we would face doom together.

Prompted by something I didn't understand, Kalanthe pushed the godsgem against the handle of Sir Branthear's axe, and the two items fused to each other, as though they had been forged in the same fire.

"Sir Erris!" Kalanthe screamed, and threw the axe at the altar as hard as she could.

It struck the magical barrier, sparks flying everywhere, but did no damage at all. Erris lurched forward, diving to catch the weapon as it fell.

"Impotent humans," the Old God gloated, looking straight at us. "Your defiance is nothing!"

Erris regained her balance, her knees pressing hard into the broken stone. She held Branthear's axe in one hand and her sword in the other, and she had a strangely peaceful expression on her face. I clung to Kalanthe as the Old God's fury turned to us. He raised His terrible will against us, but the blow never came.

Sir Erris surged to her feet—weapons in hand—as a bright green light flashed through the plaza. Its force seemed to counteract whatever had animated the Old God's warriors, because they all crumpled to the ground. Mage Ladros and the other knights were panting—bleeding—but alive.

"No!" screamed the Old God, but He was too late.

Kalanthe had distracted Him, drawn His attention from Sir Erris at the critical moment and she had used that moment to save us—to save everyone.

Surrounded by a blazing halo of green light, Sir Erris let Branthear's axe fall. She lifted the godsgem in her hand, reached through the Old God's barrier, and almost gently touched it to the idol that rested atop the altar. For a moment, it felt like the whole universe hung there in the balance of the Old God's scream and the godsgem's music, and then Quicksword brought her great blade swinging down, and the idol exploded, shattering into pieces.

Sir Erris was protected by the godsgem, still bathed in its green light. Sir Terriam was already down—alive, I was pretty sure—and Sir Uleweya dove to cover her. Mage Ladros was stationary enough that he could throw a magical shield up over himself, but Kalanthe and I were right in the path of the blast, and she was in no condition to do magic. So I tackled her, and as we fell to the ground together, I felt the scalding burn of the idol—evil even after it had been utterly vanquished—searing across my face.

It was like the deepest, warmest ocean, and Olsa was a dolphin, playing in the wake of a great vessel. Only, she was alone.

So she went looking for her friends.

＊——＊

Tarvy was cold. It was spring in Cadria, but his little room in the Thief's Court was drafty and far away from any fireplace. He kept it because it was private, and privacy was hard to come by, but on nights like this, he wished he could afford a heavier blanket.

Tarvy sits up, swearing. The room is full of brightly decorated woollen blankets in all his favourite colours. They are crushing him. They are making it difficult to breathe. He struggles free and looks down at his bed in horrorwonder. He is going to have more money than he's ever had in his life when he sells them. He shivers again.

When he sells most *of them.*

＊——＊

Branthear had put the girls to bed herself. She knew they had a nursemaid for that, but Branthear figured that everyone deserves a night off at some point. After she'd told them a couple of stories and waited for them to fall asleep, she'd gone into Edramore's old study and started trying to tidy it up. The law books were scattered all over the table. Apparently the girls' research had only involved moving the books one way, but she didn't mind putting them back. Edramore seemed to have a particular shelving style, and Branthear looked at the shelf to be sure she got it right.

The books fly out of her hands, rearranging themselves midair, and then sliding into place on the dark wooden shelves. Even the book that Branthear holds shifts in her grasp, trying to jump away. Branthear drops it, barely noticing when it flies to its place on the shelf, and reaches for a sword that isn't there. As soon as it's started, though, the magic is over. Branthear helps herself to more of her cousin's whisky and goes off in search of that strapping blacksmith lad who has been eyeing her across the courtyard these last few days while she spars.

❖ ⋯ ❖

Sir Eiris put the parchment down and pressed her fingertips to her forehead. She never used to get headaches before she was queen. She missed her friends, missed being out there with them, trying to save the day, even though she knew that she was needed here at court. She never asked the king if it was hard to wait at home while she rode out to save him, and now she knew what his answer would be.

With a sigh, she picked up the parchment again and kept reading.

Sir Erris's headache flares, pressure in the wrong direction. She sees stars behind her eyes and nearly passes out on her desk. Part of her knows that it is magic and looks around for her attacker, but before she finds anything the headache is gone. Somehow, she knows with absolute certainty that she will never have a headache again.

✦——✦

Uleweya looked at Kalanthe and decided to let the girl sleep for another hour, if she would. The horses were sturdy, but they were starting to show signs of the strain, and another hour's rest would serve them well too. Uleweya was very proud of Kalanthe's patience on this journey. A lesser knight would have chafed at every delay and pushed the horses too far, but Kalanthe let her take over and manage everything, and Uleweya did exactly that. She rummaged through the food parcel. They were out of real bread, more's the pity, but maybe if she softened the travelling bread with water, it would be more palatable.

A steaming loaf of fresh white bread appears next to the kettle that Uleweya left cooling after last night's dinner. Beside the bread, a pat of butter appears, and then a round of cheese. Uleweya pokes the bread cautiously and, when nothing happens, picks it up and breaks the loaf in half. The smell of it is perfect, but the fire in her eyes knows that it is wrong. She buries the loaf, butter, and cheese, crockery and all, and spits on the ground before she turns her back.

Terriam stood watch in the glade, even though there were several mages who were probably better qualified than she was to do the job. She couldn't do anything to help, not really. She couldn't even guard against magic, should anyone try anything. She didn't think anyone would. They were finally listening to Mage Ladros. Mostly, she was just tired. If she didn't have a friend to watch over, she would give anything for some sleep.

Exhaustion hits her in waves, stronger than anything she has ever felt before, and Terriam falls to her knees. She's asleep before she hits the ground, and no one will be able to wake her.

‹┼···┼›

In the whole of the southern desert, there is not a single grain of sand resting against anyone's skin.

‹┼···┼›

On a ship in the sea, an old sailor is suddenly surrounded by flowers with blooms as big as her head.

‹┼···┼›

Giran is far from home, but she has never been happier or felt more useful. She has much to learn. She wishes for nothing. Nothing is exactly what she gets.

‹┼···┼›

At an isolated estate on the coast of the northern ocean, a thousand new books appear in the baroness's library. Furniture cracks under the weight and the baroness's arm is crushed.

In Cadria, a sewer is finished. Three people are walled up inside until they starve to death.

It's too much for one. It's too much for one. It's too much for one. It's too much for one. It's too much for one. It's too much for one. It's too much for one.

Kalanthe.
Kalanthe!
KALANTHE!!!

. . . . **AFTER** . . . .

Kalanthe and Uleweya rode into the Mage Keep uncontested. All four horses were exhausted, but they didn't stop to hand them off to the grooms. Instead, they pressed on, up the broad avenue between the white buildings that lined the way. The deserted streets should have been unnerving, but Kalanthe didn't give them a second thought. At last, they rode into the centre of the Mage Keep, where a strange scene was waiting for them.

The first thing Kalanthe noticed, of course, was Olsa. She was impossible to miss. Suffused in green light, Olsa was hovering about ten feet in the air in the precise centre of the glade.

The second thing was the glade itself. Outside the city the last remnants of winter snow were on the ground, and a chill was still in the air; but the glade was as clear and green as the springtime, and a warm breeze was blowing off it.

The third thing was Mage Ladros, who seemed to be pitching a tent.

"What are you doing?" Kalanthe asked.

Mage Ladros gave a startled cry and then turned around to greet them. He looked so much older than Kalanthe remembered. Surely not that much time had passed.

"Kalanthe!" he said, reaching up to clasp her hand.

"What are you doing?" Kalanthe repeated. She swung down off Constance's back, and patted the gelding on the neck. Free of their riders, all the horses wandered to the glade and started eating the grass. It was probably forbidden for horses to graze in the Mage Keep glade, but Kalanthe couldn't care less about that sort of thing right now.

"It's Sir Terriam," Mage Ladros was saying in answer to her original question. "She fell asleep last night while she was standing guard, and we can't wake her up."

"How tired was she?" Uleweya asked.

"Not that tired," Mage Ladros said. "She just fell. We straightened her out and I took off her chainmail before we tucked her in, not that she noticed. I wanted to cover her because it's easier for her to wake up in the dark."

Kalanthe forced herself to pay attention. The godsgem was singing at her again, which made it difficult to concentrate on anything other than the music.

"What about Olsa?" she demanded.

"That was my fault," Ladros said. "Come inside and I'll tell you."

"No," Kalanthe said sharply. "You can tell me here. I'm not leaving her again."

Uleweya, who had travelled much farther than Kalanthe had in the past few weeks, lay down on the grass beside Terriam's tent and looked up at them.

"I've ridden much too far to miss whatever happens next just because I can't stand up any longer," she said, when the mage looked at her askance.

"I asked Olsa to come here under the pretence of testing our non-magical protections of the godsgem," Mage Ladros said. "My fellow mages were in disagreement, and I couldn't persuade them to simply throw the thing into the sea. What I really wanted was for Olsa to steal it and throw it into the sea herself."

"You can't pick up the godsgem," Kalanthe said. "It has to meet you halfway."

"I remembered," Mage Ladros said. "We had put it in a box, if you'll recall? Well, some of my fellows placed spells on the box so that if you were holding it, you couldn't move. Only nothing can contain the godsgem really, so anyone holding the box died pretty quickly."

Kalanthe looked at him in horror.

"It's been months!" she said.

"Yes, well, I could hold it," Mage Ladros said. "I held it for six months, and I was fine, but when I went to get Olsa, it took more than four weeks, and ten mages were dead by the time I returned."

"So you told Olsa to steal it," Kalanthe said.

"Yes," he said. "I had planned to have her put the godsgem into unmelting ice, to seal it against further tampering from my idiot colleagues. That's what I sent Sir Uleweya to find for me, but we'd run out of time."

"I didn't, by the way," Uleweya said. "Or rather I did, but I couldn't extract any of it. I was riding back to tell you we'd have to bury the godsgem there instead, when I got your magenote."

"I'd rather it go into the sea, regardless of the case it's in," Mage Ladros said. "Where was I? Right: I was holding the box myself when Olsa tried to steal the godsgem. I made sure that my hands were only underneath the box, so that she'd be able to open the latch and lift the lid. She was going to try lifting the godsgem itself with a spoon, I think. I'm not sure if that would have worked. Anyway, one of my previously mentioned idiot colleagues attacked her, and she knocked the box out of my hands. The godsgem flew out and she caught it."

"I remember how that goes," Kalanthe said.

She looked up at the girl she loved. Olsa looked peaceful, at least. Kalanthe had walked through a battlefield without so much as a scratch when she'd held the godsgem, so presumably nothing could touch Olsa here either. But that didn't mean she could stay forever.

"I think the first step of whatever you're planning should be to get her down," Uleweya said. She stood up again and experimentally waved her hands above her head, though she was still too far away from where Olsa had floated to really gauge height.

"I don't have a plan," Mage Ladros said. "This is up to Kalanthe."

"I don't have a plan either!" Kalanthe protested.

"Yes, but you've held the godsgem," Mage Ladros said. "And unlike Sir Erris, you talked to people while you were doing it."

"I don't remember very much," Kalanthe said. "There was music, and everything made sense."

"Let's just get her down," Uleweya said again.

"Wait," Mage Ladros said. "Before we touch her, did anything strange happen to you on the road?"

"No," said Kalanthe.

"Yes," said Uleweya. Kalanthe looked at her. "While you were sleeping one morning, I was thinking about bread, and a loaf of it just appeared, along with butter and my favourite kind of cheese."

"Did you eat it?" Mage Ladros asked.

"I buried it," Uleweya said. "It didn't look right."

"I think that was Olsa," Mage Ladros said. "Because the only explanation for what happened to Terriam that I can think of is that she wished she could get some rest, and then . . . someone made sure she did."

"It's possible," Kalanthe said. "When you're holding the godsgem, anything seems possible."

"We have to stop her before she hurts someone else," Uleweya said. "I'm going to try to get her down."

Before the tall knight could move, Kalanthe walked to the middle of the glade and looked up again. She was right under Olsa's feet, so she took two steps to her left.

"Come down, Olsa," she said softly, and Olsa floated down until she was hovering right in front of Kalanthe's face, her feet still a few inches from the ground because Kalanthe was taller.

"Well, that was easy," Uleweya said. "Tell her to wake up."

"*Ask* her to wake up," Mage Ladros amended. "Remember, she has the power of the new gods right now. We can't antagonise her."

"It's time to wake up, Olsa," Kalanthe said.

She knew it wouldn't work as soon as she finished speaking. Olsa never liked being talked to like she was a child. Sure enough, Olsa's eyelids didn't so much as flicker.

"Wake up, Olsa," she said again. And again, nothing happened.

"Keep talking," said Mage Ladros. "But whatever you do, I don't think you should—"

Kalanthe reached out with both hands and held Olsa's face.

Instantly, the light in the glade shifted so that it covered her too, though her feet remained firmly on the ground. Olsa's eyes flashed open, but Kalanthe knew that she was seeing far more of the world with them than anyone else could, and that her vision could not be trusted.

"Kalanthe!" said Olsa, in a voice as old as the mountains. "I was looking for you."

"I was in a new house," Kalanthe said. "I don't live in the palace anymore."

"That's good," Olsa said. "I know you hate court."

"You're right," Kalanthe said. "I do."

"Wait, you had to leave because you had to get married," Olsa said. Her temper was rising. "You left me."

"I'm sorry, Olsa," Kalanthe said. "I'm so, so sorry. But it's all right now. Everything will be all right. You just have to wake up."

"No!" said Olsa. She suddenly seemed like she was a hundred feet tall. "No, I won't wake up. I can't fix anything when I'm awake. Asleep I can do whatever I want."

"But who can you share it with?" Kalanthe asked. This probably qualified as antagonisement, but it was all she could think to say. "I thought that if I had my knighthood and my honour and my nobility, everything else would be tolerable. But I was wrong. I was asleep and now I am awake."

"Did your husband-to-be show you that?" Olsa said, bitterness oozing out of her. The grass beneath her feet turned black.

"Before he died, yes, he did," Kalanthe said. "He was a good man."

"HE TOOK YOU FROM ME!" The blackness spread out, creeping towards the tent where Sir Terriam slumbered.

"He didn't, Olsa," Kalanthe said. "I left on my own because I thought I had to. I owed so many people so much, and I forgot what I owed to you."

"Too many people owe," Olsa said. She was calmer, but there was a terrible distance in her voice. "Too many people are hungry. Too many people don't have what they need."

"That's why you have to wake up," Kalanthe said. She let go of Olsa's face and wrapped her arms around her shoulders. The godsgem burned against her chest.

"No!" said Olsa again. "It's sleeping that gives me all this power."

"You're killing Sir Terriam, you know," Kalanthe said. There must be a way to make her see.

"She wanted to sleep!" Olsa said.

"And now she can't wake up," Kalanthe said. "She'll starve if she doesn't wake up."

A ripple tore through the flurry of power that surrounded them, and Olsa began to cry.

"I didn't mean it!" she screamed. "I didn't mean it!"

"Then let her wake up too," Kalanthe said.

"But I can fix it, Kalanthe. I can fix everything. I can save you."

Olsa's voice was wild with love. Kalanthe bit her lip and did what she did the very best: she told the truth.

"I don't need you to save me, Olsa." She said the words, even though they killed her. "I don't need you to save me. I don't need anything."

"No!" screamed Olsa. "No! I don't believe you!"

"I don't need you," Kalanthe said. She took a deep breath. "But, Olsa, I want you so much. I want you more than I have ever wanted anything in the whole world. Please, you have to trust me."

It hung there, poised on eternity. Then, weeping, the thief who held the balance of the universe in her hands reached out with the godsgem and changed the course of worlds.

BEFORE . . . .

We used most of the medical supplies patching up Sir Branthear and Sir Erris, but there was enough disinfectant left when Mage Ladros was done with them for Olsa and me. I swabbed her cheek carefully, and she flinched.

"Sorry," I said. "I know it stings."

"It's not so bad," Olsa said. "I mean, I've touched pure evil today. I can handle a sting."

I finished cleaning the cut on her face, and then she cleaned mine. In a perfect world, we would have stitched them, but we didn't have time for that. No one, not even Sir Erris, wanted to spend the night in the Holy City, and soon we would have to leave. Sir Uleweya and I carried Sir Branthear on a makeshift stretcher. Sir Erris was limping. Olsa walked with Sir Terriam, who was awake but very, very pale. Mage Ladros had stayed behind to encourage the vines of ivy that grew through the altar platform to swallow it.

We moved very slowly back to the horses. They were fine, though spooked, and I cried into Lightfoot's mane, I was so happy to see her. I rolled my shoulders, not particularly looking forward to carrying Sir Branthear all the way back to Cadria—though of course I would do it—when Mage Ladros rejoined us.

"Let's go a bit farther," he said. "I want to get clear of the city. Then Olsa and I will go to the coast and signal for the ship to come in for us."

"Thank you, Ladros," Sir Erris said, and I knew that she was thinking of her knights and how exhausted we all were.

It was the first time she had spoken since what happened at the altar. She still held the godsgem in her hand, though it was inside an iron box at Mage Ladros's suggestion. I couldn't hear it singing anymore, and I missed the music with every part of my soul.

"Come on, Kalanthe," Uleweya said, and we picked up Sir Branthear again.

We quickly fell behind everyone else, but I didn't mind. They had their jobs to do and I had mine. Against all odds, we had survived. We were probably going to be home soon, and then I would have to face a future I had all but given up on. I was eighteen now. In another year, I would be a proper knight. In another year, I would have to repay my debt.

In another year, I would have to marry.

"Kalanthe?" said Sir Branthear.

"Yes?" I said. We didn't stop moving. "Do you need something?"

"I need you to stop thinking so hard," she said, laughing. "If you trip and drop me, I might start bleeding again."

"That's not funny," I informed her, only then I couldn't stop laughing. We had to set the stretcher down, and Sir Uleweya looked back at us with a scandalized expression on her face.

"There is something wrong with the pair of you," Sir Uleweya said.

"There is nothing wrong with Kalanthe," Sir Branthear protested. "Kalanthe is the perfect knight."

"That's the blood loss talking," Sir Uleweya said. "Can we go now?"

For an answer, I picked up my end of the stretcher, and we kept up our march after the others.

By the time we arrived, Olsa and Mage Ladros were gone, and Sir Erris had built a fire. Sir Terriam was staring into it and flinching at things the rest of us couldn't see. We set Sir Branthear down close enough to get some of the fire's warmth, and then I sat down beside her, suddenly exhausted.

"Someone please tell me what happened after you all left me," Branthear said. "All I could hear was a lot of shouting."

"I don't really want to talk about it," Sir Erris said. I didn't either.

"Consider it practice," insisted Sir Branthear. "For starters, I am going to believe you. You're going to have to tell this story a lot, probably for the rest of your lives, and since I'm going to have to tell it too, I need to know."

Slowly, and with Sir Uleweya and me chiming in from time to time, Sir Erris recounted what had happened. When she got to the part about the reanimated corpses, Sir Terriam stood abruptly and walked out of earshot. Sir Uleweya moved to follow her, but when it became apparent that Sir Terriam needed space, she left her alone.

"I can't believe you both held the godsgem," Branthear said, when we were finished. "Well, I mean, of course I believe it. And of course it was Kalanthe."

"It was an excellent throw," Sir Erris said. "I owe you a new axe, though. Yours didn't survive in very good condition, and I think we left it behind."

"Good," said Sir Branthear. "If you'd brought it, someone would have put it in a temple or some such nonsense. I'll get another one, and one for Kalanthe besides."

I almost protested, but then I remembered that I had to live through my future, and if someone wanted to give me something, I almost had to take it.

I had nearly nodded off by the time Olsa and Mage Ladros returned. They had several burly-looking sailors with them, and they helped us cover the distance back to the sea. I fell in the longboat, despite the arms that reached out to steady me, and by the time we boarded, I was nearly asleep on my feet.

It occurred to me, as we were led belowdecks, that what I really wanted was to curl up with Olsa, but when I looked around to ask her, I couldn't see where she was. Then there was a bed in front of me, and I was falling into it, and then I was asleep.

It took a few days to get back to Cadria, and I was as awake as I was ever going to be by the time we made it to the river. A barge was waiting for us there, vast and overdecorated. Beside me, I heard one of the sailors sniff, and I agreed with her. The vessel was clearly ornamental and probably barely seaworthy, but the river was calm and predictable, so we would be safe enough. It would take too long to ferry all the horses over to the barge, so we decided to disembark onto land and then board the riverboat. We bid farewell to the ship's captain and crew, knowing that they would spread our story far and wide, and stepped onto solid ground.

At the riverbank, we turned our horses over to royal grooms, and then King Dorrenta, hale and well, met us himself. For a moment, I wondered whether our meeting would be formal, but after one look at Sir Erris, all pomp and circumstance went out the window. The cheering was loud and long, because everyone enjoys it when their monarch kisses someone in public. Kissing reminded me of Olsa, and I wanted to put my arm around her, except she wasn't standing beside me and I couldn't reach her.

The boat ride up the river to Cadria was calm and uneventful. I felt like I was going to claw out of my skin, but Sir Terriam finally fell into a quiet sleep, so I made myself stay still. The royal physician saw to Sir Branthear and Sir Erris, and then to each of us in turn. She complimented me on how well I had cleaned the wound on my face, and before I could tell her that I hadn't done it myself, she was clucking about the scar.

"I don't mind," I told her.

"Knights should have a few scars," she said, which was true, but that wasn't the reason I didn't mind.

The river barge slid through the night. I slept after the physician left, and when I woke it was to the bright morning and the sound of heavy ropes landing on the deck. We were home.

Our ride into Cadria itself was the stuff of song. The city gates were thrown wide-open to receive us. The people wore flowers in their hair, and children sang. Every stitch on the city guards' uniforms was perfect. I think the cobbles had even been washed before we walked on them.

In comparison, I felt bedraggled and tired, but even Sir Branthear was allowed to sit on her horse, so I put my best face on it. Somehow, I ended up riding next to Sir Erris.

"You didn't tell the sailors that you held the godsgem," she said to me. Even though she was talking, she was still smiling and waving at the crowd. She was going to make an excellent queen.

"It never came up," I said.

"Kalanthe, you did something amazing," Sir Erris said, "You should tell people if you want. I'm not worried about being overshadowed."

"It's not that," I said. "It's just that, well, I'm not a knight yet. I won't be for a year. I'll have to go back to the dormitories and sit in my lessons and train with the other apprentice knights again. I don't need to be all that *and* the girl who held the godsgem."

"I've been thinking about your living arrangements," she said. "But we can talk about that later. I do see your point about the godsgem, though. It's one thing to be a knight and go on a Quest. I imagine it will be different for you and Olsa."

I looked around for her when Sir Erris said her name. She was at the very back, riding beside Sir Terriam. She had a hand on her elbow, like she was reassuring Sir Terriam that the noise of the crowd was all right.

"Olsa saved you as much as I did, you know," I said. We hadn't talked about it, what happened while I held the godsgem. It felt like I hadn't seen her at all since I threw Sir Branthear's axe. "I was lost in the godsgem. I don't know if you felt it, but it's very hard to focus when you're holding it."

"I noticed," Sir Erris said. "It was all I could do to remember who I was, let alone what I was meant to do."

"Olsa pulled me through it," I said. "She made me remember. When the Old God was yelling all those horrible things at you, she made me remember. And then I could act."

"And then—" Erris used the hand she was waving with to indicate my cheek. I pressed a hand to it. It was throbbing lightly, but most of the pain had faded.

"And then she saved my life." I looked up. Erris was looking at me instead of the crowd. "I want everyone to know what she did," I said quietly. "I want everyone to know that she wasn't just so much extra baggage on this Quest. There are going to be so many stories told. I want her to be in them."

"You'll be in the stories together, Kalanthe." Sir Erris said it with such conviction that I didn't doubt her for a moment.

I knew it would be hard. I knew it would be next to impossible. There was a lot I was going to have to do to make everything work out, but together we had faced the Old God and together we would go down in story and song. I didn't know how, exactly, I was going to make any of that work out, but I knew in my heart that I would keep fighting to try.

When I turned back to tell Olsa, she was already gone.

Then rise, Sir Kalanthe Ironheart, knight of the realm, hero to the King, and go into the world to fulfill your oaths."

The queen's voice rang through the throne room, and Sir Kalanthe got to her feet. Cheering echoed off the polished marble floors, and at least two people loosed ear-piercing whistles. Kalanthe was smiling broadly, and the queen and king both matched her expression. Sir Erris handed her back her sword, and two small girls came forward with her shield. The sigil was Kalanthe's own colours mixed with theirs, and she couldn't have been prouder to carry it. When she turned around to face the crowd, the cheering multiplied. Her parents, brother, and age-mates were all hollering from the front row, but Kalanthe Ironheart had eyes for only one person.

Olsa's hair was a shocking white, now. There would be no more hiding in crowds for her, unless she wore a cap over her spectacular curls. Today, her hair was unbraided and surrounded her head like a halo. Kalanthe liked the look. Triana had made a wonderful dress for her. In actuality it was a pair of wide-legged trousers, but it looked like a proper skirt unless Olsa was running.

Kalanthe was in her full armour, of course, as were her fellow knights from the Quest, including the queen. It would be the last time for a while that the queen was able to wear her armour, even for ceremonial purposes, because soon her belly would swell sufficiently that it would no longer fit.

Kalanthe stepped off the dais into the arms of her parents, who gave her quick hugs, and her brother, who patted her on the shoulder, effectively ringing her like a bell. She laughed and turned to greet her age-mates, some of whom had already been knighted. The rest would follow before the year was out, and she was happy to rejoice with them.

Then Sir Uleweya enfolded her in a bear hug, nearly lifting her off her feet in spite of the armour. Sir Branthear embraced her with a bit more decorum, and Sir Terriam, looking out from under her hooded scarf, kissed her on the forehead. She shook hands with Giran, who was staying with Sir Terriam for a time before heading back home, and then finally, finally turned to Olsa.

"You look very impressive," Olsa said.

"Thank you," said Kalanthe. "I practice a lot."

Olsa rapped her knuckles on Kalanthe's breastplate.

"You know, a year on the road with all of this, and I still don't know how you bear it," she said. "Not to mention the smell."

"The things we do for king and country," Kalanthe said. She looked at her. "The things we do for love."

"You are entirely ridiculous," she said.

"I am having a moment," Kalanthe said, as primly as she possibly could. Then she bent and kissed Olsa for the whole world to see.

The cheering went on for quite some time, and then King Dorrenta invited everyone to a celebratory feast. Kalanthe and Olsa sat next to each other and pretended not to notice the dark looks that the magistrate and the commander of the city watch kept sending their way. Olsa flinched when a lady with an emerald necklace walked past them to get to her seat, and Kalanthe took her hand.

"It's over, love," she said. "The godsgem is gone."

She had carried it to the ocean herself. After Olsa had handed it to her, Kalanthe had made the trek on foot because her horses were exhausted, and if she stopped to wait for another mount, she knew she would never go. Sir Terriam had caught up with her a few hours into her journey but had given her plenty of space. After she cast it into the sea, it was Sir Terriam who had put her on a horse and brought her back. Kalanthe had wept so hard she couldn't remember the route, and since Sir Terriam wore her hood, she couldn't give a description of the landmarks either. If someone wanted the godsgem again, they were going to have to find it the hard way. Kalanthe couldn't think of a better end to her part in this particular story.

When she'd come back to the Mage Keep, Olsa was awake and furious about being left behind, but had calmed almost immediately, mostly because Kalanthe had shucked off her travelling clothes and climbed right into bed with her. They had hardly been separated ever since.

"I know," Olsa said. "It was just so terrible for a moment there. I did such terrible things."

"And then you chose to stop doing them," Kalanthe reminded her, as she always did and always would, as long as Olsa let her talk. "I don't think there are very many people who could have made that choice."

"You would have," Olsa said.

"Yes, well, I'm a knight, you see," Kalanthe informed her. "They gave me a shield and everything."

"I love you," Olsa said. "You're ridiculous and noble and just a bit too tall for my convenience, but I love you."

"I love you too," Kalanthe said. "Even if you are short and just as ridiculous as I am."

Elenia and Carster came over to talk, thrilled at being treated like ladies at a party at the actual palace. They had taken to Olsa very well, for which Kalanthe was eternally grateful, even if Carster now had several more items on her list of things Kalanthe had promised to explain to her when she was older. By the time the meal was over, Kalanthe was feeling restless, though. She loved Cadria and Sir Erris and her parents, but she had places to be, now, and, after all, there was planting to be finished.

Their horses had been brought, along with a carriage for the girls and their nurse, and all of the people Kalanthe loved best had come to see them off. She watched as Olsa mounted up on Constance and then swung herself into Lightfoot's saddle.

"Shall we go and make a better world, love?" she asked.

Olsa smiled.

"Let's go home."

ACKNOWLEDGEMENTS

The Afterward is the kind of book every author dreams of writing. It seemed like there was no boundary between my brain and my computer when I was writing the first draft, and throughout edits, the book remained my dearest love. That said, books require a tremendous amount of work, even when the author's dreams are met and matched at every turn.

Josh Adams continues to be a true champion of my work, somehow limiting himself to a mere sigh when he called to ask how I was doing with a proposal and I told him I had written 25,000 words of something entirely different instead.

Andrew Karre told me a while ago that he didn't do epic fantasy, and I'm still not sure which one of us has pulled a fast one on the other, but I think it was me, and, full disclosure, I am probably going to do it again.

The team at Penguin has once again taken a .doc file and turned it into something beautiful I can hold in my hands. Thank you to Theresa Evangelista, Elaine Christina, and Sebastian Ciaffaglione for the pretty, and to Melissa Faulner and Natalie Vielkind for keeping everyone together.

My readers—Emma Higinbotham, Colleen Speed, Katherine Locke, Kaitlyn Sage Patterson, F.M. Boughan, Tessa Gratton, Vee Signorelli, Camryn Garrett, Sangu Mandanna—thank you for your time and your thoughts (and, um, your tears).

Thank you to everyone whose eyes lit up when I explained the premise. I had to wait for this book F.O.R.E.V.E.R. and making all of you suffer with me helped a great deal.

The Afterward began on a drive across Michigan, was written over six glorious days (with a fourteen-month break because: Star Wars), and I hope you love it even half as much as I do.